RAW
A CROSSING THE LINE NOVEL
REDEMPTION

RAW
A CROSSING THE LINE NOVEL
REDEMPTION

TESSA BAILEY

It's never too late to be redeemed

♡ *Tessa Bailey*

This book is a work of fiction. Names, characters, places, and incidents are the product of the author's imagination or are used fictitiously. Any resemblance to actual events, locales, or persons, living or dead, is coincidental.

Copyright © 2016 by Tessa Bailey. All rights reserved, including the right to reproduce, distribute, or transmit in any form or by any means. For information regarding subsidiary rights, please contact the Publisher.

Entangled Publishing, LLC
2614 South Timberline Road
Suite 109
Fort Collins, CO 80525

Entangled Teen is an imprint of Entangled Publishing, LLC.

Visit our website at www.entangledpublishing.com.

Edited by Heather Howland
Cover design by Heather Howland and Clarissa Yeo
Interior design by Jacob Hammer

Manufactured in the United States of America

First Edition June 2016

10 9 8 7 6 5 4 3 2 1

*For every single reader who came along
on the Crossing the Line series ride.*

Chapter One

Henrik could only get himself off in the shower.

Something about the white noise of liquid pelting the plastic curtain, the bathtub floor. The gurgle of the drain as it sucked down blood-tinged water, courtesy of that evening's underground fight. He was removed from the world when he stood inside the shower stall that barely allowed for his height and bulk. Even now, as Henrik stroked the erection he'd been sporting since the match ended, his elbow occasionally slammed into the hollow wall. If he kept this pace up, there would be a hole in the tile by the time he finally climaxed.

Now, that would be an interesting one to explain to his landlord.

His torment could be over in seconds if he pictured the girl. The girl. The fucking *girl*. Always with him, like fingertips whispering over his skin.

A flash of red hair and hazel eyes filtered through his mind and Henrik groaned, the flesh in his hand swelling to the point of agony. This time, the pleasure-pain was laced with guilt. The prevailing reason he escaped to the shower every time he needed to relieve the pressure between his legs. He had no right using the single memory he'd created in her presence to find completion. Not only did it make him a depraved human being, but it didn't exactly speak well of his sanity.

One sentence. She'd spoken a mere *ten words* in that light, melodic voice and that alone—that single encounter—had been enough to make him throw his career as a Chicago police officer away. Given the option of prison time or working with a team of ex-convicts formed by his captain to stop crime from the inside, Henrik had signed his soul away to that group of six devils, of which he was now the seventh.

Ailish O'Kelly hadn't asked him to destroy the evidence that implicated her in the crimes of her father, but he'd thought of the beautiful yet fatigued girl walking in the park. Thought of her in that conservative green dress, the way she'd taken his measure with just a hint of feminine appreciation. And he'd been unable to watch her take the fall. Mentally incapable. Physically repelled. No way could he see that girl in handcuffs.

So he'd burned anything that could put her behind bars. Hell, he'd taken sick pleasure in the task. Protecting her. Even if she'd never know it.

But what if she *did* know?

This was where his depravity kicked in. Henrik wasn't a man who thrived on accolades. Shit, he'd joined the dark side with his eyes wide open, knowing the potential outcome. Losing his badge, his livelihood, everyone he called a friend. Even the respect of his family. Yeah, gratefulness was never something Henrik required, but a grateful Ailish O'Kelly? His body responded to that notion in a fast, fluid rush.

He braced his left hand on the slick wall and quickened the pace of his strokes, the choking circle of his hand traveling from heavy balls to engorged tip roughly three times per second. Hell, if jerking off were an Olympic sport, he would have taken home enough gold medals in recent months to fill every closet in his apartment.

"Jesus Christ," Henrik gritted out, wishing he could finish without what came next. If he could orgasm just *once* without thinking of Ailish, maybe he could fall asleep that night without feeling like an unredeemable son of a bitch. But no, *no*, the weighted sack suspended between his thighs wouldn't be coaxed into emptying without thinking of the sweet redhead.

He always pictured them in the park, the one and only place they'd ever shared oxygen. This time, she came toward him with a knowing look, her eyelids drooping low to cover half of those bright hazel orbs that defied their plain four-letter name. *Eyes*. No, this girl didn't simply have eyes. She had torture devices. They held intelligence and inexperience at the same time, enough of both qualities to stun him silent. Closer. She was closer now. Running slender hands up and over her swaying hips. As always in his fantasies, she knew what he'd done. Knew he'd protected her name, her life. Knew he would never ask for anything in return.

But she wanted to give it to him anyway.

Henrik groaned as moisture pearled on the tip of his dick and was quickly washed away by the raining shower. No going back now. She'd reached him on the sidewalk at the park's edge and the world around them had suspended its animation. Everything frozen but the two of them, even the street sounds and characteristic Chicago wind. She stopped an inch away and slipped those delicate hands up his stomach, his pecs.

"I've been thinking about you," Ailish murmured.

The very idea of him appearing in her head sent a jolt of need to his loins, forcing him to tighten his fist and pump with more force. Apparently, his imaginary self was easy like that.

"You have?"

The gorgeous redhead gave him a shy nod. "You protected me." Her eyes raked up and down his body. Liking what she saw? Since this was his fantasy, Henrik was going with *hell yeah*. "If I needed protecting again, could you keep me safe… with your body?"

"Yes," Henrik rasped, the sincere affirmation bouncing off the shower walls. "I'd do whatever was needed. Nothing could stop me."

Black eyelashes swept down to hide her eyes before revealing them once more, the impact almost knocking him back a step. "Could you show me right now?"

Henrik's bracing hand curled into a shaking fist on the shower wall as the second self in his mind stooped down and picked up Ailish. One forearm beneath her ass was all it took, her lips parting on a whimper as both feet left the ground. She clung to his shirt collar, seeming a little unsure. But ah fuck, then she sneaked her thighs up around his hips, all slow and mischievous. Not quite snuggling his cock, but close enough that her heat reached through his fly and sucked.

Ailish stared at his mouth. "Can you show me more?" She leaned closer, her tits grazing the front of his shirt. "How you'd protect me?"

Two steps and he had Ailish crushed against the side of his police vehicle, the backs of her high heels bouncing off the doors. *Good.* Dent them. Henrik didn't give a fuck about anything but the girl gasping for breath in front of him. He savored a second of anticipation before shoving his rigid cock against the seam of her body. The seam that gave pleasure, gave life. *Give it all to me.*

"You wanted me to *show* you, Ailish."

"Y-yes."

He rolled his tongue along the roof of his mouth. "I would keep my body between you and danger at all times.

Nothing and no one would touch you but me." Using his hips, he pushed her higher up the car's exterior, mentally recording her soft cry of surprise. "Inside or out."

One of her high heels dropped onto the sidewalk. Maybe his reaction to the lost shoe stemmed from her being *that much* more naked. Or perhaps her lack of concern for the dropped footwear accounted for the surge of lust. For whatever reason, though, that forgotten high heel pushed Henrik past the line of his defenses, his consciousness whittling down to his wet manhood. *Almost there. Almost…*

Ailish beckoned him forward by licking her upper lip. "Henrik?"

"Yes, baby."

She rubbed that single bare foot against his ass. "Will you please touch me on the inside?"

"*Fuck!*" Henrik shouted as tremors racked his body. "*Ailish.*" Spurts of pent-up need left his cock in what felt like endless rushes of the tide. Forward and back until he was forced to release his flesh to support himself with both hands on the shower wall, while the remainder of his orgasm found its way free onto the bathtub floor.

The shower spray had turned lukewarm by the time consciousness streamed back in. No Ailish in front of him. No police vehicle. All gone. Should he care more about the girl than the fact that he'd never drive another squad car again? No, he shouldn't.

Did he?

Yes.

Ailish O'Kelly, daughter of Chicago's ruthless crime boss Caine O'Kelly, had vanished into thin air after the evidence against her had been destroyed, forcing the police to release her from any further questioning. Thanks to the skill set of his new teammates on the undercover squad—a squad made up of criminals like him—Henrik had been in possession of

Ailish's location for two hellish weeks.

Two weeks filled with unsanctioned boxing matches. Illegal fights a million miles away from the charity bouts he'd competed in as an officer. He'd literally needed his skull bashed with another man's fists to keep himself from going after Ailish. But his method was losing its effectiveness. A sane man wouldn't consider himself in a position to go after Ailish like some broken-down superhero without a cape. Or a badge. Not after having exchanged a single sentence. It was very likely the girl didn't even remember him.

But he remembered *her*. And staying stationary when he could have eyes on her in a day's drive? Pure motherfucking torture. If his teammate Polly's information was accurate, Ailish had left town on her own, without the assistance of her father. She could be scared. Or in trouble. Might require help, but didn't know who to ask…which could lead to her asking the wrong people.

Gut churning, Henrik reared back and slammed his already-battered fist into the shower wall, cracking the tile on impact. No more waiting.

He was going after Ailish.

For once in her life, Ailish didn't need a single thing from anyone.

It. Felt. *Incredible.*

No one was required to escort her to the supermarket or approve her chosen attire. Cutting holes in the knees of her jeans had been mission number one upon leaving Chicago. Since fifth grade, when Helen Brady showed up to a school fund-raiser with ripped Free People skinny jeans, Ailish had wanted them, too. Such a small rebellion, but to her, it was on par with, say…robbing the mob.

Something she knew a little bit about.

She wasn't thinking about that today, however, or what her father's reaction to her disappearance had been. Today was about earning an honest wage. Making money the right way, without dipping a hand into someone else's pocket and leaving them desperate. In debt. For too long, Ailish had been a witness to dishonest dealings that turned her stomach and made her ashamed. Ashamed to be an O'Kelly.

There was no shame in physical labor, however, which was why she'd chosen a farm in Wisconsin as her first stop. She had no itinerary. No plans beyond today, when she would assist the farmer's wife who'd taken a chance on hiring her. Turning soil, planting seeds, working with real live animals. Maybe she should have waited to rip holes in the denim. The manual labor might have formed them naturally. And just what would Helen Brady say about *that*?

Ailish looked out the tiny window of the guest quarters she was renting on the cheap. Her wage would cover the room and leave her with enough to purchase supplies in town. What a glorious feeling, knowing she could depend on herself for food. That she wouldn't have to touch the bloodstained money wedged inside a duffel bag, beneath the loose floorboard on which she stood, tapping her toe.

Tap, tap…tap.

A prickle climbed the back of Ailish's neck. Had that last *tap* been from her? She remained perfectly still and listened to the breeze whisper outside, laughing and shaking her head when no other sounds met her ears. Paranoia came part and parcel with being an O'Kelly, but there was nothing on this farm that could hurt her. Not unless she managed to piss off the cow. Again.

It was the loose ends she'd left in Chicago that wouldn't allow her to relax completely. With prison time hanging over her head and two dogged cops breathing down her neck in an interrogation room, she'd felt…freedom. Ironic, sure. Or perhaps that skewed outlook meant she had a screw loose. As a young girl, she'd dreamed of traveling. Swimming in the oceans of faraway places and eating exotic foods. But as her life had progressed and she'd only seldom been let outside the confines of her father's marble mini mansion? Prison had not only been a change, it had represented distance from witnessing her father's violence.

But more importantly, a chance to atone for *her* part in that violence.

Then all at once, she'd been standing on the sidewalk. Outside the police station, instead of behind the bars of a cell. For once, there had been no one to take her home. No dark car approaching. No meaty paws on her back, shuffling her forward. Without warning, freedom had stretched before her, a swimming pool in which she would sink or swim. So she'd swum…and swum. Away from her past and family name. No longer was her only option to trade one prison for another. She could finally break free.

Being her father's daughter in certain small ways, she'd assumed there would be surveillance on her after leaving the police station. So she'd done what any girl raised inside the walls of a criminal organization would do. She'd woven through businesses, leaving through back exits and jogging down trash-strewn alleys until she found a parking garage where she could hot-wire a car.

And she'd never gone home.

She *had*, however, made one quick stop at her father's "office" to procure funds. It had been risky, but entirely necessary, considering she'd had only the clothes on her back and zero job skills to speak of.

Unless you counted the talents that had landed her in the interrogation room to begin with.

Talents that would get her nowhere on a farm. Thank

God.

Creak.

Ailish went still. She knew better than to show any sign that she heard a possible intruder, but such a feat was difficult with your heart punching you in the throat.

Breathe.

Humming the first song that came to mind—"It's a Small World"—Ailish gathered her hair in a ponytail and secured it with a black band. She took the two steps required to enter the tiny kitchen and slowly removed a knife from the drawer, under the guise of slicing a green apple. When she heard another creak from the rear of the guesthouse, she only hummed louder.

It couldn't be the farmer or his wife. They usually arrived with all the subtlety of a fireworks display, shouting her name from the backs of their horses. No, someone was lurking and dammit, she'd only been in Wisconsin for two weeks. Who had found her so quickly? The cops or her father?

Which was worse?

Out of the corner of her eye, Ailish watched the back doorknob turn. Slowly…slowly. She gripped the knife's handle with such force, it made tiny chopping noises against the wooden cutting board. "Come on, just do it," she murmured under her breath. "Stop playing games."

Ailish got her wish as the door flew open with a bang against the opposite wall. It only took her a split second to recognize the two men—*hopefully* only two—and hurl the knife. It caught the taller one in his left shoulder, sticking out at an awkward angle.

Tall Man gave Ailish a look of disbelief as he removed the blade and dropped it at his feet. "Oh, you shouldn't have done that."

She inched toward the loose floorboard. "How'd he find me?"

Cautiously, a man in a vintage Cubs cap eased up beside his bleeding crony. "Your father is a very industrious man."

"Don't tell me about my father. I've known him for twenty-one years."

"All right," Tall Man said, gritting his teeth. "Here's what happens now. You get your sweet ass in the car. You don't want to know the alternative."

Ailish listened for a third person outside, heard nothing. They'd made a mistake by coming in the same entrance. "Maybe not. Tell me anyway. I want to recount it word for word to my father next time I see him."

Cubs Cap laughed without humor. "You know, you've gotten a hell of a lot more interesting since taking off. Should be a decent car ride back to Chicago."

"I'm not going anywhere with you."

Tall Man advanced, one hand plugging the knife wound she'd inflicted. Ailish halted her progress toward the loose floorboard and backed toward the front door instead. Dammit. She'd never make it. She had to leave without the money. God, she'd be lucky to escape at all.

No, she *would*. She had to. This unexpected freedom was too precious, and she'd regret not fighting tooth and nail to keep it.

As soon as Tall Man reached Ailish, she swung her fist, hoping to stun him long enough to get out the front door. It worked. Briefly. She snatched her car keys off the peg beside the entrance, threw open the door—and was caught around the waist before clearing the porch. Operating on instinct, Ailish twisted around and shoved her thumb into Tall Man's knife wound, as deep as it would go, scrambling away once more as he howled.

"*Goddammit*," the man shouted behind her, his nearing voice indicating that he hadn't stayed down long. Cubs Cap growled an order in the distance. To grab Ailish. Which wasn't going to happen as long as she was breathing. *Not going back to Chicago. Can't go back.*

Tears blinded Ailish as she sprinted toward her stolen car. Almost there.

Blinding white light filled her vision, the breath leaving her body. Pain like she'd never experienced bloomed along her forehead, behind her eye sockets. Something had struck her. A fist? When she managed to crack an eyelid, she was stunned to find herself on the ground, faceup, the two men standing above her and blocking out the sun.

"Are you out of your fucking mind?" Cubs Cap shouted, nearly splitting Ailish's head in half. "Bring her back unharmed. *That was the job*. How are we going to explain a black eye?"

"She threw a *knife* at me."

Cubs Cap paced away, throwing his hands up in the air. He jerked a cell phone out of his pocket and started to dial, but Tall Man knocked the device out of his hands. A shouting match ensued. Even in her woozy state, Ailish knew this was her chance. They were distracted and believed they'd incapacitated her. The car keys were still clutched in a death grip inside her palm, the vehicle only twenty yards away. She could get there. She *could*.

Ailish flopped over onto her stomach and started to crawl. Her elbows dug into the dirt, little lights winking before her eyes as the pain expanded inside her skull. When a foot landed on her back and collapsed her to the ground, Ailish screamed through her teeth. *Not fair. This wasn't fair.*

She was jerked up onto her feet by Tall Man—only to find a gun pointed straight at her head. "Don't," she managed through numb lips. "*Please*, don't."

"Can't bring you back like this," Tall Man said, with more than a hint of pleasure. "And can't have you talking, saying I knocked you one."

Ailish played her final card. "I have money," she whispered. "I can give you money. You won't need to go back to my father at all."

Both men tensed, like two dogs that just had a bone tossed down between them. Their expressions turned calculating. Ailish saw Cubs Cap reach for the small of his back and dived away with a prayer on her lips, expecting to feel a bullet enter her body at any second. The quiet *zing* of shots being fired through a silencer were greeted by still morning silence. Silence so loud, she swore death had found her. But she couldn't be dead if she still felt pain, could she?

Ailish uncovered her head and looked up, finding Cubs Cap staring at the crumpled body of his associate.

"You show me where the money is." He punctuated each word by stabbing his gun in the air. "Then you get the hell out of here."

Chapter Two

Henrik thundered into the squad meeting room, seeing his six teammates and one captain through tunnel vision. He'd never played video games—even as a kid his hands had been too big for the controllers—but he imagined this was how it felt. His objective was secondary to the more immediate crisis he'd been presented with, and that crisis was a sword twisting in his back. Nothing looked familiar or tangible. The walls could turn to smoke at any moment, so he needed to get the required information and get back to the objective.

If, in fact, that objective still existed.

A deafening ring started in his head, making his steps waver. He couldn't think in terms of what-ifs yet or nothing would get accomplished. Nothing would move forward, because he would turn to stone. Already, his limbs felt like they were swimming through cement as the undercover squad meeting came to a standstill around him.

Henrik found Polly, much like he'd found her the first time they'd met. Always inches away from Austin, her now-boyfriend. And always calculating. But there was a difference in both Austin and Polly since coupling up, like an unbreakable alliance had been formed. One that Henrik could freely admit was formidable with Austin's skills as a con man and master of disguises. Add in Polly's hacking abilities and they were invaluable to the squad. A fact they made no qualms about flaunting.

Henrik made sure he had Polly's attention. Then he removed the bloody knife from his pocket and tossed it on the dirty floor. "She wasn't *there*."

If he'd been in a room full of cops—or even law-abiding citizens—they would have already exploded with questions. *Where did you get the knife? Who wasn't where?* However, Henrik was in a room with Bowen and Connor, former gang members from Brooklyn. Erin, a pyromaniac and accomplished escape artist. Seraphina, a rogue cop whose revenge plans had once almost gotten her killed. Austin, a con man with a God complex, and expert hacker, Polly. So instead of asking the typical questions, they all leaned back in their chairs and waited, watching through their own unique, dysfunctional lenses to consider their play. Distantly, Henrik wondered if the smoke coming out of his ears was white, blue, or possibly a light shade of purple.

"She wasn't there," Polly repeated, having the decency to look a little pale. "But the knife *was*?"

Henrik's chest tried to cave in. "That's about right. Signs of a struggle outside, too. She's gone. And that might be her… blood, *goddammit*." He drew a long breath that hung in his neck like dangling razor blades. "Why don't you have your laptop out yet?" Incidentally, another device for which his fingers proved too large. "Get it *out*."

Austin came to his feet beside Polly, his once-nemesis. "I understand your frustration, old boy. But you're going to want to rethink your tone."

Derek blocked Austin from Henrik's line of vision. Only

then did it occur to Henrik that the captain hadn't asked any questions, either. Attempting to blend in with the team he'd built? Or had the line between cop and criminal become just as blurred for Derek as it had for Henrik? Didn't matter. He couldn't question the captain's motives now. He had to find Ailish. He'd stopped second-guessing his sanity and embraced the lunacy of finding this girl he didn't even know. And it felt good, simply allowing the need to rule him. He'd explore his motivation after he knew she was safe.

"Who are you referring to, Henrik?" Derek asked, wariness in the lines of his shoulders. "Or do I already know?"

Henrik stayed silent, giving the captain his answer.

"Jesus Christ." Derek raked a hand down his face, then turned to Polly. "You lied about Ailish O'Kelly being off the radar. You said you were working on pinning her down, but you already had."

Austin spoke before Polly could respond. "My fault, as usual." Cockiness laced the Brit's tone. "We needed leverage on Henrik, and Polly, darling genius that she is, procured it. But it was *my* plan. So direct your outrage at me, if you please."

Of course, the arrogant con referred to his and Polly's scheme to draw their own big-fish enemy out into the open last month, by using Henrik as bait. They'd made the claim to their mark, who also happened to be Austin's ex-business partner, that Henrik was willing to throw an underground fight for a big payoff. In exchange for participating in their con, Polly had given Henrik Ailish's location, the fruit borne of hours spent hacking security cameras and cell phone towers.

Bowen's chair scraped back, the ex-Brooklynite jumping up to pace, his usual restless energy a living thing inside the room. "Man, Austin. I won't ever get used to the way you talk. And I sure as shit don't want to."

Henrik ignored the verbal posturing that ensued between

Austin and Bowen—and the quiet patience with which Bowen's girlfriend, Sera, attempted to calm them—focusing instead on what Derek had revealed. "You asked Polly to look for Ailish O'Kelly?" He took a step closer to the captain. "Why? We cleared her of charges. In case you forgot, that's the reason I'm not wearing a badge anymore."

"Oh, I didn't forget. It's the same reason I didn't tell you we *are* looking for her." Derek shook his head. "You might have destroyed the evidence against her, but she's still an asset in the case against her father."

Henrik resisted the urge to check his stomach for holes. "You can't put her on the stand. They won't let her live to see the trial."

"I have no such plans." Derek paused, obviously taking Henrik's measure. "She'll be more useful to us inside the house."

"Hell no. Not happening." Henrik schooled his features so they wouldn't portray the worry eating him alive. "If she lit out of Chicago, even as a free woman, she had good reason. Caine. And he might have already gotten to her."

A hand patted him between the shoulder blades in the rhythm of "Shave and a Haircut." Erin. Had to be. His guess was proven correct when the blonde stepped into his tunnel vision. "She's *probably* alive."

Connor, Erin's ex-SEAL boyfriend, who was never far behind the blonde, cleared his throat and drew Henrik's attention. "If you hadn't found the knife, I would assume her father found her. Caine O'Kelly is a ruthless bastard, but I can't imagine he would want his own daughter killed in cold blood."

Erin tilted her head. "Not without saying good-bye first."

Henrik held up both hands in a request for silence. "No more theories. No more guessing. I need facts." He turned to send Polly a pointed look, but she already had her laptop open. Her fingers stopped flying over the keyboard long enough to flip him the bird before she went straight back to typing, while Austin looked on proudly from his lean against the wall.

"What do you plan to do with those facts?" Derek asked. "You're not operating on your own this time. You've already proven you're far from objective where Ailish O'Kelly is concerned."

There was a surge of adrenaline that always rushed through Henrik before a bout, when everything in his body went loose, apart from his fists. It happened now, the familiar slide into no-man's-land, causing his decreased vision to narrow even further, further until all he could see was the bloody knife on the ground.

But he beat back the claustrophobic feeling and forced himself to breathe, to *think*. If he displayed nonobjective behavior, Derek and the squad would have no choice but to cut him out. And this dank basement of an abandoned community center was all he had left to his name. He'd been given a reprieve from prison—sent to purgatory with other misfits just like him. Now compromises needed to be made. Oh, he *would* find Ailish. Wouldn't stop until he'd achieved that end. He couldn't, however, risk being cut out of the picture once he did.

Henrik gave Derek his full attention. "You've got it out for Caine O'Kelly. I understand. Your department has been trying to make something stick since I went through the academy." He swallowed the discomfort the next part instilled. "You need Ailish in order to do that? Fine. But we both know what I'd put on the line for her best interest. If you want to bring her back to Chicago—before anyone else goes after her with a butcher knife—I can guarantee I'm the one who'll get her here safely."

A muscle ticked in Derek's jaw. "Polly?"

The hacker punched a few more keys. "I've got a hit. Do you want the good news or the bad news?"

"*Bad*," everyone answered at the same time, except Henrik, who desperately needed some good news. *Fucking cons.*

"Is it too late to choose prison over joining this team?" Henrik wondered out loud.

Polly shrugged. "Sorry, buddy. The masses have spoken. Bad news is, Ailish is either out of money or foolish. Good news is, she's alive." The printer on Derek's desk began to spew out documents, thankfully disguising the deflated sound that whooshed from Henrik's mouth. "A big-box store north of Wisconsin ran a credit report on Ailish a few hours ago. She must have applied for a store credit card. Not too smart when you're trying to disappear, but who am I to judge?" Polly closed the laptop and examined her nails. "Anyway, she's moved north to the Great Lakes state."

Weight fell from Henrik's shoulders, allowing him to skirt the group and retrieve the printed documents. "Michigan."

"Yes," Polly continued. "When you get to her—and please note my agreement that *you* should be the one to go—make sure she keeps her cell phone off. Last time she turned it on, her father called. Good for us, because I traced her location via a cell phone tower. Bad for her if Caine O'Kelly has an employee with rudimentary tracing skills."

"God, but I love my girl," Austin murmured.

Derek considered him for a beat. "Get moving, Vance. You've got a week to get Ailish O'Kelly back here, or I'll do it myself," he said, stepping into Henrik's personal space and lowering his voice. "Listen, this department would place a lot of value on the man who finally managed to roll O'Kelly. You accomplish that? You'll have my full support to be reinstated as an officer."

In the midst of his urgency to drive like a bat out of hell to

Michigan, the captain's unexpected delivery of hope almost wasn't welcome. Too good to dwell on when his priorities were so firmly elsewhere. But the hope wouldn't be denied. Not completely. It started in his stomach and rolled out like a ripple effect. Cautious, but alive. "I don't know what to say."

"Say you'll do the right thing. Bring the girl back for your own sake." He tipped his head forward, eyebrows drawn. "And for the love of everything holy, keep it in your pants."

The first time Ailish ran away, she was thirteen. She'd walked out of her all-girls private school and saw the black town car waiting for her at the curb, the bulky man in sunglasses waiting to bring her back to the walled prison she called home. She remembered that afternoon so clearly because it had marked a week since her mother left. Just…left. Sure, the relationship between Caine and her mother had been volatile, but she hadn't even tried to keep Ailish. Hadn't even said good-bye.

Gangster. Evil. Murderer. Words her classmates whispered as they passed her in the hallways, in reference to her father. For a thirteen-year-old girl who'd just essentially lost her mother, any excuse to run away had been welcome. Run away from the male-dominated house, a father who became less recognizable by the day, her new, confusing hormones. So many ambiguities in her life and nowhere to turn. So she'd booked it, without any idea of where she might end up.

The man in sunglasses had caught up with her at the corner noodle shop. She could still remember that frigid fear of being cornered. That realization that she couldn't survive on her own, even if she got away. No money, no friends. A severe lack of social skills, thanks to her sheltered existence.

That hadn't stopped her from trying. Again and again.

If anything, Ailish's faith in humanity had been restored

since leaving Chicago. A ramshackle car dealership just outside of Green Bay had traded in her car with no questions asked, giving her a few hundred dollars on top of it, due to the difference in quality of the vehicles. The cash had been sorely needed since Cubs Hat's greed had left her broke back in Wisconsin. She didn't realize until later, when a Walmart employee bent over backward to help her apply for a store credit card, that the black eye was responsible for everyone's apparent sympathy. Not wanting to give a false impression, Ailish had explained to the employee that she was just fine. There was no need for concern. But she stopped when it became apparent her words were falling on deaf ears.

Once she'd reached the small waterside city of Escanaba, Michigan, she'd been given the same careful once-over upon walking into the cabin rental office. Based on the other clientele milling around, the cabins were rented mostly by fishermen and families looking for a quick weekend at the lake. But the woman behind the counter had handed her a key, asking only for a small deposit. Unfortunately, that small deposit had cleaned her out. Tomorrow she would need to think about a temporary job. Maybe renting fishing gear, or—

Creak.

Ailish dropped the Cup Noodles, wincing when the hot soup splashed up onto her bare legs. *Not again.*

This time, however, she was better prepared.

She jogged to her twin bed, lifted the mattress, and removed the nine-millimeter she'd stolen from Tall Man's waistband while fleeing from the guesthouse in Wisconsin. After which she'd thrown up in the dirt. Twice. Right now, though, she was sure as hell glad she'd taken the weapon.

Ailish positioned her legs shoulder width apart and pointed the gun at the cabin's only entrance. When she caught her reflection in the mirror, she deflated a little. No one looked threatening in a Disney Princesses T-shirt—courtesy of the sale section at Walmart—and no pants. She probably didn't have time to change, right?

The doorknob jiggled and Ailish stifled a gasp. Inhaling nice and slow, she steadied the gun. Ready. She was ready for whomever her father had sent. They weren't good men. They were men who killed for a living. She had to remember that.

Another creak outside on the porch. "Ailish O'Kelly?"

The booming voice startled her—and then she heard a *pop*. Followed by a pained growl. Ailish stared at the hole in the door in disbelief before transferring her attention to the gun in her hand. It was hotter than it had been a moment ago. She'd fired a bullet? How was the possible? No…it wasn't possible. She'd barely grazed the trigger.

"*You shot me?*"

Okay, maybe she *had* pulled the trigger. Oh God. What would she do if this unknown person died? Worst-case scenario, she'd planned to aim for their leg and call an ambulance while she slipped out the side window. But the bullet had fired high. "Are y-you okay?"

A long pause. "I don't know how to answer that."

Ailish set the gun down on the rickety wooden dresser before thinking better of being weaponless and picking it up again. "Who are you? Did my father send you?"

"No." A gritted curse. "I'm…with the Chicago Police Department."

Her stomach dropped. "I don't know which one is worse."

A quick expulsion of laughter. "Trust me, your father is worse. I'm here to make sure he doesn't touch you." While Ailish was processing that surprising news, the man spoke again. "He got to you in Wisconsin, didn't he? I found the knife. I thought you'd been stabbed, but now I'm beginning to think"—his breathing was becoming labored—"beginning to think *you* might have done the stabbing."

God, she absolutely shouldn't be feeling guilty right

now. "Well, you shouldn't have been sneaking around on my porch."

"There's no light out here." There was a loud *thump*, as if he'd leaned against the doorjamb. "I was checking the cabin number to make sure I had the right one."

Oh. "What do the police want now? They released me."

"Yeah, I heard." The man didn't speak for a while. "Look, I'm here to talk about your options, Ailish. We need something solid on your father, and we can accomplish that through you. It would mean an end to the running. And the end to a lot of unnecessary violence in Chicago."

A hand closed around her throat. "I can't do that. I—whatever he's done, he's my father."

"Nothing has to be decided tonight. And when the time comes, *you'll* be doing the deciding." He didn't continue for a few, heavy seconds. "I'm not here to force you into cooperating."

Holding the gun down at her side, Ailish glided toward the door. There was a certain way her father's men spoke. Rough, careless. This man reminded her more of the cops who'd interrogated her. He inspired trust, even as he represented the possible end of her new lifestyle. She knew better than to be lulled into a false sense of security, however, especially by a voice alone. Opening the door and bandaging his wound didn't pose a threat, though. Not so long as she had the gun. And her rights.

"I'm opening the door."

"Okay."

She settled her palm over the doorknob. "What's your name?"

"Henrik. Henrik Vance."

Goose bumps lifted on her arms. Something about the way he'd said his name. Like a vow that he would be giving Ailish a good reason to remember it. Beyond curious to see the man's face, she took a calming breath and opened the door. And found herself eye level with his heaving chest.

Huge. He was…*huge*. Her neck craned back, further and further, to find his head resting against the doorjamb, beneath a crooked elbow. Awareness flitted through her belly when those eyes pegged her through the darkness, holding her gaze like he was in no hurry to let it go. Nighttime wrapped around the man, giving him an air of danger, but his stillness kept it from breaking loose. He appeared to be…allowing her to get used to his size. The air of a cop, minus the knowing smirk she was used to receiving.

Realizing they'd been locked in a stare-off for far longer than was normal, Ailish forced herself to look down—and saw blood spattering the top of his shoulder. "Oh God. I shot you. I shot a cop."

Her words seemed to startle him out of some fog. "I'm only an honorary cop now. Don't even have a badge to show you." His eyebrows drew together. "You know, you really should have asked to see my badge."

"You just said you didn't have one." Did he really just stifle a laugh? Maybe he was going into shock. Lord, that was the last thing she needed. She'd never be able to drag him inside. Not without a crane or maybe a tractor. "I think you should come inside so I can try to keep you alive."

"I'll come inside when you put some pants on."

That awareness in her belly spun like silk around a fist. He hadn't even looked down, as far as she could tell. Not once. The reservations she had about Henrik thinned. Too easily? Yes. She'd grown up constantly surrounded by men, and she'd never felt comfortable with a single one of them. Why wasn't she more wary of *this* man? She would have to think about it later when blood wasn't pouring from the wound she'd inflicted.

"Hang tight. I have some leggings…" Ailish sidestepped

out of his view to riffle through the dresser one-handed, until she realized the gun was still clutched in her other hand. With a glance at the doorway, she buried the weapon underneath some underwear and quickly tugged on a pair of black capri leggings. "Okay. Come on in."

With one big hand clapped over his wound, the guy literally had to duck under the doorframe. And as soon as Henrik stepped into the light, recognition tugged at her consciousness, like a fishing line with a wiggling catch at the end. His features were unique—not the kind one came across more than once in a lifetime. Although he was at least half African-American, his distinct brow and cheekbones reminded her of the Eastern European men who occasionally met with her father to talk business. She often found their appearance bold or sharp. This man wouldn't have been an exception if it weren't for the softness in his eyes, the inviting curve of his mouth.

He was, in no uncertain terms, *dramatically* handsome. His current status of gunshot victim made his movements stilted, but she somehow knew with confusing certainty that he usually walked with a swagger. Fluent, irreverent. Confident.

Her father always said she'd been gifted with his ability to never forget a face, and Ailish was positive she'd met this man somewhere before. Seen the way he moved. Not a doubt in her mind.

"Do I know you from somewhere?"

His progress toward the bathroom halted, just a tiny stutter, but she caught it. "No. I've only seen your picture in the file. Never face-to-face."

Ailish frowned and followed him into the bathroom, where he'd flipped on the light. Hovering in the doorway, she watched him in the mirror. "Are you sure, because—" He took his shirt off. "Hhhhoshit."

Henrik passed a glance over his shoulder. "What was

that?"

"Uh." Ailish turned and lunged for her plastic bags of supplies, lined up against the wall of the main room. "I bought a first aid kit. That's what…I said. Band-Aids and gauze. Other stuff and…stuff." When she sensed Henrik face the mirror again, she couldn't help peeking up at his reflection. The man's torso was like a rock-climbing wall. Muscles so defined, they swelled out, like they were waiting to be used as footholds. Arms like cannons. But holy hell, his butt took the mother-loving cake. The very top curved above the back waistband of his jeans, like two ski slopes made of solid male muscle. She had the sudden urge to slap his backside.

How rude was that when she'd already shot him?

"You all right down there, Ms. O'Kelly?"

"*Yes.*" First aid kit in hand, she sidled around his distracting form to get between him and the sink. She cringed when she saw the ripped skin of his shoulder, but decided it could've been much worse. It looked like she'd just grazed him, thank God. "You should probably call me Ailish. Since I shot you and all."

His throat moved in a sensual slide of muscle, surely meant to hypnotize the opposite sex, but he didn't look at her. Had he really *looked* at her since coming into the cabin? She decided she would remember that.

"Ailish, then," Henrik rumbled. And finally, finally, his golden-brown gaze fell to her face. "How did you get that black eye?"

Alarm trickled into her blood at the transformation that overcame him. She would swear he expanded, like the Hulk, ready to burst straight out of his skin. As if she'd just received the injury, her fingers lifted to prod at the puffiness. Test the spots that hurt worse than others. "I think your bullet wound is a slightly more pressing issue."

Ailish could actually hear the grinding of his teeth.

"*Answer* me."

"No." She rooted through the kit for a bottle of peroxide and cotton. "I don't like being ordered around. And I'm very stubborn when I feel like it."

His breathing slowed, but he appeared quite unsatisfied with her lack of cooperation. "If you tell me who hurt you, I'll forgive you for shooting me."

Her chin dropped. "You won't forgive me otherwise?"

A moment passed before Henrik shook his head. "Uh-uh."

Ailish huffed a breath. "I don't know why I care." She unscrewed the cap on the peroxide with jerky movements and threw the cap into the sink. "Don't you wonder why *you* care so much about *my* black eye?"

"No. I don't wonder."

"*Well*." Just what the heck was that supposed to mean? "Then I guess we can't be friends, Henrik. It's too bad, because you wanted to laugh at my lame joke back on the porch. No one *ever* laughs at my jokes. And you can't even feel bad about it because we're not friends."

His expression was indiscernible. "You're nothing like I expected."

"What am I supposed to say to that?"

Henrik's throat did that hypnotic muscle slide thing again, as he planted his fists on the sink and leaned forward. Close. They were suddenly *so close* and she forbade herself to breathe in case he found oxygen intake offensive and pulled away. "Ailish?"

"Sup."

The corner of his mouth jumped. "If you tell me the blood on that knife I found in Wisconsin belonged to the man who blackened your eye, I still won't be happy, but I might be able to sleep tonight."

Wariness blew across her senses, but its presence had

little to do with an honorary cop asking her about witnessing a stabbing. It was more about wanting to tell him everything she'd been through since leaving Chicago. Maybe even *before* leaving. She'd never had a confidant before, and his eyes were so stabilizing. *Everything* about him was. But she'd been raised to keep her mouth shut at all costs. "I can't tell you that."

Henrik inclined his head, face betraying his obvious satisfaction. "Baby, you just did."

Chapter Three

Yeah. Despite the promise Henrik had made to Ailish, there was no way in hell he was sleeping tonight. There had been a significant part of him that wondered if the initial impact of Ailish that day in the park was all in his head. That his memory of her beauty, the husky notes in her voice, had been embellished over time to justify what he'd done to keep her out of prison.

Oh no. She actually had the nerve to be *better* than his memory. He'd expected quiet dignity. Or caginess. Why wouldn't the daughter of a violent crime boss be cautious and jaded? Instead, however, she was this irresistible fucking combination of wit and innocence, rolled together in an adorably sexy package. And after fantasizing about her for months, here they were, crammed inside a bathroom, Ailish in pajamas with no bra underneath, him without a shirt. If this were one of his fantasies, his next move would be pushing her forward over the sink, tugging down those tights that clung to her ass, and railing her from behind.

This was not one of his fantasies, though, and Ailish didn't know him from a hole in the wall. She shouldn't have let him into the cabin without some identification, let alone be pressing her body up against him as she tended his wound. Her lips were pursed as she worked, blotting away the excess blood with breathy little apologies that made him feel like a bastard for the creative ways he'd dreamed of screwing her senseless. Yeah, she definitely wouldn't want to be in such close quarters with a man who'd imagined her kneeling enough times to sustain permanent rug burns.

Couldn't he have pictured her doing something innocent at least once? Knitting, picking flowers, reciting poetry... anything.

He should leave the bathroom now. Fix his own bandage and pop a few Advil. But dammit if his feet weren't buried in concrete, refusing to carry him away from Ailish. Her scent reminded him of summertime, all sunbaked and fresh. God, he couldn't inhale it fast enough. She had a twitch, too. It was so subtle, most people probably didn't even notice it, but every couple minutes, her right eye did a little half wink. Like a wince, but a million times cuter.

Unfortunately there was nothing cute about his cock at the moment. Between finding Ailish gone in Wisconsin, driving back to Chicago, then immediately turning around and speeding north to Michigan, there had been scant time for stroking off, a task he'd been performing on a regular basis since the day she'd spoken to him in the park. Had it been three days since he'd found her missing? Four? Having the object of his lust so close was a recipe for disaster in his restless state. Already, moisture crowned on the head of his dick where it laid swelling inside the right leg of his jeans. He should move away now. This was a job. He'd come here to protect her, not assuage his sick infatuation.

A waterfall of red hair got in the way of her ministrations so she shoved it back over her shoulder, sending a waft of summertime into the air. "How did you find me, Henrik?"

Oh fuck. Don't go saying my name. "We tracked your cell phone to a tower about eight miles from here. This was the closest rental park, so I took a chance. A phone call from my superior convinced them to be helpful at the front office." His hand flexed at his side with the need to adjust himself. *Don't do it. She'll notice.* "We need to destroy your phone as soon as possible. If we tracked it, someone else could do it, too."

"My father, you mean," she murmured, before ripping a piece of white medical tape with her teeth, nearly wrenching a groan from Henrik. "You keep saying *we*. Who is we?"

"I work with an undercover squad." His voice emerged like a growl rippling through a dark tunnel. "Sort of an unofficial branch of the police department. We're not technically cops, we just do their dirty work."

"And I'm considered dirty work?"

"That's not what I meant," Henrik said. "There's nothing dirty about you."

She looked up at him through a sea of black eyelashes. "You'd be surprised."

Even though he was fully aware she couldn't possibly have meant the rejoinder to sound sexual, Henrik's hungry thoughts had a hard time processing it any other way. Jesus, he needed to get some air before he did something embarrassing. Or against the rules. But the depraved man on the inside, the one who finally stood in front of the woman who'd robbed his concentration for months, wanted to press her into acknowledging an awareness between them. To prove he wasn't alone. "Some men might take what you said as an invitation, Ailish. Are you always so reckless?"

"Invitation for wha—" Her head came up, gaze focusing on him. "Oh. Well." Her gulp was audible. "I guess you're not talking about a party."

I'm going to hell for wanting to corrupt this girl. "No. I'm not." *Deep breath.* "But I should be. I should be talking to you about anything *but* invitations. Like your favorite pizza toppings or scary movie."

"Pepperoni and *Poltergeist*," she whispered. "But to answer your first question...yes. I am reckless. *And* stubborn. We've only been friends for five minutes and you already know my two greatest faults."

It must have been the way she couldn't stop staring at his mouth, but God help him, he stepped closer, careful to keep his hips angled away, so she wouldn't feel his erection. "You forgot about dirty."

"No, I didn't." Her cheeks went pink, and Henrik couldn't help dipping his head, letting his mouth hover over her right one, just to feel the radiating heat. They flushed even pinker. "I didn't forget, but if I tell you my third fault, you might think the bad outweighs the good. I've already shot you, Henrik. I haven't really had a chance yet to put my best foot forward."

Ailish's logic made him desperate as hell to kiss her. He wanted to tug her chin down and get his tongue so deep, she'd moan and press her thighs together. "Put your best foot forward tomorrow. Right now, I want your third fault."

"You won't like it."

His lips brushed her cheek, and she gasped. "Let me be the judge."

This was bad. Very bad. He'd been in her presence for twenty minutes and already he inched toward breaking the rules. She was a potential asset under his protection. In his care. Touching her could jeopardize the case, his job, and the possibility of earning back his badge. His good name. Worse, she didn't know a disgraced cop stood in her midst. She didn't know what he'd done on her behalf. For all he knew, that knowledge would make her run screaming in the opposite direction. *Shit*, though. It just felt so goddamn perfect to be this close, to hear her breath racing in and out.

"Henrik, I'm—" Her words cut off abruptly when she stepped too close. One of her thighs rubbed against his dick, and those eyes shot wide. Henrik focused on staying very still. Focusing on *not* slamming her hips up against the sink and humping her pussy through the thin tights. He could come that way. *So easily.* God, if she knew his thoughts, she would be horrified. Any second now, she would slap him. Or sprint a hundred miles an hour from the bathroom. Right?

Wrong.

Ailish smiled.

She lifted her hands and clutched handfuls of her hair, excitement dancing across her features. "Is that for me?"

Ailish was an unrepentant tease.

It was her third and most heinous fault.

Junior year of high school, she'd fallen behind in her advanced literature class. Words had never been her strong suit. Numbers. She'd always loved numbers much more. Thankfully, her private school had an active tutoring program with college-aged teaching students looking to get work experience. Ailish's tutor, Chris Nussbaum, had been on the skinny side and always wore the same green hoodie. But she'd liked him. He'd obviously liked her back, too, because he'd made his move during their third literature lesson, taking her innocence on a wobbly wooden desk while tutoring sessions continued in the next room.

The experience had been less than satisfying, but she hadn't exactly expected to reach the Promised Land on attempt number one. Trying would be fun. Or so she'd thought. Late one afternoon, the driver sent to pick her up from tutoring had caught Ailish and Chris sharing a kiss behind the school. Her father had been informed of her budding attachment to Chris, and she'd never seen him again, except in the pictures he'd posted on Facebook of his time in Saint Anthony's Hospital ICU. He'd credited a fall down the train station steps, but Ailish had known her father's men were responsible.

Severe guilt caused Ailish to swear off men. But doing so had *really* pissed her off. She'd felt powerless. Small. Until one day she'd caught one of her father's men checking out her butt and shaking his head in the reflection of the car's passenger side door. A tiny ball of fire had lit in her belly. And she'd regained a little power each time it happened. She filed those hungry expressions away and withdrew them late at night when she felt restless. Knowing she'd turned a man on, starved him a little, was enough to excite her. Enough to push her over the edge as her heels dug into the mattress, as she kicked at the sheets. And as an added bonus, her actions didn't put anyone in the hospital.

Ailish hadn't been teasing Henrik *at all*. She'd been too focused on his injury to notice much else, but he had all the classic symptoms of a teased male. His fists were balled, his breathing uneven. The bulging line of his arousal was *breathtaking*, a damp spot marking where the head sat, wedged inside the leg of denim. All because she'd been standing close to him? Ailish's heart sped up. Imagine how he would react when she *really* turned it on.

"You shouldn't be smiling right now."

"I know." She chewed her bottom lip. "Isn't it awful?"

Suspicion tempered the heat in his gaze. "What's the third fault?"

Thrills raced up and down Ailish's back, weaving into her hair. "I like to torture men, Henrik. Maybe your undercover squad should have sent a woman."

She knew her nipples were in hard peaks by the way he shuddered while looking down at her breasts. "I don't understand."

Ailish dropped her attention to the vee of his legs. "Are you sure?"

"Eyes up," he rasped. "An answer, please."

Never having been required to put her affliction into words before, it was difficult for Ailish to form an explanation. "I've learned to be satisfied when a man wants me. But…I don't actually let him. Have me, that is."

"Jesus Christ." Henrik's laughter was chock-full of pain. "I deserve this. That's the fucking kicker."

"*Why* do you deserve it?"

He raked both hands down his face. "You don't want to know, Lish."

She wanted to push, but her stubborn nature wouldn't allow it. If he didn't want to tell her, she wasn't going to beg. "You have a pet name for me already. Can I come up with one for you?"

"I'd prefer you didn't."

"Why?"

"Because I might like hearing you say it a little too much." His attention was locked on her mouth. "I can't have this conversation with a hard dick, Ailish."

She sucked in a breath. "Do you have a plan to make it soft?"

His crack of laughter made her jump. "That plan can't involve you."

"Why?"

"*Damn*, you ask a lot of questions."

Ailish's shoulders sagged under the weight of disappointment. "Oh *God*. I have a fourth fault now, too?"

Henrik's sigh blew her hair back like a stiff gust of wind. "While I'm with you, Ailish, I'm working. There are lines I can't cross."

Even knowing it was a little evil, nothing could suppress

the pop of excitement in her belly. She was alone with a man—a gorgeous man—who wanted her. But had to keep his hands off. It was a tease's paradise, and they were both screwed. Or *not* screwed, depending on your point of view. "We can't sleep together."

"No." He dropped his needful gaze to her breasts again. "We can't."

She executed her best nonchalant shoulder shrug. "Oh."

"You're smiling again."

Ailish couldn't stifle her chuckle. Man oh man, she really liked this big ol' bruiser, and they'd only just met. He deserved a fair warning about what he was getting himself into. "Henrik, you should probably put as much distance between you and me as possible. I really like that you want me. And I probably won't be able to help trying to keep it that way." She drew a lazy circle on his abdomen with her index finger, watching in awe as the ridged muscle shuddered under her touch. "For instance, I'd love to tell you I'm wearing cheap white panties and you can see clear through them in the right light."

His body did this kind of *heave*, right at Ailish, flattening her backside against the sink. Their mouths were suddenly so close, she could feel his hot puffs of breath on her lips, feel his chest lifting and falling where it met her breasts. "I don't like hearing that you've talked to other men that way."

"I haven't," she whispered. "I don't. I usually just—"

"I do *not* want to know."

Henrik made a subtle move, just a downward roll of his hips that dragged his erection over the crotch of her leggings. But it wasn't really subtle at all because he stopped right over her clit and nudged forward. She nearly jumped out of her skin, it was so unexpected, her body's deluge of need so extreme. "*H'oh boy.*"

His mouth sifted through the hair covering her ear. "Tease me as much as you want. Just don't try to send me packing again. Are we clear?"

"I told you I don't like being ordered around."

He rasped the stubble of his jaw against her neck. "You'd love the way I do it."

Ailish's outrage was shattered when Henrik pulled away, leaving her to sag back onto the sink. "You're not the only one who can tease." Her mouth hung open as he backed through the doorway into the bedroom. "Where do you keep those see-through panties?"

What had just happened here? She couldn't deny her curiosity over wanting to see what he did next. Not very many things surprised her, but this man—he couldn't seem to stop. Brow knit, Ailish pointed toward the top drawer of her dresser. She watched as Henrik remove a single pair, examined them a moment, and stuffed them into his back pocket.

"I'll be watching the cabin, but you won't see me until tomorrow morning. We'll talk then about why I've been sent and your potential role in the investigation." He paused at the door. "You're safe, Ailish."

Finally, she found her voice. "What about you?"

He arched an eyebrow.

"Men who anger my father don't last long. Especially when I'm involved." She hugged the bathroom's doorframe. "Maybe that's the real reason I think you should put distance between us."

"What did I say about trying to send me packing?"

"I can say whatever I want because you just stole my panties."

He held up a shiny black device. "*And* your phone. Say good-bye."

"This friendship is over."

His laugher followed him out the door.

Ailish frowned at the entryway for a moment before shutting off all the lights and slipping into bed. Time to consider the real matter at hand. Henrik was here to take her back to Chicago, to operate against her father. A terrifying possibility. Despite her father's overprotective nature, he wouldn't hesitate to mow down his own daughter if he perceived her as a threat. Running away with his money had already accomplished that task to a certain degree, but if he realized she was working with the cops? It would be the ultimate act of betrayal.

Could she believe Henrik Vance when he said cooperating had to be her decision? What if the police had really found new evidence against her to use as leverage—and this was just a ploy to bring her in peacefully?

She might have escaped her father, but she hadn't escaped the one very important lesson he'd imparted. Trust no one.

Ailish had to get away from Henrik Vance.

Chapter Four

He'd expected her to make a break for it overnight. But as Henrik was quickly learning, Ailish had no intention of meeting his expectations.

From across the campsite, Henrik watched Ailish hang clothes to dry on the provided line, the secret smile on her face indicating she enjoyed the task. He'd wager she was humming. God, he wished he were close enough to hear which song. His mind started to conjure guesses, even though it would likely be a song he didn't expect, knowing her.

Knowing her? *Easy, man.* He'd only been acquainted with the stats from her file until last night, and those surveillance notes had done nothing to give him accurate insight.

Caine O'Kelly was known for having an irrational, hair-trigger temper that usually led to people dying—often members of his own crew. Ailish's decision to leave Chicago might have been impulsive, but she clearly knew how to play the long game. Was hanging laundry her way of sending a signal that she wouldn't bolt?

Clever girl. Too bad he wasn't buying it.

Henrik needed to be on his toes. In more ways than one.

So, the girl was a tease, huh? He'd never been teased. Not without immediate follow-through. If there was mutual interest in sex between him and a woman, they typically ended up sleeping together in short order. Not that he slept with armies of women, but when Henrik got the urge, he sought women who weren't after anything serious. For a long time, that decision revolved around his job. The demanding hours and danger he faced every day.

Then Ailish had approached him in the park, opened her pretty mouth, and every belief he'd had went from dried cement to loose sand. Since that day, there had been no other women to speak of. Now here he was. A man aching for one woman, unable to have her. But kind of hoping she'd show him a little more of that teasing nonetheless. The verdict was in—he'd lost his fucking mind.

Henrik needed to get his shit together before approaching the cabin. He'd taken his edge off last night in the backseat of his truck, winding her panties around the base of his cock and jacking off the remaining flesh. As his hand slipped up and down, he'd thought of Ailish answering the door in her underwear as she'd done, but this time she'd braced her hands on the doorframe and swayed her hips. Dipped low and eased back up, back arched to push her ass out. He hadn't hit a peak that heavy in a long time, making him wonder if he didn't mind a little teasing.

Even so, the day would be torture. Already the devil on his shoulder was urging him to bring her inside and see who could hold out the longest. Jesus. His job was to keep her safe, and that needed to take priority over his neglected johnson.

Get your head in the game, Vance.

Loins girded, Henrik climbed out of the vehicle and crossed the dirt courtyard to where Ailish was hanging a pair of smiley-face boxers. And humming the *Addams Family* theme song.

He opened his mouth to ask her where she'd managed to rustle up a Disney princess T-shirt, ugly boxers, and see-through underwear all in the same place, but she spoke first, without even looking at him. "I was wondering how long you were going to watch me." She sank her teeth into her bottom lip as she turned. "Did you like what you saw?"

Fuck. Two seconds and his resolve had already waned. *Focus. This is about her life.* Men had already come after her. Henrik was the only object standing between her and the next ones. "Talk to me about breakfast, Ailish."

"Pancakes, sausage..."

"Good. Do you have those things in your cabin?"

She clipped a sock to the line. "I have Cup Noodles and some beef jerky."

After fifteen hours without food, Henrik's stomach chose that moment to growl. Which made Ailish drop the clothespin in her hand, face lighting up like he'd just announced she'd won the Miss America pageant. Until that moment, he hadn't noticed her black eye had been covered with some type of makeup. He was grateful, since looking at the injury made him ill. Had she done it more for his benefit? Or her own?

"Was that your *tummy*?" She leveled her disbelief at the body part in question. "I didn't know they could be so loud."

"I have a *stomach*," he corrected. "Not a tummy."

Ailish gave a low whistle. "Don't take this the wrong way, but you're kind of a grump in the morning." She went up on her toes, then back down. "I just thought of your pet name."

"I told you I didn't want one." His stomach growled again, and she stifled a laugh with her hand. "All right. What's the nickname?"

She stooped down to retrieve her box of clothespins and skirted him with a smug expression. "I'll tell you when I'm ready." Halfway up the cabin steps, she stopped and turned.

"There is a diner about a mile from here, if you need to take care of the lion living in your stomach."

"Only if you come with me."

"Was there a please in there somewhere?" She tucked a lock of hair behind her ear. "I need you to say please, Henrik. I've been shuffled around and crammed into quiet rooms my whole life without one person asking me where I wanted to go. I want breakfast, too, but I'll starve right here on these steps before agreeing without a please."

He had two reactions to her speech, both of them equally potent. Rage at the ones who'd stolen her choices. Admiration that she'd spoken her mind, even though it appeared she hadn't had a lot of practice in that arena. "Please, Ailish. Will you come to breakfast with me?"

"I don't have any money."

He didn't like the note of distress in her voice. "I'm buying."

She stared off over the dirt courtyard for long moments, wheels whizzing in circles behind her eyes. "You can buy me breakfast, but I'm going to keep a running tally of our financial relationship so we stay on even footing."

It sounded like something she'd learned from her father, but no way in hell would he say that out loud. Instead, he wondered at her particular reasons. Did she dislike being in someone's debt, even for the price of eggs? Or was she afraid of feeling guilty when she attempted to cut and run? Didn't matter. She needed to eat more than instant soup. In fact, now that he knew what she'd been subsisting on before his arrival, anxiousness ate at his gut. "Fine. Keep your tally."

Her shoulders lifted and fell on a satisfied sound. "That negotiation went well, didn't it?"

"I went just fine, Lish."

She finished climbing the stairs. "I wonder if you'll still call me that when you realize I've decided to call you Growler."

Henrik only smiled after the door had clicked shut behind her. No sense in two of them being aware she'd already gotten to him. "My truck is this way," he called through the closed door.

"I have to change into something better," Ailish singsonged back.

Oh, he didn't like the sound of that. When she stepped out onto the porch in a short, loose skirt and a skintight T-shirt a few minutes later, his foreboding proved accurate. *Jesus*, those thighs. There was so goddamn much of them showing. Enough that if she bent over, they would have a situation on their hands.

On her way to the truck, she winked at him, and he groaned.

Apparently the teasing had begun.

Ailish hadn't allowed herself to wish for decent food over the last couple weeks, because eating noodles would have been an even bigger letdown. But now that so many yummy items were listed on the menu in front of her, she wanted *all* of them. Good thing the diner was packed full of people or Henrik would hear her stomach growling loud enough to match his. That would never do.

She'd woken up before dawn this morning and started to pack her things, but decided one day to hear Henrik out wouldn't hurt. After all, they'd barely scratched the surface of why he'd sought her out. Or what exactly this honorary undercover squad expected her to do. She *hadn't* stayed because she found him interesting and wanted to know more. That hadn't even factored into the equation.

Ailish took a sip of orange juice to get the lie's taste out of her mouth. "What are you going to have?"

"All of it," he answered, without missing a beat.

She fell back in her chair. "Oh, thank God. Me, too." Right on cue, the waitress showed up and took their order. It quickly became apparent Henrik had a different definition of *everything*, in the sense that he actually meant it. He ordered darn near every item on the breakfast menu, while Ailish got French toast, bacon, and eggs. "There really is a lion living in your stomach, isn't there?"

"Tell me what happened in Wisconsin."

"Lord, you are such a cop."

His coffee mug paused halfway to his mouth. "How's that?"

She gave an exaggerated sigh. "You do that thing. Where you ask abrupt questions to throw off the person being interrogated. It's not very polite when we're having a breakfast date."

He shook his head slowly. As though he were issuing a warning. "It's not a date, Ailish."

Trying to hide her embarrassment, Ailish reached for the sugar container and picked through the offerings. "That wasn't polite, either. Two friends can have a date, can't they?"

His voice was gruff. "Do you usually wear skirts like that for your friends?"

Even as a butterfly flapped its wings in her middle, Ailish let the truth tumble out. "I don't have any friends."

For what seemed like an hour, Henrik stared at her, leaving her words hanging in air, before snatching up his coffee and draining it. "Wisconsin. Please."

"That's better." Ailish prayed her cheeks hadn't fallen victim to the Redhead's Curse, when they lit up like two blazing bonfires. What on earth had possessed her to tell Henrik that hideously sad detail of her life? "Two men entered through the back door of the guest house. I threw a knife and hit the tall one. They chased me out the front door and—"

The waitress showed up with their breakfast. It was a good thing, too, since she hadn't thought through her recitation of events very well. When the waitress left again, Henrik made no move to touch his food, so she continued. "The man who I hit with the knife gave me the black eye. His partner in the Cubs cap was upset, since they couldn't take me back to my father injured. So he shot the tall man."

Henrik narrowed his eyes. "And then Cubs Cap—the shooter—let you go?"

"Yes," she answered, a little too brightly. "Better to come back empty-handed than with damaged goods, I guess."

He winced in the process of picking up his fork. "Don't call yourself that."

"Lighten up, Growler."

"Jesus, here we go." Henrik took a bite of pancakes and Ailish became a little mesmerized by the chewing movements of his mouth. The way his Adam's apple bobbed when he swallowed. "Ailish. Tell me the truth now."

She shook herself. "Huh?"

"The truth. Why did the man let you leave? If he'd taken you home with an injury, he would have gotten a pass for taking down the man who delivered it."

"You don't know that."

Henrik took another bite while considering her. "I'm not going to let it go."

Ailish stabbed her fork into her French toast, cut off a bite and put it into her mouth before she could say something mean. Like what a lousy breakfast date he was turning out to be. Henrik seemed to read the sentiment in her eyes, however, because he let loose one of those category ten sighs that she felt all the way across the table. "Okay, my turn. What does your squad want from me?"

"Specifically?" He watched her like a hunter watches a deer in the woods. "Information about the Bookie Cookie."

Ailish choked on a bite of eggs, but held up a hand when Henrik all but dived out of the booth to reach her. "I'm fine. I just…" She accepted the orange juice he offered and took a long pull. "I know Chicago PD was interested, but I didn't realize she was on *your* radar."

Henrik sat back down, looking slightly green. "You know who she is?"

Tread lightly, girl. "I've heard my father speak about her." She thought of the grueling hours she'd spent in the interrogation chair. *I can't go back there.* And it was entirely possible Henrik wanted to put her right back in that situation, despite his assurances to the contrary. "I was transporting money for the Bookie Cookie when I was arrested, but my father has always been the middleman. I couldn't help the police then, and I can't help you now."

"If you were to go home…" Henrik broke off, appearing to gather himself, before starting again. "If you were to go back to your father's house, would you be in a position to aid the investigation?"

Her skin felt too tight. "Why are you talking like a robot?"

"I have a job to perform," he enunciated. "But I don't have to like it."

Ailish could barely process that explanation, assaulted as she was by visions of men stripping out of bloody clothing in her home's foyer. Being told to remain in her room for the evening while meetings took place downstairs. Meetings that her solid wood bedroom door didn't always muffle completely. "I don't have to like it, either."

"Ailish—"

A man stopped alongside their booth, interrupting the stare-down between her and Henrik. The newcomer held out a newspaper to Henrik, seemingly oblivious to the fact that he'd intruded on a tense moment. "You interested in the sports page? Thought I'd offer instead of throwing it out."

Jaw flexing, Henrik took the paper with a nod. "Thank you."

Little multicolored pieces trickled in from her memory bank, forming a bigger picture in her conscious. Henrik holding a newspaper...those hands, loosely gripping the sides...surrounded by green. That couldn't be right. Could it? Ailish focused on his hands and let the image spread out farther. Henrik in navy blue. A color he hadn't worn since arriving last night.

"I remember where I saw you before. I remember." She was frozen in her seat, a chill settling over her skin. "In the park. You were reading the newspaper." Her fingers rose to massage the hollow of her neck. "You were wearing a badge and a uniform. Standing right next to a police car."

He stayed very still. "Ailish—"

"What is this? Are you cop or not?" Reminding herself she hadn't told him anything that could implicate her in a crime, she tried to remain calm. But she couldn't deny feeling hurt, which was silly. She'd only known him for a matter of hours. Her lack of experience with making acquaintances gave her an unbalanced perspective on what was normal. That was all. This man could very well be there to dupe her into confessing things that could put her away for a long time.

"Please stop looking at me like that."

She threw her paper napkin down on the table. "Like what? Like you're kind of maybe a liar?"

He shook his head. "God, you can't even insult me properly. How did you stay so goddamn sweet in this world, Ailish?" Apparently he didn't expect her to answer—not that she could while processing what he'd said—because he plowed on. "Stop looking at me like you're just seeing me for the first time."

"That's how it feels."

He visibly centered himself. "When you saw me in the

park, I was still a cop. I am not a cop now. The department took my badge."

Huh. She hadn't been expecting that, but her paranoia still didn't quite allow her to believe him. "Why?"

"I can't tell you that."

Ailish started to slide out of the booth. "I'm leaving."

Henrik had a good head on his shoulders, because he didn't try to argue with her. He removed his wallet, tossed a handful of bills onto the table, and trailed after her as she sailed through the diner. They didn't speak again until they were outside in the parking lot, giving her time to think. To formulate a plan. Her father would have called what just happened a game changer. When a man lied to you once, he would do it again without fail. Caine might have taught her a lot of skewed philosophies, but *that* wasn't one of them.

She started to open the passenger side door, but Henrik's hand slapped onto the car's exterior to stop her. "I'm not a cop. I told you that up front, and it wasn't a lie."

"But you *did* lie about meeting me before." Trying her best to ignore the way his body heat seemed to increase as he crowded her against the car, Ailish searched his expression. "You do remember seeing me that day, don't you?"

His head fell forward. Both hands lifted as if they were operating against his will to cage Ailish between his body and the truck. "I remember."

Pain sparked in her chest. "I'm just supposed to believe it's a coincidence that you're here now? After you were watching me in the park?"

"That's not...*no*. It wasn't like that." His shoulders were bunched, laden with tension. "They stripped me of my badge after I saw you in the park. But instead of prison time, I was put to work on the squad. I never...actively worked on your or your father's cases prior to now. Even now, my involvement is unofficial."

Had he moved closer? Like...*way* closer? She couldn't breathe without getting a nose full of man. Maybe she should stop trying to store it away like a squirrel stocking nuts for the winter. He was a possible enemy, and she should *not* want him to keep on crowding her.

"Look at me, Ailish. I'm on your side. If you don't believe anything else, believe that one thing."

She wished like hell she could just trust him, but she'd already decided on the best course of action. This taste of freedom had addicted her, and she wouldn't give it up. Wouldn't lose the ability to make her own decisions because of one beautiful man. "Was there a please in there?" she murmured.

Henrik's eyes closed, but when he opened them again, a fire had lit in their depths. "Fuck, baby." His belt buckle pressed against her belly button. "I don't know if I can keep myself from kissing you much longer. Not with all that sweet coming out of your mouth."

"Maybe you should wait until we get home." She arched her back, letting Henrik see the points of her nipples, reveling in his groan. "In case you get carried away and need somewhere to lay me down."

His breath heaved out. "Stop talking like that."

Ailish made a figure eight with her hips. "If you kiss me, you'll want to get your hands under my skirt. You can't do that in the parking lot."

"I'd like to prove you wrong."

The thickness in his voice settled in her belly like syrup-soaked marshmallows. God, she wanted to provoke him more. Her nature was singing and pawing, trying to get loose. But in order for her plan to work, she needed to be home. Needed to be with him in private.

Ailish crossed her wrists behind his neck. "Take me back to the cabin?"

Chapter Five

Jesus. If any more of Henrik's blood ran south, he'd be seeing double.

Ailish sat beside him on the bench seat of his truck, her hand resting on his inner thigh. Her breast flattened against his right triceps. They could both see the tented fly of his pants, so there was no pretending it didn't exist. It was *right. There.* Growing more swollen by the minute, as if trying to tempt her hand into making that final journey and giving him a good hard stroke.

The morning had not gone according to plan. Their encounter in the park had been months ago and so damn brief, *no one* should remember it. No one, save himself, who'd read between the lines of her statement and heard a cry for help. A cry he'd been powerless not to answer. Now he knew why. Some intuitive part of him had seen the goodness inside her. She couldn't hide it. The very idea of her behind bars with hardened criminals turned him inside out. Thank God he'd gotten rid of the evidence against her. That was the only sentiment he could muster.

Unfortunately, the girl was pissed as hell at him, despite her attempts to prove the opposite, by all but climbing onto his lap and giving him the world's most brutal erection. Even worse, he'd set himself way back in the trust department by not admitting he remembered seeing her in the park that day. He had a lot of work to do, especially if she was going to feel secure enough to testify.

As of now, Henrik was pretty sure Ailish was compiling a mental list of ways to leave him sputtering like an asshole in the dust, so returning to Chicago with her in tow seemed unlikely. But he would do his job and protect her until a decision was reached. There was a twisted part of him that hoped Caine would send a couple more men their way, just so he could send the man a message. No one touched Ailish on his watch. And *someone* would be paying for her black eye. Since the man who delivered the injury was dead, it would need to be Caine. The man who'd sent violent men to retrieve his own daughter.

Henrik released a pent-up breath. If he allowed his protective streak toward Ailish to build, there wouldn't be a hope of resisting her when they got back to the cabin. And his dick needed to stay where it belonged. Inside his pants. Already she was suspicious of his motivation, and sex would only increase that distrust. Make her question his intentions.

What exactly are *your intentions?*

As they pulled into the rental campsite, Ailish's hand inched higher on his leg. "Almost there."

You're telling me. "I told you last night, Ailish. We can't."

Okay, he'd barely managed to convince himself with that utter lack of conviction, let alone Ailish. "You said you wanted to kiss me."

"Wanting and doing are two different things."

"Now you're talking about doing." She clucked her tongue. "Make up your mind, Growler."

Jesus, she was so damn cute, he almost threw the truck into park right there, on the side of the road, just so he could tell her so. "I changed my mind about something. Last night, you said you don't usually talk to men...the way you spoke to me."

"About my see-through panties?"

"Yeah, that." He sounded like someone was strangling him. Probably because he could already feel the subsequent regret from his next question. Not to mention they were having a casual conversation about her underwear. "What *do* you usually do?"

Ailish ran her fingertips up the inside of his arm. "Little touches like this. Or straightening a tie when it's not really crooked."

Henrik stuffed down the urge to clap a hand over her mouth, make her stop talking about what she did to entice other men. But finding out what made her tick was more important.

"There was one man who worked for my dad who had to leave the room whenever I ate a Popsicle. I think he hated me a little."

Christ. Henrik might have actually felt bad for the guy if he didn't wish him permanent blindness and non-opposable thumbs. "Why do you do it?" he managed.

"Because they kept me confined. Ran my life. I needed a way to feel like I had *something*...some kind of weapon." Her touch slid ever so slightly higher on his jeans, the very tip of her middle finger brushing his cock. "Since I couldn't date, I learned to be content with being wanted."

"Yeah?" he rasped. "You must be pretty damn content."

She turned her face into his neck...and just exhaled. "No. I don't think I'd be content with just teasing you. I'd want more."

Regret didn't even begin to cover what he felt for leading

them into this little question-and-answer period. He hadn't thought it possible to need her more, but she'd slammed her foot down on the accelerator pedal of his lust like a Formula One driver. The remainder of his functioning brain zeroed in on two things she'd said. *I couldn't date...I learned to be content.* "Ailish, baby, are you a virgin?"

"No," she said, her focus on his mouth. "But I don't think that one guy in high school would be an even match for you."

It was lucky they had just reached the parking area, because Henrik might have crashed the truck otherwise. He shoved the car into park, his intention to get out of the vehicle to calm himself down. Breathe through the wild arousal his body had been gripped with. Yeah, he just needed to get out of the truck. *Now.*

Henrik yanked Ailish onto his lap sideways and fit her snug ass right over his cock. Then he gripped her hips and moved her in a circle, groaning at the friction, the openmouthed look of awe on her face. "No, Ailish, he wouldn't be a match for me. Because once I'd been inside your body, you sure as fuck wouldn't be referring to me as *the guy* afterward. I'd be *the man* whose name can still make you sweat through your clothes. The man whose name makes you cross your thighs and palm your tits. Don't ever speak about me in the same breath as the guy. Ever again."

Her wide-eyed shock lasted a few beats before her spine snapped straight. "Was there a pl—"

"Please." Lord, this girl was going to drive him crazy. "All right? Please don't ever do it again."

Ahhhh then Ailish just melted into him, her bottom doing this half scoot, half drag on his lap and wrenching a curse from the depths of his soul. With his harsh sentiment still hanging in the air, her lips settled against his. Light, light, like fog rolling in above lake water. Hell broke loose inside him despite the gentleness of her kiss, however, his bones expanding, the organ guarded by his rib cage booming, *booming*. He could actually see the white flag of surrender lifting. To the kiss. *Just* a kiss. Pulling away—especially when she suddenly seemed so unsure—was beyond his capabilities where Ailish was concerned.

Henrik licked along her bottom lip. "Part your lips for me and I'll give you a kiss." He cupped her right knee and squeezed. "But you keep your thighs together. If you open them up like you want more than my mouth, I'll stop."

"Okay," she whispered, appearing dazed. "For now."

It was on the tip of his tongue to issue another warning, but she mimicked the way he'd licked her bottom lip...and Henrik fell into the abyss. He released her knee in favor of bringing her head close, close as possible, until their mouths were meshed so tight it was an effort to work his lips. And fuck, it was well worth the effort, because she tasted like coffee and fruit and hazy afternoon sex. He couldn't even recall a time he'd experienced afternoon sex, but this is how he'd always imagined it. Slow and greedy. Mouths picking up speed, lips growing slick. Hands that grew steadily more demanding, the way his were. Twining in her long red hair, tugging, growling in answer to the way she gasped at his treatment.

She did this goddamn thing, running her fingertips over his nipples. Jesus, had he ever *liked* that before? He sure as shit did now. Even more when she seemed to sense he wanted more...and she scratched at them through his T-shirt. As if those two disks had a direct line to his cock, the swelling between his legs increased, but the flesh had nowhere to go with Ailish sitting right on top of him. Unless he moved her skirt just a little to one side and *made* room. *Don't do it.*

If he shoved her legs apart, there would be a wet spot on her panties. He knew right where it would be. And he'd want to palm that wet cotton and slide it up and down her clit. If he allowed himself that privilege, he wouldn't stop until her back was bumping against the steering wheel.

"No more," he growled at her mouth. "That's enough."

"Not enough," she panted, her fingers fidgeting with the collar of his T-shirt. "You haven't given me enough yet." Those hazel eyes were packed full of challenge as she twisted around in his lap—choking the breath from his lungs—and pushed open the driver's side door. She hopped out onto the dirt ground and threw a sultry look over her shoulder that had the impact of a right cross. "I guess I'll just take care of the rest myself."

Oh *fuck* no. That hadn't just happened. Ailish had warned him. She'd told him teasing was her thing, but he hadn't expected it to put him on his proverbial knees. Not when she came across so innocent and sympathetic. She sure as hell wasn't sympathetic toward him right now—because he was going to need a medic just watching her walk. That short floaty skirt of hers swung up beneath her ass with every step she took toward the cabin, lapping at the underside of those cheeks. Cheeks that had been wiggling around on his hard dick a few seconds ago. God*damn*, she moved like she wanted it. Wanted it bad. And apparently he'd been programmed with the responsibility to give it to her.

Resist.

Across the courtyard, two men stood looking under the hood of a truck, but when they caught sight of Ailish, their heads whipped around faster than a washing machine spin cycle. Henrik didn't bother biting back his growl as he shut off the truck and followed Ailish toward the cabin, transferring eye contact between the two men as he went. *Yeah, she isn't staying alone, so don't even think about it.*

Henrik reached the cabin door just as Ailish pushed it open. He expected her to walk straight in, but instead she did the worst thing imaginable. There was a white envelope on the threshold with the rental company's logo and the word

"Invoice" stamped on the front. So naturally, Ailish bent over to pick it up, without even having the decency to bend her knees. And after an hour of being hyperaware of the garment's abbreviated length, Henrik knew what would be exposed to anyone who happened to be watching outside. His only option was to step forward and hide her backside with his lap and upper thighs.

"Motherfucker." The shield of her skirt was gone, leaving only the barrier of his jeans...and almost nothing to the imagination. A warm pussy and taut thighs that looked flexible enough to spread with ease. She was curved to take a man the roughest way possible, and his body responded with rampant enthusiasm. Because of the innate sweetness she cloaked herself in, Henrik had never allowed himself to fantasize about taking Ailish in this position. He was a large man and was well used to holding back half his strength during sex. But Christ, presented with a stance that would be so easy to maintain with two steps forward, where he could push her facedown onto the bed and take, *take*...his composure tilted and swayed.

After an eternity Ailish straightened, a move that slid her cheeks down his erection. Instead of stepping away, she pushed up on her toes and arched her back, fitting into the notch of his lap, but in a standing position this time. And if he'd been wearing handcuffs, he would have broken straight through them. Nothing could keep his right arm from wrapping around her waist, lifting her higher, using her body to place pressure on his throbbing cock. Ailish made a little mewling noise that sounded like his name, and he lost it. He fucking lost it.

Henrik kicked the door shut and walked Ailish farther into the cabin. "Hands on the dresser." As she followed his instructions, Henrik pulled her hair aside to attack her neck with bites. "You want to tease me, you do it right."

He could see her reflection in the bathroom mirror, just a couple yards away. There was no trepidation or indecision on her face, just the fading of relief…the beginnings of bliss. This girl really did love acting the temptation, and maybe that should have irritated him. Or made him worry for the future of his sanity. Right now, it only turned him the fuck on. She was *his* naughty girl to endure. Bring it on.

"Tell me how it feels when you come," he breathed into her ear. "It'll make me so fucking hard."

Ailish's body dipped on a moan, but he caught her, instructing her with a growl to get her hands back on the dresser. "It can get harder than it is now?"

"It gets so damn hard, Lish." His mouth moved in her hair, harassing the back of her neck, her shoulders. "That few minutes before I let it bust, you would be screaming for me to stop into your pillow. But you'd be spreading your legs wider for it. You wouldn't want to let all that hard go to waste. I wouldn't let you, either."

"Oh…oh wow." Their bodies breathed together—in and out in heavy gulps—for long moments before she spoke. "I… it always starts in my knees. I don't know if that's right or not, but it does. Like a ticklish feeling."

"Mmm." Henrik's left hand slipped down the back of Ailish's thigh, massaging the back of her knee, savoring the shaking whimper his touch produced. "Keep going."

Her head fell to the side as Henrik licked across her shoulder. "H'ohhh. That feels…" He watched her hands flex on the dresser, would have smiled if he wasn't in pain. "Um. I-I squeeze my thighs really tight around my hand…"

Fuck me. "You always use fingers on that pussy, Ailish? Nothing else?"

"Nothing else."

A growl broke free without warning. Henrik slid his middle finger up the back of her thigh, slowly, so slowly, and felt Ailish hold her breath. Until finally his palm curved around the left side of her ass, rubbing the flesh beneath her skirt in circles. "My fingers are a lot bigger than yours. It would be more of a fucking than a fingering if I put my middle one down the front of your underwear. You could ride it just like a dick."

Ailish pushed her backside into his hand on a moan and he squeezed, hard enough that she shot back onto her toes. With the depraved half of him rising to the surface, Henrik leaned back and lifted Ailish's skirt, getting his first full look at her almost-bare backside. *Shit.* The girl was beyond fine. Not that her attractiveness was breaking news, but the cheap white cotton panties almost killed him. They covered everything, but hid exactly nothing. Those pretty palm-sized cheeks that had probably never been smacked, never been propped up in the air. God he wanted to be the first *everything* for that ass.

And hell, that was before she started to dance. She tossed that red hair back and started rocking her hips side to side, muscles flexing in her thighs and calves. For just a moment, Henrik was able to tear his rapt gaze from the temptation of her bottom to seek her reflection in the bathroom mirror. *Jesus.* Eyes glazed over, lips held prisoner by white teeth, she was the razor's edge of temptation. Her expression of ecstasy alone would be enough to get Henrik off for a lifetime's worth of showers, but combined with the standing lap dance she was treating him to? He'd be lucky to make it out of this situation alive.

Need just a few more minutes of this...then I'll stop...

Henrik smoothed his hand down one side of her butt. "Giving me a private show, Lish? That's real nice." He had no control over the slap his hand delivered, or the groan that sailed past his lips when her flesh shook a little in response. "I'm going to put my cock up against it again. You ready for that?"

He watched a shudder run down her back. "Yes. Please."

There was no help for him. Ailish was begging for contact with those swaying hips, that blissed-out look on her face. And *dammit,* if his erection grew any more, he'd bust through the zipper of his jeans. Friction equaled survival for him at this point. Maybe one last reminder to keep his fucking head was futile, but Henrik's common sense issued the warning anyway as he stepped forward and—

"*Ahhh. Christ.*" When their lower bodies connected, Henrik reached past either side of Ailish to grip the dresser. She worked her tight ass on his lap, giving him the dirty kind of treatment a man gets in a private room at a strip club. The difference being, she wasn't going through the motions. Her goal was to coax him into coming, draining right into his jeans. A little more of her dance and it would happen, too. He'd been dreaming of coming for Ailish since that day in the park. A significant part of him wanted to show her, too. *This is what you do to me*. But her parting shot in the car chose that moment to reverberate in his skull.

You haven't given me enough yet.

The girl might get her kicks out of teasing, but he had a feeling she just hadn't gotten something better yet. It was time someone fixed that oversight.

Henrik fisted a section of Ailish's hair and tugged her head to one side, traveling up the side of her neck with bared teeth. "Feel how big you made me?"

Her nod was vigorous. "Yes," she breathed. "I feel it."

He openmouth-kissed the spot between neck and shoulder. "You're a hot little tease, aren't you? You like knowing I could unzip my jeans, give myself a couple pumps and spill all over that pretty ass. Huh?" His palm connected with her upper thigh. *Crack.* "But I told you last night. I told you you're not the only one who can tease. Didn't I?"

Without giving her a chance to answer, Henrik turned

Ailish around, and seeing her dazed expression up close almost made him lose his train of thought. And it became imperative that he replace that confused arousal with satisfaction.

My responsibility. Mine.

Henrik maneuvered her toward the bed, using his body to guide her down onto the mattress, wasting no time fitting his dick into the notch of her thighs. *Just for a few seconds. Just a few.* Ailish was all wide eyes and shallow inhales of breath as she looked up at him, innocence so at odds with her seductress side.

Braced on his elbows, Henrik leaned down to kiss her mouth, rocking his hips forward just as their tongues met. *Goddamn.* Starbursts went off behind his eyelids, the lower planes of his stomach shaking. Somehow he found the will to end the kiss, to stop simulating the act he wanted to commit with her. "The difference when I tease, Alish?" Henrik eased down her body, lifting the hem of her T-shirt as he moved lower. "There's a reward at the end."

"What?" Her legs moved restlessly beneath him. "I—"

She broke off on a cry when Henrik bit down just inside her hip bone, nearly jackknifing off the bed. He pressed her back down onto the mattress with a palm to the chest and soothed the fading bite mark with his tongue. Then he *sucked*. He sucked the spot until it turned red, until the opposite leg tried to hook behind his neck and he was forced to pin her knee. "Breathe, Ailish," he rasped. "I'm just getting started."

Henrik moved across her body, giving the other hip the same treatment, before licking his way to the middle. Her belly button. It lifted and fell beneath his mouth, as if every part of her body had been programmed to tempt. To tease. So he gripped her hips to keep her still, noting that she stopped breathing above him.

Eyes trained on her face, Henrik hardened his tongue and stabbed it into Ailish's belly button, savoring the surprised whimper she let fly.

"Oh, we can do better than that." He slipped a hand up her rib cage to knead her breast. "Who has you on your back?"

"You. H-Henrik."

"That's right." He pushed his chin into her pelvis and moved it side to side, holding her down when she tried to fly off the bed again. When she calmed a little, he scraped his stubble against her right hip. "We're going to make sure everyone in the park knows it, too. Hold on to the sheets while you get a full body fucking from my mouth."

Chapter Six

Flames were engulfing Ailish's body. Impossible, right? It *seemed* impossible when he'd only put his tongue in her belly button. But God...*God*. There was an electric current underneath that tiny hollow corresponding to the female flesh between her legs. The first drive of his tongue had elicited arousal that usually took Ailish ten minutes to achieve. It felt like the beginnings of an orgasm. Her stomach tightened like a fist; the insides of her thighs quivered. More, she wanted more.

But this was her opportunity to get away. She'd more or less orchestrated this moment. Or at least, she'd planned to get Henrik distracted so she could make her move. Now, though? Now—

Henrik pushed his tongue into her belly button again, a slow slide of wet pressure that sent liquid to the juncture of her thighs. In preparation for a man. The harder he pushed, the more gravity built at her center. Ailish's fingers dug into the bedspread, twisting the rough material. "Oh my God. What are you d-doing?"

He shushed against the soft skin above her panty line before scooping two hands beneath Ailish's body to cradle her bottom, massaging both sides in tandem. "The only thing that matters," he grated, running his tongue around her navel, "is it's getting your pussy wet as fuck. I can feel the wet against my chest. Making me want to yank down these panties and give you my dick. What matters, baby, is you want more."

It hadn't been a question, but she answered anyway, her brain scrambling to remember the plan. *The plan, Ailish.* "Yes, I want more."

She did, too. Maybe more than getting away. And that realization is what jolted Ailish. Henrik looked so massive, so sexy, covering the bottom half of her body. A formidable male packed with shifting muscles. His hands were spread on her skin, the tips digging into her flesh and creating indentations. Their desperation felt equal. Heavy and immediate. They were in this together.

No. *No*...she needed to *separate* herself.

Henrik flexed one of his pectoral muscles and it ground against her core, hardness against soft. Hearing her own scream, Ailish slapped a hand over her mouth. Oh Lord, she'd never experienced a buildup like this on her way to an orgasm. What would it feel like? If it felt anything like the lead-up, she would implode. Henrik moved his chest muscles in tight up-and-down movements between her legs, his tongue making repeated advances into her belly button. Each stab into that shallow valley made her vision grow bleary, turned up the intensity of her stomach's quickening.

"Oh. *Oh.* You have to stop. It...I don't know what's going to happen."

His only response was a tighter grip on her bottom, his thumbs digging into the underside in what resulted in—shocker—another newly discovered erogenous zone. Arousal rushed in from all sides, like a car sinking into a river with all four windows open. It scared her. Shame followed that mental confession. After being such a tease, she couldn't even handle the tables being flipped.

Henrik's teeth sank into her hip. "I'll tell you what's going to happen." His lips skimmed their way back to the center of her belly, starting those torturous drives into the hollow once more. "You're going to get off while I fuck the bed, pretending I'm giving it to you doggy-style. And between now and the next time we touch, baby? You're going to wonder what I can do when I actually let myself attack that pussy. *That's* what's going to happen."

His blunt speech made her nipples tighten, sent her heels burrowing into the bed. *So close. So close*. But worry held her body back. Henrik would own her afterward. Ailish could sense it. She couldn't allow him to overwhelm her like this—to know he could do it whenever a situation arose where she needed placating. He'd lied to her. His intentions weren't clear. If she dropped her guard too much, she could end up imprisoned again, whether it be with her father or the police.

Dammit, this is going to hurt.

Ailish kept her attention trained on Henrik as she slipped a hand across the bed to feel around beneath her pillow. Cool metal greeted her knuckles, and she turned her hand over to grip the gun. Her resolve wavered when Henrik laid a kiss on the white material of her panties, pulling at the waistband with his teeth. If she just lay back, she would hit her climax in seconds. A climax she *craved*. But the fear of returning to Chicago, the possibility of a future planned by others, propelled her into action.

In one fluid motion, Ailish pulled the gun from beneath her pillow and pointed it at Henrik. With the opposite elbow, she scooted back on the bed to get outside of reaching distance. An ex-cop—especially one as large as Henrik—would be well capable of disarming her, and then the real trouble would begin. "Don't move," she said, sounding embarrassingly out of breath.

Still poised on his stomach, Henrik watched her through narrowed eyes. "Ailish, put the gun down. Now."

Was there a please in there? She knew better than to ask that out loud—and it made her throat ache at the reminder of their running joke. How many people could you have a running joke with in less than twenty-four hours? Probably not many, but speculation did her no good, since she'd already pointed a gun at him. For the second time. Very slowly, Ailish placed one foot on the floor, then the other, careful to keep the gun lifted and level. "I have to go now, Henrik. Just let me—" He pushed off the bed and stood at his full height, which muddled her thoughts for a beat. "I'm not going back to Chicago. Just let me leave."

They were facing off across the bed, but Henrik took a few steps toward the end, as if he would round the furniture in her direction.

"*Stop*," she ordered, wishing away the panic in her voice. "You didn't learn anything from the first time I shot you?"

"The first time was an accident." His tone was forged in steel, but did she detect a note of…hurt? "You don't want to run from me. I'm here to keep you safe. Just let me do that. Please."

His *please* made her hand droop, just a little, before she jerked the weapon back up. "That's exactly what I would say to someone I wanted to keep in line. I have a lot of experience being spoken to like that, you know? Twenty-one years." She retreated a step when he took one forward, sand granules shifting in her belly. "You know, I got caught on purpose. By the police. I *wanted* to go to prison."

Henrik became a statue, his mouth the only part of him that moved. "What did you say?"

Good question. She'd never told anyone. Had barely

acknowledged it to herself. But there was something intimate and permissive about holding a gun on the man who'd just had his mouth all over you. And nothing would stay behind the dam anymore, truth needing to flow. Be gone. "I gave the police what they needed to put me away. I couldn't be a witness anymore to my father's actions. Every day, I felt sick. Even prison was better than my father's house. But they just let me go. I still don't *understand* it. I needed that chance to atone." It felt incredible, letting go of her misery. She'd kept it inside so long. "I was trading one cell for another, but I never thought I'd be free. I am, though. I'm going to make up for my wrongs by being a good person. Someone who's nothing like my father. And if there's even a chance you'll take me back to a cell, I have to get away from you. It's…it's nothing personal."

He finally shook himself out of his eerily still state. "It's been personal since I walked in here last night. Like it or not." His gaze raked down her body, snagging on her bare thighs. "You just had your ankle hooked around my neck. Was that an act?"

"No," Ailish answered without hesitation. "I like you, Growler. I wish you hadn't lied to me, because now I have to question everything you've said."

His expression reminded her of an athlete who'd just lost a game at the buzzer. "I didn't want you to know I'd been kicked off the force."

"Why not?"

He moved a few steps closer, his big barrel chest heaving in and out. "Because I like you, too, baby."

Ailish wanted to shout at her heart for having the nerve to lift, at her gun hand for starting to tremble. How could she feel *anything* but nerves? She was running out of space, and she was on the wrong side of the bed. They needed to reverse sides if she wanted to make it to the door. Only she could barely see the door around Henrik's wide shoulders, his tight jaw.

Loathing the whimper that passed her lips, Ailish cocked the gun. "Stop coming toward me or I'll *shoot* you."

"No, you won't," Henrik murmured. "You know you can trust me, even though I fucked up. You can feel it."

Irritation blindsided her. "Kind of like I should be able to trust my own father, right?" She swallowed hard and climbed onto the bed, sidestepping her way across the pillows. "I don't know what trust is—I only know what I was taught to think. Maybe someday I'll understand what trust means, but I won't be able to learn anything if someone puts me in a cell. Or returns me to my father for good."

Rage slashed over his features and for a second, Ailish thought he might dive onto the bed to retrieve her. "I'd never let either of those things happen."

"Why? *Why* do you care so much? You barely know me." The gun was getting too heavy. She had to get away soon or her arm would drop. But it was suddenly imperative that she learn the answer to her question. It had been nagging at her since last night, and she'd only just acknowledged it. "This is just your job. I'm a job to you." She nodded once. "Right?"

His stare penetrated, reached inside and rearranged vital parts. "Ailish—"

The cabin door burst open.

A gun was leveled at Ailish.

"*NO*," Henrik roared. "*NO!*"

When Henrik was nine, his older sister Danielle took him to a carnival. As a preteen, she'd wanted nothing more than to gossip with her friends, and looking after Henrik had seriously cramped her style. Sick of listening to the girls talk about girl things—and tired of feeling like a burden—Henrik went off by himself, buying his way into the haunted house with his last ride ticket. He'd found nothing about it scary, even recognizing a few of the zombies from around the neighborhood. But there'd been this one bloodcurdling scream that had stuck with him. The recorded sound had swooped down on him as he exited the haunted house—and after hearing it only once, he could recall it perfectly.

His family believed he'd joined the force to follow in the footsteps of his father, a retired Chicago cop, but that wasn't 100 percent true. Something about fear itself made him uncomfortable. Henrik rarely experienced the emotion himself, but he hated seeing it on other people's faces. Or hearing it in their voice. To him, being a cop meant preventing and alleviating fear. That goal had always been general, not focused on any one person, until Ailish. She'd sucked every ounce of that driving force and commanded it for herself, without even realizing it.

She'd hidden it as best she could, but her terror had shown through in that interrogation room. Although he hadn't been working the case, he'd talked his way onto the opposite side of the two-way mirror. He'd wanted to tear the roof off the precinct every time they were aggressive toward Ailish. Instead, he'd come back later that night and used a stolen code to break into the evidence locker.

That haunted house scream from Henrik's memory sliced through his head now, deafening him until he could only hear a distant ringing. He was back in that makeshift carnival ride, the ground tilting beneath his feet, the air sticky with sugar. Ailish's expression went from curiosity to dread, making waves crash into the sides of his brain. Gun. Gun pointed at Ailish who liked him but couldn't *believe* him and he was already losing her and *no, no, no, please don't let this be happening*.

Time sped up again as Henrik launched himself across

the bed and dragged Ailish beneath his body. Muscle memory had him pinning the wrist holding the gun, but his mind zeroed in on her. Breathing. Okay, she was breathing. And moving. Alive. She was alive.

"*Erin*," Henrik shouted over his shoulder. "Put the goddamn gun down."

He watched as his blond teammate mimicked his order in a false man voice before holstering the weapon inside her jacket. "Maybe you didn't notice, but she had a gun pointed at you first. I thought I was saving the day, as usual."

Connor stepped into the doorway behind his girlfriend. "What the fuck."

Erin leaned back against Connor. "Sorry, baby. I couldn't wait for you to come back from the bathroom. Mafia Princess Runaway here was going to put holes in Henrik. Now they're just cuddling, though, which is nice." She reached up and scratched his beard without looking. "That's where we're at."

Connor grunted and entered the room, his sharp gaze running over everything in the space of seconds. The ex-SEAL raised an eyebrow at Henrik and Ailish's position on the bed, reminding Henrik he was probably crushing Ailish. Or maybe not, since her fingers were drawing circles on the side of his neck.

"Are you okay?" Henrik asked Ailish.

She nodded. "Are you?"

Good God, this girl was confusing. Until a minute ago, she'd been pointing a gun at him. Now she was asking after his well-being? "I've been better."

"Right." She wet her lips. "I'm not going anywhere now, am I?"

"I really don't want you to."

Ailish cast a sidelong glance at Connor and Erin, the latter of whom was perched on the dresser, hand cupped around her ear, making no attempt to disguise her eavesdropping. "I guess you better introduce me to your friends, then."

Hating the resignation in her voice, Henrik allowed Ailish to scoot out from beneath him. She stood, smoothed her skirt, and held out a hand to Erin. "I'm Ailish. It's nice to meet you. I forgive you for pointing a gun at me, since you were just trying to protect Henrik." She heaved a sigh. "I wouldn't really have shot him. Are you going to shake my hand?"

Erin looked slightly pale. "I'm working up to it."

Not wanting Ailish's feelings hurt, Henrik bent down to whisper in her ear that Erin had difficulty being touched due to a past trauma, but Ailish surprised him by giving Erin a firm nod. "Okay. Let me know when you're ready."

"Thank you," Erin muttered, scrutinizing Ailish with increased interest.

Connor stepped forward and shook Ailish's hand. "Connor."

Erin hopped off the dresser. "He's my—"

"Boyfriend," Connor finished for Erin, amusement flaring in his stoic face. "I'm her boyfriend. Sorry we gave you a scare."

Ailish's answering smile would have knocked the wind out of Henrik if he had any wind left. "Oh, you're a couple. How nice."

Needing some form of contact with Ailish, Henrik laid a hand on her hip, relieved as hell when she didn't step away. But that relief did nothing to keep him from reeling. She'd been arrested *on purpose*. Had *wanted* to serve prison time, in order to ease guilt she likely didn't need to feel. And he'd been the one to set her free. How would she react if she knew?

"What are you doing here?" he asked Connor and Erin, ignoring Ailish's disapproving look. Right now he needed to be distracted from images of her getting hit by a damn bullet. And the fact that she'd been in the process of leaving when Erin and Connor showed up. Knowing he could have tracked her down or followed was of little comfort when men were out there looking for her.

Before the door had burst open, he'd been on the verge of telling Ailish everything. How he'd destroyed the evidence, how he'd been unable to cope with the idea of her in prison. So yeah, he also needed a distraction from the possibility that after he confessed everything…she still would have left.

Connor gave him a look rife with meaning. "Talk to you outside?"

Fuck. He'd known something was wrong. "Yeah."

Ailish drew his attention by laying a hand on his forearm. "I—thank you. For trying to protect me." She stared at the bed behind him. "I've gone my whole life without having a gun pointed at me, then it happens twice within the space of a week."

He tilted her chin up with a finger. "It won't happen again as long as I'm around, Ailish."

"I don't think that will be for long," she murmured.

His brows drew together. "Why do you say that?"

Her eyes cleared, as if she'd broken free of a trance. "If Connor and Erin just wanted to talk, they could have called your cell." She glanced at Erin, who was shuffling her boots in the doorway. "You're here to take his place, aren't you?"

"Guys." Erin divided a look between Connor and Henrik. "Let's keep her."

God, I want to. Ailish's intuition and his teammates' lack of denial sent a prickle up the back of Henrik's neck. "I'm not going anywhere without her."

"You'll want to hear me out first," Connor said.

Henrik ground his teeth together and started toward the porch, but Ailish kept a hold of his elbow, drawing him up short. "Have your talk in front of me."

Erin let out a low whistle in the doorway, turning Ailish's cheeks pink. When she stepped close to him and dropped her voice, it took a massive strength of will not to back her into the bathroom and kick the door shut behind them. Just to have her to himself. "You can fix the...gap between us right now by not leaving me in the dark. I've been in the dark a long time and I-I resent it. Don't make me resent you, too."

"Ailish." Henrik tipped his head forward and breathed. *Shit.* She didn't know what she asked of him. This could repair the trust issue he'd created between them, or it could make an even bigger one. Depending on what Connor had to tell him, his involvement with her release from custody could come barking right into the open. With her safety at stake, he couldn't risk her panicking, thinking he had a fucking screw loose, and taking off. Or resenting him even more for taking away the decision she'd made for herself.

Hell, maybe he did have a screw loose, because half of him was tempted to reveal everything and let the chips fall where they may. Unacceptable when lives were at stake in Chicago the longer Caine O'Kelly was a free man.

"You ready, man?" Connor prompted from the door.

Henrik let his hand drop from Ailish's hip. "I'm sorry."

He strode away, but not before seeing the disappointment break out across her pretty features. Swallowing the guilt, he stepped out onto the porch and closed the door behind him. "What's up?"

"Oh, a few things." Connor held up a finger. "One, Caine O'Kelly has been calling in all debts. Every one of his regulars from the south side to North Park has been paid a visit, O'Kelly looking to get what's owed to him. Four bodies have turned up since yesterday morning, all with ties to the O'Kelly gambling ring."

"The ones who couldn't pay up."

"Verdict is still out, but that's the idea." Connor shook his head. "This kind of behavior is unusual, even for O'Kelly."

Henrik felt sick. "The increase in violence is connected to

Ailish disappearing, isn't it?"

Connor regarded him a moment, as if he didn't want to deliver the remaining news. "It would stand to reason, considering he just issued a reward for knowledge of her whereabouts. A fucking big one."

"Jesus." Henrik's impulse was to reenter the cabin, gather Ailish up and find somewhere less exposed, somewhere not even his teammates could find them. But he'd just snapped what little bond he'd built between them in two, hadn't he? "We need to move her soon. If he's that desperate to find her, it's only a matter of time." When Connor said nothing, Henrik stared out over the courtyard. "There's more, isn't there?"

"Yeah. Enough that Derek didn't think we should lay it all on you over the phone." The ex-SEAL cleared his throat. "Look, Caine has approached two officers, separately, since Ailish split. Asking about his daughter, why no charges were filed. It's likely Caine thinks she cut a deal with the police."

Henrik closed his eyes and focused on breathing in and out. "So that reward he's offering…it could very well be a bounty. On his own daughter."

"Possibly." For a moment, they remained silent until the ex-SEAL spoke up again. "When Caine approached those officers, he asked about you specifically, man."

"Me?" Henrik's mind landed on the only possible reason. "The department kept my involvement quiet, but not quiet enough to keep it from Caine. Maybe he already has a friend on the force."

"Money talks louder than honor."

"Yeah." Henrik turned and braced his hands against the wooden railing. "Or maybe we're wrong about Caine hunting Ailish. If he's got a cop in his pocket, he could already know I destroyed the evidence against his daughter." Henrik laughed without humor. "Maybe he wants to offer me a job."

Beside him, Connor leaned against the railing. "Either way,

we need to know. Derek wants you and Caine in the same room. That's why me and Erin are here."

Henrik pushed off the rail and started to pace. *Goddammit.* Ailish had been right. They wanted him to leave her. Already, the idea of driving away and leaving her behind made his skin feel too tight. "No, I need to be here."

"One night, man. You know Erin and I won't let anything happen to her."

He didn't want to hear it. Didn't want to consider leaving. "Even if I agree, how the hell am I supposed to get into a room with O'Kelly?"

Connor gave him a meaningful look. "I think you know."

At Henrik's sides, his hands flexed into fists.

Chapter Seven

He'd left. Not even a casual good-bye from the man who'd made love to her belly button less than an hour before. If that didn't signal she'd made the right decision in attempting to run, nothing did. She *really* shouldn't be so worked up over Henrik's lack of verbal communication, but her usual logic appeared to be lacking where the big ex-cop was concerned. Just as she'd been in her father's home, Ailish was once again a prisoner. Wasn't the definition of crazy to expect a different outcome from the same scenario? So Henrik appeared to be attracted to her? That didn't mean his own goals didn't take precedent over hers.

Yet since hearing his truck pull away, she'd vacillated between outrage and guilt. Why would he say good-bye to the person who'd threatened him with a loaded weapon? He was probably thrilled to be rid of her.

Screw that. She was glad to be rid of him, too. At the end of her pacing, Ailish kicked the cabin door, hard as she could, and listened to the conversation between Connor and Erin cease on the porch. Erin opened the door and swaggered in a moment later, Connor watching her backside appreciatively from his lean against the porch railing. Nighttime had fallen, and Ailish looked out at the courtyard and lake just beyond with envy. If this was freedom, freedom was overrated.

"You rang?" Erin said, making her way to the tiny kitchen where she flicked on the stove burner, running her hand over the flame.

"I need to get out of here."

Erin flipped off the burner with a gusty sigh. "Enough said. Let's go."

Ailish straightened. "What? Just like that?"

"If anyone knows how hard it is to be confined, it's this girl." There was a note of gravity in her voice completely at odds with her somewhat giddy expression. "Leave Connor to me. I'll meet you outside in five. For a *walk*. We're not driving to Canada. Tonight, anyway."

Not needing any more encouragement, Ailish knelt down to retrieve her tennis shoes from under the bed. She crammed them onto her feet, doing her best not to eavesdrop on the muffled conversation taking place on the porch, especially when Connor's voice dropped in timbre and Erin moaned. It made Ailish think about that afternoon, what she'd done with Henrik. Her memory continued to replay the way he'd restrained her knee, squeezing it in his grip, even pinning it to the bed at one point to keep her from closing her legs.

He'd been so...commanding. Confident in every movement of his body, his...tongue, and oh, his *teeth*. Even though her abbreviated sexual exploration with the literature tutor four years ago hadn't technically been satisfying, Ailish had always held the experience close. Treasured those too-short minutes of a man's weight, frantic hands, the evidence of lust moving inside her. However, Henrik had shed light on a sad truth. Ailish had never been with a *man*. Not like him.

She'd actually sneaked into the bathroom to change her

underwear afterward because the cotton had been clinging to her flesh. And once she'd pulled down the wet pair, leaving her bottomless in the small bathroom, she'd been powerless against the urge to touch herself. Face buried in one of the hanging towels, she'd finished in minutes, replaying the scene with Henrik in her mind's eye. Not just what he'd done with his skillful mouth. No, she'd thought of that part of him he'd kept behind his zipper. The part she'd felt against her bottom. A moving image of Henrik releasing his erection had sent Ailish hurtling past the finish line with a silent scream.

Feeling flushed at the memory, Ailish stood and curved a hand over the doorknob. Had it been five minutes? *Ready or not, here I—*

Oh, Connor and Erin definitely weren't ready. For Ailish to make her exit, anyway. They were definitely ready for *something*. Erin had her legs wrapped around Connor's waist and the man was using the porch railing to keep his girlfriend stationary as he thrust into the notch of her thighs. They were still fully clothed, thank God, but that detail did nothing to stop Ailish from being horrifyingly turned on.

"I-I'm so sorry," Ailish stammered, stumbling backward into the cabin. "I'll-just—"

"Wait." Erin blew out a shaky breath against her boyfriend's neck. "It's okay."

"The hell it is," Connor grated.

With a secretive smile, Erin whispered something in Connor's ear that had his head dropping forward onto her shoulder. One shaking hand started to curl around Erin's neck, but it dropped onto the railing instead with a *bang*. After a long pause, Connor finally spoke. "You've got fifteen minutes for your walk. Any longer and I'll come looking."

Erin lowered her legs from around his waist. "Thank you, baby." She winked at Ailish, exertion showing in her striking face. "Let's go."

Ailish and Erin followed a marked path down to the lake's edge, Erin having produced a Zippo lighter from her pocket to illuminate the path. It didn't escape Erin's notice that a shiny silver Ruger was stuffed into the back of Erin's waistband, but decided not to question it. After all, Ailish had her own Glock tucked inside the deep pocket of her jacket.

"Are you and Connor…always like that?"

"Like what? Ready to bang?" Erin's smile looked spooky in the orange glow of the lighter. "Pretty much. Ain't it grand?"

Ailish's laugh was swallowed by the darkness. "Yes. I guess it is."

They reached the shore of the lake and headed toward the lit picnic area in the distance, the wet gravel crunching under their feet. "Have you and Henrik checked each other's oil yet?"

"What?" Ailish winced at her high pitch. "I—we only met yesterday."

Erin appeared to find that answer amusing. "Don't worry. Connor and I didn't wait long before checking under each other's hoods, either." A touch of seriousness entered her expression. "People like us—cons—we've seen how fast good things get taken away. We move on a different schedule than everyone else."

"Henrik isn't a con," Ailish said. "Even though he did something wrong, I know cons. I've lived with them all my life. He wouldn't have committed a crime without a good reason."

The blonde glanced over, eyes full of speculation. "He hasn't told you?"

"Told me what?"

Erin stooped down and snatched up a piece of driftwood, running the flame of her lighter along the underside. "Sorry. It's not my story to tell. Would you settle for hearing about the time I robbed a clown college while it was in session? Talk about a circus."

Ailish laughed, despite being denied access once again to the knowledge she wanted so badly. Having another person—a woman her age—to speak with was too priceless, though, and she wouldn't squander the opportunity. Who knew when she might get another one? Breeze blew hair in Ailish's face, and she didn't even bother pushing it behind her ear as Erin relayed a crazy tale that couldn't possibly be true. By the time Erin finished the story, Ailish's cheeks hurt from smiling.

"You did *not* get away on a unicycle."

"Hey, you use what you've got." Erin shivered. "And what I've got is nightmares. Word to the wise, if you've ever got a dozen clowns in full makeup chasing you? Don't look back."

"I'll try to remember that," Ailish murmured. Dammit, they only had about two minutes before they needed to be back at the cabin. Just enough time to push for some kind of information. Most pressing of which was… "So. Where did Henrik go?"

As if she'd been expecting the question, Erin showed no reaction. "Back to Chi-town to handle some business. He'll be back in the morning." Using the lighter, Erin flickered the light beneath her chin, making her face look like a jack-o'-lantern. "Unless something *terrible* happens."

Ailish's stomach tumbled out onto the gravel. "Just when I was starting to like you," she managed as Erin chuckled. "I gathered he went back to Chicago, but what is he doing there?"

Erin stopped at the entrance to the path, conflict in the lines of her body. "Look, I don't agree with our captain's call to keep you in the dark until we have your agreement to cooperate. If they pulled that shit with me, I'd have already split and left a bonfire behind. We're asking you to work *with* us, but Derek is too busy worrying you'll end up working against us." She took a rubber band out of her pocket and fixed her blond hair up in a ponytail, her movements jerky. "I'm not sure if you're aware of this, but your father is kind of a dick."

"I'm aware."

Erin's lips twitched. "Right. Well, Derek is worried about your loyalties potentially shifting. Out of fear or…paternity." She turned and started up the path. "But he hasn't met you like we have, so I'm making a judgment call."

Fighting the impulse to cheer over the badass liking her enough to break a few rules, Ailish drew even with Erin. "Thanks, I appreciate that. Don't feel pressured, though, okay? If you don't want to tell me anything—"

"Are you actually trying to talk me *out* of enlightening you?" Erin's face was a mask of disbelief. "How'd you manage to stay this way in your father's world?"

A pang struck Ailish in the chest. "Henrik said the same thing."

They completed the rest of the path in silence. Erin lingered at the end, but stopped walking as they could both see Connor in the distance and she obviously had more to say. "Henrik went back to Chicago for a fight." She used one finger to push Ailish's dropped chin back up. "Your father has been taking a heavier interest in his gambling operation. Since *you* left, actually." Erin eyed her a moment, but shook herself and continued. "Henrik is planning on getting some face time with the man. A disgraced cop could be a valuable asset to a man like Caine. All that intel, friends in the department…"

"*No*." Ailish felt like she'd been sprinting, only to slam full speed into a brick wall. "I don't want Henrik anywhere near my father. He can't be trusted. One minute you're his best friend and the next…you're disposable."

Erin reached out and patted the air above Ailish's shoulder. "Henrik can take care of himself."

God. She *knew* that. But she also knew her father better

than anyone. Henrik's team didn't know the half of what they were dealing with. The morning couldn't get there quick enough. Knowing Henrik could be facing her father right that very moment made Ailish twice as upset he hadn't said goodbye.

"I'm ready to shake your hand now," Erin said without preamble.

Ailish's head came up. "What?"

Erin ran a hand down her ponytail, her gaze trailing over to a waiting Connor. "I couldn't shake your hand earlier, but I think I can now."

"Okay." Ailish put her hand out and waited. It took a minute, but when Erin finally grasped her hand, Ailish was surprised to feel a sense of much-needed comfort infiltrate her breast. Especially when Erin laughed under her breath and squeezed harder, like maybe she was experiencing the same sensation. "I've made two friends in less than twenty-four hours. What do I have to complain about, huh?"

"Make it three," Connor rumbled as he approached.

They walked back to the cabin in silence, but Ailish's mind was anything but quiet. Erin's earlier sentiment circled back to replay in her head. *People like us—cons—we've seen how fast good things get taken away. We move on a different schedule than everyone else.*

Maybe that was true. The connection she'd experienced with Henrik seemed anything but new. It felt...cultivated. Rich. She wanted to lie down and revel in her attraction to his rough-cut body, his deep voice, how he didn't flinch at her lack of social skills, but seemed to appreciate them. Maybe even share them. And Erin's words made sense on more than one level. Ailish herself fit right in with the undercover squad of criminals. They thought she'd been arrested for being in the wrong place at the wrong time, having been pressured into transporting money and crucial documents for her father.

How would they react if they knew she'd earned her stripes as a potential future con by helping her father in more ways than one?

Henrik fell back against his corner of the ring. Perspiration poured down his face, chest, and arms, mingling with the red welling on his knuckles, before dripping onto the mat. Since his fight was third of the night, he couldn't tell which sweat belonged to him and which belonged to the last contenders. There was a cut over his eye that seemed intent on blinding him with blood, but he swiped it with the back of his hand, ready for the bell to ring. *Ring, motherfucker.*

Yeah, he couldn't deny the fight felt good. Here in this place, a warehouse basement in Back of the Yards, men didn't disguise their nature, so he wouldn't bother doing it, either. When he'd boxed for the Chicago Police Department, participating in good-natured sparring and charity matches, he'd never felt satisfaction being declared the winner. There had been no retribution in the eyes of his opponents, as there was in this place. Men hell-bent on having the demons bashed from their skulls, night after night.

Maybe he was one of them, because every blow he landed, every blow he received, felt like a cleansing. A momentary blocking of everyone and everything he'd lost. Relationships. A career he'd spent a decade building. A family he'd embarrassed and dishonored by breaking his oath. Friends who looked at him the same way they looked at handcuffed perps. Most of all, his opponent's punches gave him a split second of peace from thinking about Ailish. Not just her safety, although that alone was enough to paralyze him if he dwelled too much. No, it was more. It was knowing she'd eventually see a man who could so easily abandon his honor…and realize she could do so much better.

Wasn't it ironic that his ticket to earning back his good name was to put the woman indirectly responsible for his downfall in danger?

Henrik scanned the crowd through one eye, his other having puffed up in the last thirty seconds. Bloodthirsty men laying odds, taking bets. Money and drugs exchanging hands. Dirty deals being made. If crime was a machine, this place acted as the control booth. When he'd first started coming here, they'd sneered and spit at him, hating him for having worn a uniform. He'd been the enemy. Now? They didn't so much as flinch when he stepped into the ring. In fact, he'd become a favorite for never once hitting the mat. Yeah, he fit right in now, didn't he?

If he got his badge back, would they loathe him once again? Instead of him loathing himself?

Not if something happened to the girl.

Ding ding ding. Henrik rolled his neck side to side, hearing it pop. The man with whom he'd already gone four rounds ambled into the ring's center, using one hand to massage the other. With blood pouring from his nose and two swollen eyes, he was in far worse shape than Henrik, but fire still lit his expression. It took more than a few right crosses to put down a bare-knuckle boxer in this joint, and Henrik never let his guard drop for that very reason.

Just as they were closing in on each other, someone caught Henrik's attention in the crowd. A man whose face he'd seen plastered around the precinct since his rookie year as a cop. Caine O'Kelly. Wearing a black turtleneck, the older man leaned forward in the front row, hands clasped loosely between his legs. He wore a smirk, but there was speculation in his dark eyes as he watched Henrik.

A left jab snapped Henrik's head back on his shoulders, but he was grateful for it. Staring any longer at Caine would arouse suspicion, and he needed to keep his head in the fucking game. For Ailish. For his new team that didn't believe him a disappointment to the calling. Henrik dodged a right cross and buried his fist in the other man's stomach, gritting his teeth upon feeling a snap beneath his knuckles. As he'd come to expect in this type of fight, however, his opponent stayed on his feet, merely appearing more determined than he'd been at the round's outset.

"Fuckin' cop," the man spat, blood droplets emerging from his lips.

"Haven't you heard?" Henrik jabbed once before attacking from the right. "They don't want me anymore. I'm free to kick your ass any time you want."

His opponent responded with a head butt that compromised Henrik's vision for a split second, but he rallied fast enough to block the fist hurtling toward his face. In his peripheral vision, Henrik saw Caine O'Kelly stand up from his front row seat and saunter toward the ring's edge, propping an elbow on the mat. That was all Henrik needed to remind him what he fought for. This man had kept a beautiful butterfly in a cage for twenty-one years, not allowing her to make friends or explore her obvious potential to be something more than a mobster's sheltered daughter. And those were the facts Henrik knew to date. Ailish hadn't even confided what her life had been like prior to running from Chicago. Maybe she never would. But if he wanted a *chance* to find out, if he wanted the opportunity to protect that butterfly, it started with winning this goddamn match.

A roar simmered in Henrik's throat, then broke free in a tremendous cyclone of noise. Even his cocky opponent fell back a step, the cheering and bantering from the sidelines dulling to a murmur. He wasted no time in launching his offense, juking to the left, the right, before coming in with a left uppercut that connected with his opponent's chin. The crackle of bone was drowned out by the crowd's renewed energy. Dozens of arms snaked in through the ropes, slapping the mat as they whistled and demanded more.

As the other man dropped, his eyes gone blank, Henrik saw Caine O'Kelly instead. He wore the same expression, smug but curious, as he slow-clapped from the sidelines. Although now he was impressed.

Good, asshole. Come and get me.

Henrik turned from his crumpled opponent—who was being attended by his boys—to collect his gear from the corner. The operation's unofficial manager shoved a stack of money into Henrik's gym bag as he ducked under the ropes and headed for the bathroom to clean off the blood and sweat. When the rusted bathroom door swung open two minutes later, Henrik didn't even look up. He knew who it was.

As Henrik bandaged a particularly nasty gash on his right hand, Caine O'Kelly's wingtips stopped in his line of vision. The man smelled like expensive, freshly smoked cigar. Henrik himself enjoyed a cigar from time to time, usually with his father on a holiday, but he'd never touch another one. Not as long as Ailish was around to possibly smell it on him.

Henrik retrieved a roll of white medical tape from his bag, ripping off a piece with his teeth. "Help you?"

Caine laughed, and if Henrik had hair on his head, it would have stood up. "That's what I'm here to find out." The older man removed a cell phone from his jeans, using a finger to scroll as he spoke. "You know who I am?"

"You know who *I* am?"

White teeth flashed in the other man's face. "Come on, now. Everyone here knows who *you* are, Officer."

"Ex-officer. And I could say the same about you."

Caine tilted his head. "And yet you're being kind of a prick."

"Kind of?" Henrik wound the white tape around his

middle finger. "I guess I'm losing my touch."

A tense silence ensued before Caine laughed loud enough to create an echo in the small bathroom. Henrik allowed himself to show a hint of amusement, but on the inside he was thanking Christ Ailish bore no resemblance, physically or otherwise, to her father. "Look, I've got a woman waiting for me, so I'm going to make this quick," Caine said. "I don't completely buy this cop-turned-lowlife act you're trying to pull off. But if it's legit, you could be valuable to me. Especially with that uppercut." He shifted closer, the leather of his wingtips creaking. "You like getting paid to use your fists? You could make a lot more collecting debts for me. There's been a…change in management. I recently found out I've got a lot more money coming my way than I thought."

Henrik couldn't stop his upper lip from curling. Maybe he hadn't fallen as far as these people just yet, because his skin crawled at the idea of being this man's glorified flunky. "Not interested."

Caine arched an eyebrow. "Oh no?" He dropped a number higher than Henrik's salary when he'd been a cop. "That doesn't interest you?"

"I have to think about it," Henrik said, his lips feeling numb.

The older man seemed to grow a few inches, getting right in Henrik's face. "No. *I* have to think about it. You will be the one doing the impressing, not the other way around. Are we on the same page?"

Henrik crossed his arms and propped a hip against the grimy sink. "How are you expecting to be impressed?"

"I'm not expecting shit from you. You haven't earned that privilege yet." Caine rubbed a thumb along his jawline. "But you were still one of the boys in blue when my daughter went missing, weren't you?"

"Yeah," Henrik responded in a flat voice, using all his

willpower to avoid strangling the old man. "I heard she split."

Caine eyeballed him for a heavy moment. "Use whatever connections you've maintained. Prove you've got some value by finding my daughter and bringing her back here — alive. *Then* we'll talk about that job." He started to exit the bathroom, but paused. "I'd hurry. You're not the only one I've got looking for her."

Chapter Eight

Ailish stared out the window of their cabin, willing Henrik's truck to appear. Having been allowed to take another walk this morning, she felt far less stir-crazy, but as eleven o'clock came and went, her nerves began to whir, anxiousness taking up residence in her stomach. Had Henrik met her father? Oh God, she hoped not. Nothing good could come from an association with Caine. Only pain and loss.

With a heaved breath, Ailish turned from the window to find Erin and Connor facing off across the bed, much like she'd done with Henrik yesterday afternoon, before he'd left. It appeared her two temporary protectors were equally ready for Henrik to return so they could be alone.

Yes, sexual frustration was alive and well in cabin nine.

Ever since Ailish and Erin had returned from their walk last night, Connor had been pacing, splitting his glowering attention between the cabin's perimeter and his smiling girlfriend. Knowing a thing or two about teasing men, Ailish could see the effect of Erin leaving Connor unfulfilled. This was different, though. Her own teasing had never ended in the men touching Ailish, merely with Ailish touching herself. She'd seen Henrik with the same starved expression just yesterday when she'd been beneath him on the bed, his mouth doing wicked things to her body. Actually, she couldn't *stop* seeing it.

This unrelenting yearn to feel Henrik's weight press her down into the bed again had combined with her fear he wouldn't return...and created resolution. No more teasing, no more trying to get away. She had to trust her gut where Henrik was concerned. If he would only—

Wheels crunched along the dirt outside and Ailish rushed back to the window. Behind her, Connor muttered *halle-fucking-lujah* and Erin laughed, but after that Ailish could only hear the rushing in her own ears. As Henrik climbed from the truck and strode toward the cabin, her mouth ran dry. She absorbed every detail of him, some heating her blood, others adding fuel to her worry. The jeans riding low on his hips, the way his thin white T-shirt conformed to his muscular abdomen and thick upper arms...yeah, those details made her fingers itch to touch. Made her want to sit on his lap and tempt his erection. Conversely, she hated the tape around his knuckles, his sliced lower lip. The puffiness surrounding his right eye.

Without any prompting, her palm slapped the windowpane, making Henrik's head lift. She frowned at him, and although she couldn't hear him through the glass, she knew he sighed. Actually had the nerve to look disappointed at her choice of welcome. Well, too bad.

As soon as Henrik opened the door, Connor grabbed Erin's hand and vanished through the exit, obviously headed back to their own cabin. Ailish couldn't be more grateful. She had a few things to get off her mind, and all of them were directed at the man who had the nerve to look better in a T-shirt than any fitness model she'd seen on the cover of a health magazine.

Henrik closed the door and leaned back against it, thumbs slipping into his belt loops, the picture of resignation. "Hey, Lish."

Oh no. Was it possible for a man to make you wet in just two words? *Yes.* Because Henrik had just done it. Heaviness descended between her thighs, even more powerful than yesterday, because she'd just had a full night of creating scenarios where he didn't come back. Relief bisected desire and she couldn't get across the room fast enough.

A second before she reached Henrik, his resignation transformed with surprise, but then...*God.* Then there was just a man wanting to fuck. *Needing* to fuck *her.* Ailish's knees almost gave out before he snatched her off the ground. Her stomach remained quivering in the air as he lifted her, turned, and rammed them both against the door. They moved as one unit, her thighs hugging his waist, bodies interlocking like two sides of a broken heart.

"*Jesus*," he groaned, lifting two fingers to her mouth, his eyes riveted as he pushed them deep past her lips. "I missed this little mouth. You got something to say, huh? Too bad. I can't watch your lips move right now without wanting to get some part of myself between them. You understand what I'm talking about?"

Ailish nodded, whimpering when he thrust against her mound. As if her body started to operate on pure, erotic instinct, she sucked on his fingers and was rewarding with a grind of his hips.

"You think I won't put you on your knees in that Disney Princess T-shirt, baby?" he breathed in her ear before licking along the rim. "You're wrong. I'll even use it to wipe your chin afterward."

A sensation she could only equate with lightning drilled Ailish in her midsection. The force of it made her eyelids fall, her head list to one side as if she'd been struck by the ball of electricity. But at the apex of her thighs, she'd never been more alive. More awake. The walls of her core clenched together, missing a part of Henrik she'd never even felt there. A part so huge and hot behind the fly of his jeans, she couldn't help writhing up and down on it, sucking, sucking his fingers like she'd been born for that sole purpose.

"I'm going to take my fingers out of your pretty warm mouth now, Ailish, but listen to me first." His brown eyes were darker, richer than she'd ever seen them and rife with intention. "I can't take you playing with me right now. Maybe tomorrow we can try to fuck through our clothes again to get your tease body off. But not today. On top of missing the hell out of you, I've spent the last twelve hours knowing I almost made you come on that bed. If I'd been punched in the face until I blacked out, I would have woken up thinking about how you panted and gasped, like it was just about to happen. So if you're going to let me lick your pussy right now to make up for it, nod once and I'll give you back your mouth, so you can scream."

Ailish was nodding before Henrik even finished speaking. Oh God…she could barely see the room around them, her vision had gone so fuzzy. He was the only solid part of her surroundings, so firm and capable as he turned and threw Ailish onto the bed, where she bounced once. Positive her mouth was hanging open, she pushed up on her elbows and watched him strip, revealing that brick-house body, inch by inch. Arrogance didn't typically appeal to her in men, but she loved the crap out of it in Henrik. He tossed that T-shirt aside, knowing full well his muscles shifted with every movement.

"Get your panties off." He unsnapped the button of his jeans and unzipped. "I'm going to show you my cock, baby. I'm going to show you how I jerk it when I think about you. And then I'm going to get between your legs and taste how wet it made you."

Ailish hooked her fingers in the sides of her underwear, lifting up her bottom to tug them down. When it became obvious Henrik wouldn't proceed until she completed the task, Ailish hurried through the process, throwing her panties onto the floor and waiting. With a meaty fist, Henrik drew the flesh out of his jeans with gritted teeth before kicking off his pants and kneeling on the bed's edge. Ailish moaned at the sight of him, this powerful man holding his arousal, like it was causing him an untold amount of pain—and his eyes accused her of being the culprit.

"Lift your knees up to your chest." He bent down and kissed the inside of her thigh, *so* close to her center. "I want to watch it get wet."

Once again shaken by the knowledge that she knew nothing about real, primal urges of men, Ailish hesitated only a second before she followed Henrik's order. Her stomach hollowed and shuddered at his reaction, the intensity with which he watched Ailish reveal the spot between her legs in such a new, intimate way. Being this exposed in broad sunlight should have unnerved her, but no. There was trust beneath the heat, keeping her balanced. That balance was short-lived, however, because when Henrik thrust his hips up and back, pushing his arousal through the opening of his fist, Ailish's equilibrium wavered. "This…is what you do when you think of me?"

"That's right." His grunt turned into a growl. "Nothing I thought of before now is this good, though. I'll never be able to look at your hair again without wanting to see how well it matches your pussy."

Ailish's neck loosened all its own and her head hit the bed. Her hands were hooked under her knees, keeping her legs elevated, but she wanted to turn onto her stomach. Wanted to wedge the ache in her loins up against the palm of her hand. This was *too* much, this up-close-and-personal view of Henrik stroking himself. It made her stomach tighten, strained her calf muscles.

Maybe she'd expressed herself out loud, because one of Henrik's hands gripped her shoulder, the other one sliding beneath her hip. And then he flipped her over, drawing a strangled scream from her mouth. Her hips were jerked up, leaving Ailish on her hands and knees. She could see herself reflected back in the windowpane, but refused to believe it could be her, this girl with tumbling hair and a swollen mouth. Her bottom poised straight up in the air…and a man running hands over that backside, slapping it gently.

Her breath shook out. "I thought…are y-you going to…"

"Fuck you?" Henrik's reflection dipped, and then she felt it. His tongue licking up the center of her most private flesh. "No, I'm just getting a taste." Another flicker of his tongue, this time against her entrance. "*Mmmm*, Lish. You taste like you need to come as bad as I do."

"I do," she whispered, the muscles in her thighs clenching. "*Please…*"

His palms smoothed down to her thighs and back up. "You're going to suck my dick after I finish you." He spanked her right buttock, then thrust his hips up between her thighs so she could feel his stiff erection. "I've thought about it the whole drive home. That pretty little red head bobbing up and down while you're still wet between the legs from my mouth."

Ailish's fingers twisted in the bedspread, her nipples forming tight peaks as she imagined servicing the commanding man touching her so intimately. Reverently one minute and harshly the next, with long licks of her center, tight cracks of his palm. Tingles were already beginning in her limbs, starting in her knees as usual. Being positioned on her hands and knees lifted the heaviness below her belly button and made it more effective somehow, like a delicious weight pressing down, urging her toward the finish line. "*Henrik.*"

A response wasn't forthcoming, and suddenly Ailish couldn't care less because he dropped to his knees and yanked her body closer to the bed's edge. His lips tugged at the flesh of her core, opening her up for his hardened tongue, his thumbs digging into the cheeks of her bottom and massaging as he battered her clit. Was it possible for a man to slap a woman with his tongue, enough to cause a sting? Yes. *Yes*...she could hear the sound of it connecting with the place between her thighs, causing explosions of lust throughout her middle. With rough hands, he pushed up her backside, exposing her more, giving his greedy mouth more access.

Ailish heard herself moaning and didn't bother trying to stop. Nothing had *ever* felt this good. So *good*, she was begging him to stop in order for her to savor it, this moment before her own touch was no longer satisfying. This is what she'd been craving without even realizing. "Oh God...I'm going to..."

With a guttural sound, Henrik hooked his forearms beneath her thighs and lifted Ailish's lower half into the air. His mouth never stopped nipping, licking, devouring. His beard scraped along her inner thighs with every flexing of his jaw, and Ailish mentally checked out, became nothing more than a vessel for pleasure that was about to shatter from exceeding maximum capacity.

"Oh...oh, Henrik...*yes.*"

She peaked while her legs were suspended in midair, which gave her no anchor, save the unbelievable mouth sucking at her clit. Tremors sizzled down both sides of her body, meeting in the middle. Her knees slipped down to Henrik's chest, both of her ankles held in a death grip. So powerful, this man. She could only withstand—it was her sole purpose at that moment. To survive the most intoxicating pleasure she'd ever experienced.

At least, until Henrik flipped Ailish onto her back, threw her ankles over his shoulders and made her experience it again. And again.

Henrik needed to stop licking Ailish's pussy sometime today, but *Christ*, the girl tasted sweet and fresh. Her thighs hugged both sides of his face as he took another drag of perfection, felt a little aftershock shiver through her stomach. *Never want to stop.* His hands shared the sentiment, kneading any and all flesh he could find. Her thighs, her scalp, her shoulders…that ass. He could make her come one more time. *Just one more.*

"No more," Ailish whimpered, her narrow hips twisting under his grip. "Please…you need me…let me."

You need me. God, no exaggeration there. He'd driven a hundred miles an hour to get near Ailish this morning, all the while hating himself for bringing the stain of Chicago along with him. Where he'd been last night, the man he'd interacted with…that shit had no business in her orbit. At the same time, though, he'd needed to see Ailish to get clean again. Needed to see her and acknowledge that she hadn't been returned to her father, simply by virtue of the possibility being voiced. No way in this life he would let that happen.

"*Henrik*," Ailish screamed, thighs clenching so tight he could barely hear that beautiful sound leaving her mouth. His goddamn name. *Yes.* She was coming again and Henrik lapped at the dampness like a dirty dog that hadn't been given water in weeks. So good. So *good*. Slippery and warm and smooth and *his*.

This time, when she pushed his face away with her hands, Henrik went, sinking back on his heels. As she sat up on the bed and pushed messy red hair out of her face, Henrik had to restrain himself from diving back on top of her to get his tongue in that pussy. God, he was fucking *addicted*. A certified Ailish addict. He actually might have tried to convince her to lie back and take more of his mouth, if his dick wasn't throbbing like a motherfucker against his thigh.

As if she'd read his mind, those hazel eyes glassed up, her lips seeming to go puffy under his regard. Lord, he shouldn't have come to her so damn hungry. His already-potent drive was amplified after last night's unfulfilling fight, after the frustration of being on a deadline to figure out how to keep her protected. She looked like a sacrifice waiting for him to pillage, and shit, he wanted to. His lust had been penned in like a zoo animal and now it stalked, back and forth.

"Lie on your stomach," Henrik half shouted, before taking a deep breath and repeating the order in a calmer manner. *Bring it down a notch. Or maybe ten notches would be better.* Henrik looped a hand around his cock and stood, watching Ailish crawl forward and arrange herself facedown on the bed. Without a verbal warning, he curled his hands beneath her arms and dragged her forward, bringing her face even with the edge. His heart was being beat with a mallet and bouncing back with twice the strength, just looking at her taut backside, the slightness of her form, the proximity of her mouth to his ready dick. The urge to overpower and take was fierce, but he battled it back and focused on her eyes. "I haven't been with anyone since that day in the park, Ailish."

Henrik didn't realize he'd said the words out loud until Ailish's expression changed, went soft, before sliding right back into aroused. She liked hearing he hadn't been with anyone and hell, didn't that make up for showing a portion of his hand? Damn straight it did. Her hips writhed on the bed, cheeks gone pink. The girl looked ready to mouth-fuck him into another time zone.

"You going to give me a nice ride on that tongue, baby?"

Mischief lurking in her gaze, Ailish nodded, one hand

reaching out to tug his legs closer. No sooner had his knees bumped the bed frame than Ailish surrounded his cock with wet heat. Oh God. Henrik ordered his body to keep him upright. Ailish had never been intimate this way with a man—he could tell by the way she explored—and Jesus, that made his balls tighten like nobody's business. Her mouth was virgin territory, and the first taste would always be him, no matter what. *Mine. My mouth.*

At first, she seemed fascinated with the head of his dick, the ridges, how they felt gliding over her tongue. Henrik was more than okay with that, because as soon as she took him deeper and those lips expanded to accommodate his girth, it would be a too-quick road to relief—

Fuck. That thought had formed too soon, because his fast little learner wanted to get all of him inside her mouth—at the same time. She choked twice, but wouldn't stop trying to reach his base. Over and over. Until nothing could stop Henrik from assisting her, pumping his length into the smooth entrance of her mouth. He leaned over her prone body and took two nice handfuls of her ass, squeezing the flesh as he thrust.

"Goddammit *yes*. You like having your mouth fucked, baby?" He snatched up Ailish's hands, crossing her wrists at the small of her back, that submissive position turning up the volume on his lust. "Can you tell how much I love fucking it, you cock-hungry girl? I'm going to bust like a motherfucker and it's all your fault. So greedy and hot and tight. *Suck it harder.*"

Ailish moaned around his flesh, burying her feet in the bed to push closer, to take more of him. She pulled at his restraining hands, but Henrik refused to release her. Every buck into her mouth made her pretty ass shake, and yeah, that little shudder was going to bring him to the end, sure as shit. Ahhh, then he pictured those hazel eyes looking up at him, determining whether or not he was pleased, and a Goliath tightening occurred beneath his navel.

"I can't hold on. I can't...just *stay right there.*" His head was assaulted with a wave of delirium, his balls trying to climb inside his stomach. "Fuck, *fuck*, Ailish. Your mouth is killing me. Just clamp down with those lips, baby...*yeahhh.* That's real goddamn good. Feel how bad I want inside you. All the damn time." He couldn't pull out yet. It felt too good, so he held his breath and delivered shallow pushes into her waiting mouth, groaning in a voice so foreign, he almost couldn't recognize it. *Have to pull out. Too much inside me for her to take.*

Adrenaline and animal instinct combined in a white-hot pool, twisting him down into the vortex they created. With his remaining sliver of clarity, Henrik removed his erupting cock from Ailish's mouth, held her down on the bed with a fist of red hair...and came on her bare back, as far down as he could reach, roaring his satisfaction until he'd spent himself completely.

When reality surfaced, Henrik realized how punishing his grip was on Ailish's hair and immediately let go, soothing her scalp with his hand and rasping an apology. They were equally out of breath as Henrik walked to the bathroom and retrieved a towel, cleaning the evidence of his pleasure off her beautiful body upon returning to the room, watching her turn over and stretch out like a contented cat. The bed creaked as Henrik lay down beside her, examining her expression for a hint of what she was thinking.

"I was rough, Ailish." He trailed his lips down her temple. "There's an apology dying to get out of me. But I'd have to apologize every time. I'm a big man to begin with, but it's you, baby. I...*need* your body to remember mine when we're done. Need it to feel reminders every time you move. And I need it so damn bad." His palm molded to her hip, tugged her closer. "If you want me inside your body—if you want me to fuck you—we might need to work up to it."

Just when Henrik was about to panic over Ailish's distant stare, she turned onto her side and spoke. "Um. W-when can we get started on that?"

Wait. Had he heard her right? Yeah...*yeah*, he had. A smile was pushing free behind her lips, those already-flushed cheeks deepening with even more color. Oh man. The landscape of his insides shifted, like two fault lines parting and relocating after an earthquake. This girl. She was either going to be his reason for living or the reason he died. It was all right there, shining in front of him like a spotlight.

Ailish went up on an elbow, making her tits sway like two tempting pieces of mouthwatering fruit, hidden beneath her shirt. "Henrik?"

Disliking the note of worry in her voice, Henrik leaned in and kissed her mouth, long enough that his cock started to harden again between their bodies, ready for another round. Pulling away from the promise of more Ailish wasn't easy by any stretch, but they needed to talk. His career and her freedom—possibly her life—were on the line and they needed to be part of the solution together.

He wasn't ready to tell her about the evidence he'd destroyed. Not quite. His feelings for Ailish had been given far more time to cultivate and strengthen, whereas she'd known him a grand total of two and a half days. He couldn't risk her backing off when she realized he'd *already* given up everything. Time and patience were required here. Once they were free of danger and she'd spent more time with him, he'd reveal the full picture and pray she understood. Pray she didn't resent him for taking away her choice.

"We need to talk, Ailish."

She tugged on a strand of hair, eyes suddenly evasive. "Okay, but there's something I need to tell you first."

Chapter Nine

Pitiful, Ailish. A man gives you a bushel of orgasms and you're ready to open the dam, allowing every secret to escape. Maybe she should have waited until her feet were on solid ground again, because right now, they were somewhere near the ceiling, performing a languid ballet dance. Wow. Henrik hadn't apologized for being rough, but it hadn't been required. Turned out...she *liked* being treated that way. It shouldn't have come as a surprise, really, after having a penchant for tantalizing men, that when one snapped and took what he needed, it felt like the ultimate payoff.

Ailish wouldn't kid herself that sex—or as far as they'd gotten—with just anyone would be so mind-blowing. It was Henrik. In the midst of his aggression, there'd been cherishment. And it had been directed both ways. Which had to account for her immediate need to get closer, reveal the things she'd stored inside for so long, with no one to confide in. Now, though, with sweat beginning to cool on her body, the implications of what she wanted to tell Henrik grew like Jack's beanstalk and wrapped around her neck. What she had to say could change everything.

No big deal. Play it cool. Ailish reached up and traced the abused skin around Henrik's eye. "Who did this to you?"

Dark eyes watching her closely, he turned and kissed the inside of her wrist. "I thought you had something to tell me."

Ailish sat up and snagged one of the bed pillows off the bed, holding it against her body. "That's right. You left without saying good-bye yesterday and I haven't forgiven you for it. What are you going to do to win back my favor?"

The corner of Henrik's mouth twitched. "Why do I get the feeling you're trying to change the subject?" When Ailish said nothing, Henrik sighed and moved into a sitting position. "'Good-bye' is a word I don't like associating with you."

"Oh." Ailish sniffed, her irritation vanishing in a puff of smoke. "I thought you were going to say you couldn't do good-bye properly in front of Connor and Erin."

Henrik looked back at her over his shoulder. "Mmm. That too, baby."

Warmth snaked into her belly, around her hips. Being near Henrik was like having a lasso around your middle that tightened without any warning. "Did you beat up the man who punched you in the face?"

His shoulders stiffened. "Do you really want to know that?"

"I grew up around violence, Henrik. I hate it, but I'm not scared of it."

Henrik's big body shifted on the bed so he was facing her. Ailish tried and failed not to let her gaze stray to his lap, where his erection lounged on his inner thigh. H'oh Lord. *We might need to work up to it.* No kidding. "I won the match, Ailish. But I don't want you thinking of me as a man who uses fighting as an outlet."

She moved a little closer on the bed, running a fingertip over his bruised, taped-up knuckles. "I thought it was just an excuse to get close to my father." At the mention of Caine, Henrik's jaw clenched. "But you fight because you like it."

It took him some time to answer. "It's hard to explain."

"Try."

He turned his hand over so Ailish could stroke his palm with nimble fingers. "There's so much...pretense everywhere. So much we can't see. But in the ring, it's clear-cut. Two men after one thing. No bullshit."

Guilt tracked up Ailish's spine, but she mentally shook it off. He hadn't been entirely truthful with her either, had he? She dipped her chin. "Two men after one thing. What is it?"

Henrik's brows drew together, as if he'd never considered the answer out loud before. "It's not always the same thing for every man."

"What is it for you?"

Silence passed. "A reminder that, if I can feel pain, I'm still real. I'm still there. No matter what I've lost." Abruptly, Henrik stood and pulled up his jeans, perusing her as he fastened them around his hips. "Are you going to ask me what happened with your father?"

Ailish was still transfixed by Henrik's explanation of feeling pain, so the change in topic threw her for a minute. "I was stalling."

Henrik half smiled. "You say exactly what you're thinking, don't you?"

"Not always," she murmured, tossing aside the pillow to tug down her skirt, but Henrik beat her to the task, pushing aside her hands to slowly replace the garment for her. After her clothing was back in place, big hands slipped down her thighs to apply pressure to both knees, moving them apart. Wide. Wider.

Henrik dipped his head, looking over what he'd revealed for so long, Ailish could feel herself getting wet again before his eyes. "A little forewarning. I'm going to have your pussy again for dinner tonight, baby."

Ailish's stomach hollowed out. "Why do I get the feeling you're changing the subject?"

"You're nervous about asking me what happened in Chicago. I need you to know everything is going to be okay." He cradled her neck in one loose hand and guided Ailish back onto the bed, before climbing on top of her fully clothed. Even so, her body was so sensitive from his mouth and hands, the rasping of his jeans along her flesh filled her with shock waves. When her breath started to wheeze in and out, a laugh rumbled through Henrik, who supported himself on two elbows. His amusement eventually gave way to focus, though. "Ailish, your father offered me a job."

In an instant, her nerves were pulled tighter than an archer's bow. Although Henrik's bulk made it impossible, her body tried to jackknife off the bed, moving on pure instinct. "No. No, Henrik. You didn't…take the job, did you?" She wet her lips. "The money isn't worth your soul."

His expression shifted with disappointment. "If I take the offer, it will be in the interest of my job as an undercover player, Ailish. Not because I think it would be a wise career move."

He was offended, but she didn't have the room to care just then. Something worse was coming, she could feel it. "He wouldn't offer you a job without a test of loyalty. What did you promise him?" Ailish whispered the final word, already knowing what the answer would be. She yearned to pace, but he'd obviously pinned her down for a reason, *dammit*.

"You know what he asked of me." Henrik leaned down, bringing their faces an inch apart. "But I can't do it, Ailish. I can't do anything that could result in you being hurt, baby. Do you see that?"

Ailish commanded her body to relax, but it wouldn't. She was still battling the fight-or-flight urge. Because he might have laid a bombshell on her, but she had a nuclear weapon. "What choice do you have but to offer me up if you want to go undercover?"

"I'll find another way. Do you hear me?" Briefly, he closed his eyes. "I haven't told the squad—or my captain—yet. We have time to figure this out."

"We. We?" Her eyes started to fill with moisture, but she willed them away. "You don't know who you're teaming up with."

His gaze narrowed, a new awareness hardening the powerful lines of his body. "If you've got something to tell me, get it out in the open now. But I'm telling you right now it won't change anything on my end. Nothing will."

She shook her head back and forth on the bed. "You're so sure." Her breath escaped in stages. "Your captain is targeting Caine's gambling operation. He wants to bring my father up on charges of racketeering. But what if I told you the police could charge me with the same thing?"

Henrik stopped breathing above her. "You moved money one time. There is no longer any evidence of it. You're in the clear."

"No." A rippling started along her insides, creating sharp edges and peaks. "The morning we had breakfast, you told me the Bookie Cookie was the main target. She runs the operation behind the scenes, formulating odds and managing debts. But no one has gotten access to her, only heard the name passed around among my father's inner circle." Again, she resented Henrik for pinning her down, because she desperately wanted to hide her face. "I'm her. I'm the Bookie Cookie."

A denial clogged Henrik's throat, refusing to be swallowed.

This couldn't be real. How had he missed this? He stared down into her innocent face, her demeanor the opposite of hardened. No, she was fresh and untainted by the life she'd been born into. That judgment would never be swayed. This couldn't be possible, could it?

"Say something," she whispered.

"I'm waiting for you to tell me you're kidding."

Her body moved in a shrug beneath him. "I wish I could." She turned her face to the side, giving him a view of the pink blotches decorating her neck. "The way I see it, you have two choices. Take me back to Chicago and let your friends interrogate me until I give them what they want. Or drag me back to Caine where he can lock me up. Force me to create numbers that could end in people dying or losing their life savings. Just *pick* one."

Another section of the big picture clicked into place. "This is why you wanted prison time," he murmured. "You're the oddsmaker."

"*Yes*," she sobbed.

God, the heartsick resignation in her usually buoyant voice was going to kill him. He'd been thrown the fuck off, yeah. No sugarcoating it. But it was time she learned that when he promised her something, he meant it, come hell or high water. And both were headed in their direction, make no mistake. "I'm not going to do either of those things. Are we clear? I'm still here. I'm still looking at Ailish. And I know you ran away so you didn't have to be a part of that shit anymore. I thank God for it." She turned hopeful but wary eyes on him. "So now we're going to get you clear for good. Okay? You with me?"

She scrutinized him. "I don't know how I can be with you when I don't understand where your conviction comes from. About me. I just told you I'm a bad person—as culpable as my father—and you barely flinch."

"Not as culpable. Not even close. And you let me worry about my convictions, all right? The thing about convictions is they run on faith." He rubbed their mouths together, relieved as hell when her lips stayed soft, pliant. "Now I need you to have it in me."

Ailish lifted her knee, dropping his hips further into the cradle of her thighs. An uncontrived move, but one that got his juices flowing like a swift river current nonetheless. "I'm trying," she said, her tone tinged with frustration. "It's not a familiar concept to me."

"I'm a patient man, baby. Except when it comes to your body." He took her hands and lifted them above her head. "So here's what we're going to do." A slow thrust of his hips made her lips pop open. "We're going to take a shower so I can wash off the road, while looking at you naked. And then we're going to start seeing our way clear of this. *We*. Do you understand?"

"I understand you're high-handed." She lifted the other knee and curved her feet around his ass, rubbed them up and down, shifting his hard-on against her pussy. "Can I think about the rest after we shower?"

That was all Henrik needed to hear. He hauled her clinging form off the bed, took two steps to immerse them in the dark bathroom, and kicked the door shut. He'd taken a shower that morning, didn't necessarily need one now. But he wanted to see Ailish in the place where he'd pleasured himself to her memory countless times. Wanted to see the suds sliding down her tits, water dampening the little red patch of hair shielding her sweet spot.

And shit, Henrik needed a moment. Derek wouldn't be understanding about Ailish's hidden identity. Even if the captain was taking an uncharacteristic break from being a hard-ass, he would want to use Ailish to the team's advantage, citing the greater good. A safer city. Goals

Henrik understood and shared, but not at the cost of Ailish's freedom or happiness. Hell, now that she'd run and apparently left Caine in the lurch, her life was even more at stake than before.

That scary realization had Henrik propping Ailish—legs still circling his waist—up against the bathroom wall and stripping off her shirt. Two cherry-tipped tits bounced in front of his mouth and yeah, he choked out a *hallelujah* in their honor. They were sweet and young and made him feel fucking dirty, no denying it. Big breasts had always done it for him, but never again. Give him Ailish's I-can-take-or-leave-a-bra sized sweethearts any day of the week and he'd rejoice like a sex-starved lecher.

It only got better when he sucked one little cherry into his mouth and Ailish moaned, back arching, fingers digging into his shoulders, like she felt the tug down below. The one that would slick up her pussy, make her ready for what was in his pants. "Fuck yeah," he growled, taking another merciless pull. "I can't wait to watch you ride me topless, climbing up and down my dick, crying about how deep it reaches." He palmed the breast he'd been sucking, spreading moisture with the pad of his thumb. "You know that long, thick vein that runs along the underside of my cock, Lish? You should, since your tongue gave it a bath earlier." He pushed up with his hips and let her drop, that tight body sliding down his erection. "I'm going to make you shake those tits while I'm inside you, so you can feel that vein throb."

For the space of a breath, Henrik thought he might have scandalized her, so he was unprepared for Ailish to unbutton his pants. She made quick work of the zipper, before her hand disappeared through the opening to wrap around his cock. She pressed four fingers against the vein in question, eyes going bright with excitement. Knowing what was coming didn't prepare Henrik for Ailish to shake her tits, just a few quick twists of her body that made them sway one way, then the other. It didn't matter that he'd spent himself only minutes before. Pressure built at the base of his spine, warning him. *Again, again.*

"You're right," she breathed. "It does throb."

Henrik yanked her forward with an arm around the waist, attacking her mouth with a hot, slippery kiss as he walked her backward toward the shower. Without allowing her mouth to escape, he shoved aside the plastic curtain and fumbled for the shower handle, kicking off his jeans as the water began to pelt the shower basin. Desperate to touch Ailish, he tested the temperature long enough to know it wouldn't burn them, before running his hands down her back and lifting her into the tiled shower stall. Barely having the presence of mind to close the curtain behind them, Henrik accomplished the feat nonetheless, enclosing them in wet, heavy darkness. It was like being trapped inside one of his own fantasies, except this was an experience for all five senses.

The girl wore nothing but a skirt, and the material was damp in seconds, conforming to her pussy and thighs like clear plastic wrap. Water sprayed onto her tits, slid down her legs, beaded on her parted lips. He watched as her inquisitive gaze ran down his body, snagging on his arousal, before rising again. Her fingers fumbled with the hem of his wet T-shirt, lifting it as far as she could over his head, before their height difference prevented her from lifting any farther.

She left the shirt plastered against his collarbone to run smooth palms up and over his pecs. "I like that you're so much bigger than me. I like that you ask permission... but you don't really need it," Ailish said, her voice lacing in between the shower spray. "Can I climb up and get closer to your mouth? It doesn't seem fair that you're always having to bend down."

Ah, Jesus. Now was not a good time for his heart to lurch and splatter against his ribs. He was man enough to admit she'd scared him, revealing her role in Caine's operation. That admission had made it more difficult to keep her guarded. And when she said things like *can I climb up and get closer...it doesn't seem fair*, he wanted to gather her up and let his remaining walls crumble to the ground. It also made him want something else really goddamn bad. "If you climb me, baby, nothing is going to come between me and that pussy. I just came not ten minutes ago and that means I could go for an hour right about now. You won't walk straight for a week."

Henrik couldn't remember having been compelled to speak so crudely to a woman in his entire life. It made no sense that the one he would do anything to keep should bring that side out of him, when he should be proving his worth. Proving he could be affectionate. Or maybe it made perfect sense, because Ailish loved it. Henrik could tell by the way her eyelids fluttered a little as he spoke, the way her hands slid down the sides of her hips, lingered there. "I guess you should come down here, then," she said.

Don't have to tell me twice. Henrik snagged Ailish's left hand from its perch on her hip, trapping it above her head. When he swooped in to capture her mouth, she did this little pull-away move, tease that she was, which only made him hotter and more eager. She paid for evading him with a punishing kiss, the kind that had been created as a prelude to fucking, heads tilting to get maximum access, teeth bumping. With water sluicing down their faces, not a care was given about being messy, tongues licking against each other in desperation.

His balls weighed down between his thighs, as if his body knew shower time equaled relief. He had no choice but to drop his right hand and cup them, massage them in a steady rhythm so unlike the frenetic kiss happening above.

Ailish pulled away, sucking in huge gulps of breath, her wet head falling back against the shower stall. "Oh...my *God*. Does everyone kiss like that?"

"Everyone wishes they kissed like that."

She looked up at him from beneath dripping eyelashes, wildfire brightening her cheeks. "You're very arrogant sometimes."

He bent down and sucked her lower lip between his teeth, releasing it when she whimpered. "How do you know I wasn't complimenting *you*?"

"Were you?"

"Ailish, this mouth." He pushed a thumb inside, groaning when she swirled her tongue around it and pulled. "It kisses me so good. Sucks between my legs like it's trying to win a prize. Huh, baby. It's all you, isn't it?"

Henrik took a fistful of red hair and tugged to the side, laying gentle bites along her exposed neck. "Oh, I don't know about that," she breathed. "I...your mouth is no s-slouch, either."

His lips curled into a smile against her throat. "Ailish, baby?"

"Yes?"

"Wrap your hand around my cock"—he rolled his hips against her upper stomach—"and beat me off."

Fuck. Henrik loved the way she didn't even take a second to hesitate or feign surprise that a man would want his dick stroked. Especially by a wet, naked Ailish. She simply fisted his erection and used the water to slip her hand in sleek moves, root to tip. Although there really was nothing simple about it, because she watched his face, moaning at whatever she witnessed there.

"Tighter grip. *Tighter*," he growled into the shower

spray, unable to keep his hips from pumping. Unable to stop himself from closing his eyes and imagining he was thrusting into Ailish's lithe body instead. *Ahhh shit*, if he didn't live long enough to see his hard flesh dipping between her thighs, to feel her accepting his girth, he would consider his life incomplete. "God, baby. I've never been this horny in my fucking life. If we're in the same room, I'm thinking of a way to get your hand down the front of my jeans. Remember that. It's not going to change anytime soon, so I hope like hell you like working my dick."

"I love it." There was a shudder in her voice. "I love watching what it does to you. You look like…you're dying."

His laughter was pained. "And you like watching me die?"

The pad of her thumb massaged the tip of his arousal, and his groan tore through the shower stall. "Yes," she whispered. "I think…I think I like this kind of violence. A lot."

Her husky tone battered him over the head with lust. That hand slipping up and down his thickness, her expression of awe, the shower spray coasting over her tits. It was everything he'd ever dreamed of, multiplied by a thousand. "This kind of violence is a two-way street," Henrik rasped against Ailish's temple, lights starting to wink behind his eyes. *I can't be the only one to finish.* Her pointed nipples and harsh breathing told him she needed, too. Need, need. It was a red cloud obscuring everything around them.

Henrik's right hand released his balls, eliciting a shock of pleasure/pain deep in his stomach. *Worth it. Need to touch her.* His touch slipped around the curve of her hip, down between the valley of her ass, stopping to press a thumb to that tempting back entrance. When she jumped at the near-invasion, releasing a feminine gasp, Henrik had to close his eyes against the surge of renewed desire. *Depraved* desire.

A vision assaulted him of Ailish facedown on the bed, her bottom propped higher with a couple pillows, watching him nervously over her shoulder as he worked into that forbidden place. It would be an exercise in self-control, letting her get used to him gradually, being planted inside her without moving.

God. Don't think about it or you'll come.

When his fingers continued their journey to the heaven between her thighs, Ailish's body relaxed for only a moment before arching like a spooked kitten. "Is your clit nice and sensitive from my mouth?"

"Yes," Ailish moaned, her hand flying up and down his ready-to-burst flesh, driving him insane. "T-touch me there, please."

"I'm going to *live* here. You understand?" His hips started to piston into her closed fist, his middle finger traveling over her nub, back and forth. "I'm this pretty clit's new favorite person. Same way I want your hand down the front of my pants at all times? I'm going to want a suck of this baby right here. Getting dressed, eating a meal, talking? Yeah, I'll be thinking of getting my mouth inside your panties to get you off."

Ailish's thighs squeezed together, but since he was touching her from behind, she couldn't close them around his hand, couldn't ease the pressure of his torture. And Henrik did nothing to make it easier for her, worrying that tiny bud until she cried out, her head thrashing on the wet wall. "Stop...*more*."

"Which one is it?" he taunted, licking water off the underside of her chin. "Stop or more?"

"*More.*"

Henrik slid two fingers into Ailish's damp opening, catching her resulting scream with his mouth, mastering her in two places at once. Never having been inside her before with any part of his body, now was a time for gentleness, but Henrik couldn't pull it off. Not with her whimpering into his mouth, the swells of her ass cheeks flexing against his wrist. "You like that, don't you? Like being full of me? Get used to it." He pushed deep and lifted, bringing Ailish onto her tiptoes. His tongue traced the outline of her mouth as he admired her passion-glazed eyes. Those pretty tits were shaking against his chest, making him starved for a suck of her nipples. "That wasn't a suggestion, Ailish. Get used to having me inside you. Move your hips around…make my fingers feel at home."

"I…ohhhh." Doing as he asked, she worked her hips in a haphazard figure eight, tiny whimpers breaking past her lips to get him even more worked up, if such a thing were possible. "I like it, I like it, I—" She broke off in a moan when Henrik found her G-spot, tickling it with a crooked middle finger. "*Oh my God.*"

Henrik was fast losing control, his lust reaching epic proportions, spurred on by her uninhibited behavior. He could feel the blood rushing in his veins, the release kindling in his gut. If they didn't finish soon, he would drag her out of the shower, throw her down on the floor—wet and buck naked—and come inside her from behind. Without a care or a condom. And dammit, she deserved better than that. Deserved better than to be thrust into by the hungry beast he felt himself turning into. Most of all, he only got one chance for a first time with Ailish.

Barely able to speak around the need banked in his throat, Henrik pushed a third thick finger into Ailish and went in for the kill, stroking that spot along her inner wall with rough fingers. "I don't remember asking you to stop hand-fucking me, Lish. Get that hand moving so I can come all over those legs again."

As if his treatment inside her body had paralyzed her

limbs, it took Ailish a few beats to begin pumping his flesh again. *Ohhh,* but when she got going, his orgasm built almost immediately, raking down his spine and clawing its way through his abdomen. "Henrik...I'm going to...."

"Go on." He licked into her mouth for a wet kiss. "I got you. I always got you."

Her body stiffened before starting to shake. The hand that wasn't busy working his climax free slapped at his chest, her nails digging into him as she cried out. When Ailish hit her peak, she opened her eyes, and it was like looking through two windows into paradise. Henrik wasn't even sure she could see him, even though her attention was locked on him. God, she gave herself over, as though there were nothing in this world to lose, and it was fucking spectacular. Throw in his name being chanted over and over on her lips like a prayer, and just then, in that shower, Henrik witnessed the sexiest, most breathtaking sight of his lifetime.

Warmth greeted the palm wedged between her legs—Ailish's climax—sending him catapulting into a deep ravine he never wanted to climb out of. Henrik pressed his face against the wet shower wall and roared as his hot seed decorated Ailish's shaking legs. "Next time you get all of me," he groaned. "I don't like knowing I haven't let loose inside you."

Henrik felt her bones beginning to liquefy, so he gritted his teeth and held her up, even as his own release racked his body. They stayed locked together for an unknown amount of time, their breathing mingling with the pelting shower spray.

Ailish's lips moved on his shoulder as she spoke, her voice sounding throaty from screaming. "Henrik?"

"Yeah."

"I don't think we're meant to be friends."

He'd thought his heart was done ricocheting around his chest for the moment, but obviously he'd been wrong. Damn, he fell harder for this girl with every passing second. That was saying something, considering he'd already thrown his sanity overboard just to get close to her. "And that upsets you, baby?"

She gathered the moisture on his shoulder with her lips. "No. I think this is better." A brief pause. "Don't you?"

"Hell yes, Ailish. Don't ask me things like that with doubt in your voice."

Her uneven nod calmed him. "What do we do now?"

He pulled back to lift her chin. "Now you wait for me here while I make a few calls. Okay?"

There was no hesitation in her agreement. Looking back later, he would kick himself for not finding that odd. He probably should have included a *please*.

Chapter Ten

Ailish stared at the door that had just closed behind Henrik. He hadn't shared the identity of who he would be calling. Or what he would say. Trapped between him and the wall of the shower, she'd never trusted anyone more. Then again, she'd been relying on him for pleasure during those stolen moments—and oh boy, he'd delivered. If she allowed herself, she could get lost in the memory of how his fingers had touched her so intimately, the intensity of his breathing. But she couldn't go there, couldn't get lost in that winding path. Because Ailish couldn't shake the sitting duck feeling that made her skin prickle.

Every time she took a step in the direction of trusting Henrik, he shut her out. It reminded her too much of a childhood being shoved out of rooms while the men talked. Being hushed at the dinner table while her father spoke in a low tone into the receiver of his phone. There was an undeniable urge to put her faith in Henrik. How could anyone be that convincing a liar? When they were touching, she couldn't tell where Henrik ended and she began. Her troubles slipped down some invisible drain and there were only his capable hands…and that mouth. The one that spoke to her the way no one had ever dared.

Now however, sitting alone in the quiet cabin, she could only see the road map that detailed her situation in black and white, with none of the gray areas created by Henrik. Two squiggly red lines extended from the *You Are Here* mark. One led back to Chicago, and one led to more breathtaking freedom. She'd actually told Henrik she was the Bookie Cookie, a position that made her valuable to the police in so many ways. She had enough information to shut her father's outfit down cold, and Henrik would need some serious motivation not to hand her over.

She hadn't been enough motivation for her father to remove himself from a violent, unstable lifestyle. She hadn't been enough reason for her mother to stick around. What chance was there that this near stranger who had so much to gain would actually see a reason to choose what was best for her? Not a good one.

Ailish's gaze strayed to the duffel bag Henrik had brought in from the truck, just before he'd left to make his mysterious phone calls. He'd taken out a fresh T-shirt and she assumed it contained more clothes. She shouldn't snoop through someone else's property. No, she shouldn't.

Whistling under her breath, Ailish slid off the bed and into a cross-legged position, eyeballing the bag a second before dragging it over. She unzipped the top and peered inside. Clothes, just as she'd assumed, but it wouldn't hurt to look a little deeper. She pushed a hand down the side of the folded garments, freezing when she connected with something cold and metal. After a moment of debate, she pulled out the pair of handcuffs and let them dangle in the air, her stomach seizing as reflected light from the window hit the cuffs, creating shadows on the floor.

Slammed by a sense of urgency, a driving desire to get away from the cuffs, away from the man who could use them to restrain not only her wrists, but her livelihood, Ailish jumped up from the floor. She had no idea how long Henrik would be gone, but she had a feeling it wouldn't be long. A glance out the window told Ailish that he'd left Erin to guard the door, another sign that something was wrong, right? If he didn't trust her to stay in the cabin, that was proof the distrust went both ways. She wasn't crazy to be paranoid.

Don't think about the soft way he speaks to you, asking for your trust. Don't think about the way he touches you like a man experiencing silk for the first time.

Ailish swiped a hand under her nose and dived for the plastic bags she'd saved as a makeshift suitcase, shoveling handfuls of clothes into them. Her toothbrush, her wallet. She slid the bag handles up her arms to rest in the crook of her elbows while turning in a circle, looking for anything else that might come in handy. The gun. Still beneath the pillow. After grabbing the weapon and making sure the safety was on, she took a deep breath and pushed open the door.

Erin turned with a blank expression, as if she already knew what was coming. "Ahhh. Princess Runaway has emerged from her chambers," Erin said, without even glancing at the gun in Ailish's hand. "I'm guessing this isn't about taking another walk."

Ailish tossed Erin the handcuffs from Henrik's bag. "Put one end around your wrist and the other around the porch rail." Both hands free, she gripped the gun and lifted. "I'm really sorry, but I have to go."

The blonde twirled the cuffs around her index finger. "These things are child's play. I'll be out of them in fourteen seconds."

Confusion eclipsed her urgency. "But Henrik has the key."

Erin looked sympathetic. "There's a lot we don't know

about each other. For instance, I didn't know you were afraid of heights."

"What?" Ailish's brow wrinkled. "I'm not afraid of heights."

"No." Erin's nodded at Ailish's jean shorts. "Your zipper is, though." The second Ailish dropped her gaze, Erin pulled her own gun, shrugging at Ailish's outraged gasp. "Whoops."

"That was messed up."

Erin shifted side to side in her boots. "I don't respond well when someone threatens to handcuff me. Even for fourteen seconds."

A pain started in Ailish's stomach. Disappointment in herself, regret for threatening Erin, worry that Henrik would return soon. "Look, just give me a head start. Two minutes, that's all I'm asking."

"What am I supposed to say to the Hulk when he returns? Not to mention my boyfriend." The blonde shook her head. "Neither one of them is going to believe you got the drop on me. I'm too much of a legend."

Erin was right, but Ailish could see that the other girl *wanted* to let her go. It was there in her shadowed eyes. "Look, I have nothing to offer, so I'll have to owe you one. That's the best I can do. Just…make it look like I slipped out the side window or something."

She let the gun drop and Erin did the same. "Henrik isn't someone you need to run from."

"He hasn't proved that yet."

Erin found something about that statement remarkably funny, but in the end she just sighed. "You've got two minutes."

Relief swamped Ailish. "Thank you."

"Don't thank me just yet. Henrik will find you and I wouldn't want to be you when that happens." Erin pursed her lips. "You better go—he said he'd be back in twenty minutes."

Ailish threw another thank-you over her shoulder and

stole down the porch. She didn't slow once she reached the crop of trees surrounding the cabins, but picked up her pace. Her destination was the main road, but when she saw three female campers piling into a Jeep, she drew up short.

"Hey, are you heading into town?"

"Yeah." They eyed her curiously. "You need a ride?"

An image of Henrik returning to the cabin and finding her gone filled Ailish's mind. Would he feel betrayed? Resigned? *The thing about convictions is they run on faith. Now I need you to have it in me.* When he'd said those words to her, she'd come so close to believing them. Even now, there was a voice urging her to go back. But then she thought about being promised college by her father, being promised dance classes as a preteen, promised she could go out and have an honest job outside the confines of her home, the operation. None of those promises had come to fruition. In fact, she couldn't remember a single time she'd put faith in another human being and had them deliver.

I would never do anything that could result in you being hurt, baby. Can't you see that?

Ailish ignore the pressure in her chest and jogged toward the Jeep. "I would love a ride."

Henrik's finger rested on the green call button of his cell phone. As soon as he pulled his thoughts together, he would call the captain—and it wasn't going to be an easy conversation. Not by any stretch.

The faint, addictive taste of Ailish on his lips made Henrik eager to return to the cabin and replenish his intake of her. *More.* He wanted more. It was unbelievable how much he craved her with every breath. On his walk to the lake where he'd finally found cell phone reception, he'd wondered if the constant starvation for Ailish would ease a little once he'd been inside her body, but the theory had been laughable. His need would only increase—there was no way around it.

Stop thinking with your dick and focus.

Right. He was about to go all in—again—for Ailish, and he couldn't give any quarter when the captain balked at his demands. If the conversation with Derek didn't go the way he needed it to go, Henrik was prepared to take Ailish somewhere safe where she couldn't be tracked. Just remembering the fear in her voice when she'd talked about going back to Chicago made him anxious, a little crazy even. There was only one way he would consider taking Ailish back to Chicago, and both Derek and Ailish needed to be on board.

Henrik hit call. He didn't have to wait longer than one single ring before the captain answered, his tone brisk and distracted. "Derek Tyler."

"Captain, it's Henrik."

A slight pause. "I hope you're calling me from the road, with Ms. O'Kelly in your passenger seat."

Right to the point, as usual. "Not yet, no."

Another, longer pause wherein Henrik could hear a leather creak, signaling the captain leaning back in his chair. "All right. Why don't we start with last night? Did you make contact with Caine O'Kelly?"

"I did." Henrik willed the knot in his throat to shrink. "He offered me a job with his crew. But I need to prove I'm an asset first by tracking down his daughter and returning her home."

Derek's laughter rang hollow. "I've never been more sure there's a leak in my department. O'Kelly wouldn't assign you that specific task unless he knew you'd thrown yourself on the sword for his daughter. I hope you weren't followed from Chicago."

"You know damn well I made sure I wasn't followed. And

yeah, it's possible someone clued him in. Although I didn't get the impression he'd made the connection between his daughter being cleared and me losing my badge." Just saying the words out loud caused an unpleasant tightening at the back of his neck. "He's not the kind of man who plays games. He would've called me on it."

A rapping noise in the background, like knuckles on wood. "I'm afraid to ask why you're really calling."

"You know why," Henrik said. "I'm not sacrificing her to that son of a bitch."

"Are you talking about me or O'Kelly?"

Henrik switched the phone to his other ear. "That remains to be seen." A breeze from the lake blustered a pile of pine needles into a mini cyclone, a few feet from Henrik's feet. "If you can offer her a deal, I might be able to convince her to provide information about Caine's operation. But she better walk out of the station afterward. *Without* a police record."

Henrik could sense the captain's dissatisfaction. "What information does she have that I'd be interested in? I'd be a fool to agree to a deal without any knowledge beforehand."

"You'll have to take my word for it," Henrik said. "I'll go undercover with O'Kelly and do the dirty work. But I need her protected to my satisfaction while I'm inside. Caine has men looking for Ailish as we speak and I'm not convinced he wants her unharmed. But you need to find me something else of value to offer O'Kelly, because it's sure as shit not going to be his daughter."

"What if I don't agree to that? Connor and Erin are a phone call away. They can bring Ailish in just as easy."

"You'd put two of your squad members in danger like that?"

"In danger from you?" Derek blew a breath down the line. "You haven't been thinking straight since this girl showed up. You might be doing yourself a favor bringing her back to dear old dad."

Henrik's hand tightened on the phone. "You don't want to suggest that again." Against his better judgment, Henrik gambled with a rumor he'd heard years ago about the captain, knowing it could be his trump card if true, even if guilt was already weighing down his shoulders. "Your own wife stole fifty grand from another version of O'Kelly once, didn't she? Would you have returned your wife to that man just to create an opportunity to go undercover?"

"Don't you *ever* speak about my wife again." Derek's voice vibrated down the line. "But while we're on the subject, my wife didn't have the ability to make an entire city safer the way Ailish does. You're impeding an investigation, Vance, and in case you don't realize it, you haven't hit the bottom yet. I can make that happen. Or I can make the reverse happen."

No way was he backing down now or bowing under scare tactics. "I've given you my terms. Ailish comes back to Chicago and cooperates—*outside* her father's house—in exchange for a deal, or you lose her as an asset completely. What is it going to be?"

When a full minute passed, Henrik wondered if the captain had disengaged the line, but he finally spoke. "Just answer me one thing. Is she worth losing the chance to be reinstated? Because there's no guarantee Caine gives you a shot without her in tow, and that would stop this investigation cold."

The sunshine above glowed too bright. Being reinstated would mean eventual approval once more from his family, a return to normalcy, and the career he'd been groomed for since birth. Exactly what he wanted, and yet he delivered his answer without hesitation. "Yes, she's worth it and more."

Derek's sigh was sharp. "Very well. She'll get her deal, but I want you both back here by tomorrow morning. In the meantime, I'll find something to offer O'Kelly that isn't his flesh and blood."

Had the captain's agreement been a little too easy? Derek Tyler had always been a man of his word, though. Hell, he'd given Henrik a second chance, and that alone demanded as much loyalty as he could give without sacrificing Ailish. "We'll be there."

As Henrik hung up the phone, he was already walking back up the path, eager to be close to Ailish. Eager to explain the deal he'd worked out with the captain. She would be safe. *Always.* When he'd left the cabin, her disappointment over being kept in the dark had hung in the air like smoke, but he could clear it away now. It might take some convincing that the squad could keep her safe until O'Kelly was put away, but they would get there. If anyone could keep Ailish hidden and protected, it was a crew of cons with access to police department technology.

When the cabin came into view and Henrik saw the door wide open, no sign of Erin, an uncomfortable sensation whispered down his back, forcing him to pick up the pace. The blonde walked out a second later, lighting a book of matches one by one and dropping them to the ground, where she put them out with the toe of her boot.

"*Ailish,*" Henrik bellowed, just as Connor stepped out of the cabin behind Erin, narrowed eyes fastened on his girlfriend. Bad sign. That was a bad fucking sign. "Where is she?"

"She sneaked out while I was using the bathroom." Erin pointed toward the wooden area to the cabin's left. "But I think she went thataway..." She tapped a finger to her chin, then pointed it the opposite direction. "Or maybe that way."

"*Dammit.*" Henrik dug the keys out of his pocket and sprinted for the truck. He'd left his stomach somewhere on the dirt courtyard, the blood rushing through his veins so fast, he felt dizzy. His fury that Erin had let Ailish slip away was eclipsed by frustration at himself. This was on him. When was he going to learn that Ailish wouldn't blindly trust him without a reason? Now, twenty minutes might have ruined any chance he had to help her, to…keep her.

No. No, he wouldn't let that be the case.

He stomped down on the gas pedal.

Chapter Eleven

Ailish was being followed. Not by Henrik, although she suspected at this point the man was hot on her heels. Not by Erin or Connor, either. No, the hair on the back of her neck was in permanent prickle mode because of the white sedan she'd seen three separate times since arriving in town. It had passed by once as she entered a convenience store and been parked across the street when she walked back outside. The same women who'd given her the ride to town were driving to a fishing boat rental center and had agreed to take her along, but they were taking their time shopping for supplies. Hunkered down in the backseat of their Jeep, Ailish watched the white sedan through the rearview mirror, where it sat with the motor running half a block away.

In addition to her quick convenience store run, Ailish had bought a one-way ticket to Detroit at the adjacent bus station, hoping it would throw anyone looking for her off the scent. She was learning, getting better at getting lost and staying that way. And while it gave her a sense of accomplishment to be problem-solving on her own, making her own decisions, a knot continued to tighten in her stomach. Had running away from Henrik been smart or impulsive? There was no denying that Henrik wanted to keep her physically protected, no matter what gray areas existed between them. Now, with the white sedan idling in the rearview, Ailish couldn't help but wonder if she'd made herself more vulnerable by trying to be strong and independent. The kind of person she'd always hoped to become when she could get free of Chicago.

When the white sedan left its spot at the curb, intuition had Ailish sinking down further onto the vinyl seat, until her knees bumped the front row. *Pass by, please just pass by.*

It didn't.

Ailish stopped breathing as the white car pulled into the now-vacant parking space behind the Jeep, creeping forward slowly and nudging the bumper.

"*Shit*," she whispered, rubbing damp palms against the hem of her shorts. Staying low, Ailish reached an arm through the console and locked both doors of the Jeep, before peeking out the curbside window and noticing that the busy sidewalk had cleared somewhat since she'd reentered the car. No witnesses. No one to help her. Not that anyone could if the person behind the wheel had been sent by her father. They were well versed in the art of snatching people off the street, and they didn't usually *care* who was watching. *Dammit.* Ailish dropped a hand and pulled out the T-shirt-wrapped gun, tearing away the cotton with shaking fingers and flipping off the safety.

Both the passenger and driver side doors of the white sedan opened, two men stepping out of the vehicle whom she instantly recognized. They were longtime associates of her father, had even driven Ailish to high school on occasion. Men who had stood guard outside her bedroom for months after her failed attempt to run away. Like most of her father's men, they thought her a nuisance. Or they *had*, until she'd grown up and begun employing a different method of acting out. Teasing. Something for which their resentment had been plain—and just then, Ailish wished she could go back in time and have a stern talk with her past self.

That regret snapped her spine straight. She'd been a veritable prisoner inside her own home, and these men had been complicit with her father in maintaining that situation. It would be a cold day in hell before she went anywhere with them. And she damn well wasn't going to regret things she'd done in the past. Learning to accept herself for all her faults was part of her newly discovered freedom.

Ailish took a steadying breath as the two men drew even with the Jeep's back windows. She focused on the more intimidating of the pair—Gordy—and allowed her index finger to rest on the gun's trigger. When Gordy spotted her hunkered down in the backseat, he threw his head back and laughed, joined by his partner a moment later. His reaction lit indignant sparks in her gut, but Gordy's reaction told her he hadn't seen the gun, at least.

Gordy's partner, Vick, rapped his knuckles against the window, making Ailish's heart go wild, her throat refusing to let her swallow. They were both attempting to open the front Jeep doors when Ailish's unlucky companions emerged from the convenience store, their arms wrapped around brown paper bags as they chatted. Their stride came to a dead halt when they saw the two men, however.

"Hey, that's our car."

Ailish could barely hear over the pounding of her pulse, but when the three women started backing away on the sidewalk, she knew Gordy had said something threatening. Guilt over leading three unsuspecting Samaritans into her problems tried to invade Ailish's fear, but she tamped it down. *Deal with it later.*

Gordy pulled a handkerchief from his right pocket and

wrapped it around his fist. "Come on out, little girl, or we'll drag you out," he growled, his voice cutting right through the stillness inside the Jeep.

Only a small hesitation on Ailish's end had Gordy lifting his fist, obviously intending to punch through the glass. Knowing once they gained entry to the car, she would be out of luck, Ailish raised her gun, just before Gordy could connect with the glass. He stopped cold, staring at her weapon, almost in fascination. Then the corner of his mouth ticked up.

"Oh shit, Vick. Someone grew a pair since leaving Chicago, huh?" He jerked his chin toward the opposite side of the Jeep. Ailish only had to turn her head slightly to see that Vick was now pointing a gun at her through the glass. Nowhere to go. She couldn't fire or she'd be fired on. Trapped. Again. *Dammit.* Even if they were under orders to bring her back alive, they wouldn't hesitate to return fire if she pulled the trigger first. They were stone-cold criminals first, loyal to her father second.

"I can pay you," Ailish shouted, using the first stall tactic that came to mind. "Just get me to an ATM." If she could just buy herself some time to get away. Or…or for Henrik to find her. *Please God.* As soon as she acknowledged that second possibility, the guilt would no longer be held at bay. This is why he'd had her guarded inside the cabin, why he'd been so protective.

"If we take you back, we'll be made men, little girl. That means we'll get to *send* people on these shit jobs, instead of doing them ourselves." Vick tapped the muzzle of his gun against the glass. "I'm looking to fish for a lifetime, not eat for one day. Get the fuck out of the car."

What were her choices? She didn't have any. But if she went with them now, she would at least have chances to escape on the way back to Chicago, right? But dammit, she hated surrendering to these men. *Loathed it.*

She licked away the sweat that beaded her upper lip and smoothed a finger down the gun's trigger. It was obvious that neither Gordy nor Vick liked being exposed on the street with weapons and were starting to get nervous. Maybe all she had to do was wait them out. They were shifting on their feet, getting restless, scanning the street with calculated eyes.

Just as a glimmer of hope started to appear, it was doused by glass exploding to her left. And then to her right. An arm snaked in through the passenger-side window to unlock the door, a split second before a hand wrapped around her right ankle. The passenger seat slid forward on its track and Ailish was yanked off the seat, the back of her thigh scraping over the bolted track, making her scream out in pain, alarm. Enough alarm to lift the gun and point it at Gordy's head.

Everything went still. So still.

Horror kept Ailish from immediately pulling the trigger, however. She didn't want to be like these men. Didn't want to be a murderer. "Please," she said through clenched teeth. "You never saw me."

Gordy leaned down, his face hovering right in front of the gun's barrel. Unconcerned, possibly even excited by the weapon pointed in his direction. "Pull it. I dare you." When Ailish still couldn't bring herself to tighten her finger, he laughed. "You always were a tease."

He fisted the front of Ailish's shirt and jerked her out of the car. She stumbled right into Vick, who still held his weapon, tucked just inside the opening of his jacket. Passersby ran in the opposite direction, vanishing into shops. Good. At least they wouldn't be punished for being witnesses. Gordy propelled Ailish toward their white car, still idling at the curb, but before she could open the door and climb into the backseat, a truck roared down the street. Henrik's truck. Followed by another dark blue SUV—Connor and Erin?

Refusing to let relief process itself—her friends were now

in danger because of her—Ailish went on pure instinct and ducked behind the white sedan, just as the truck and SUV drew even with them. In her peripheral vision, Ailish could see that Vick still pointed his weapon at her, but he dropped to his knees, then down to the concrete before Ailish could even raise her own weapon. Red bloomed on the front of his shirt as his gun clattered to the ground.

Tires squealed as Ailish was scooped up from behind, two hands curling beneath her armpits. A quick over-the-shoulder glance told her it was Erin.

"*Come on.*" As gunfire volleyed between Henrik's truck and Gordy from his position ducked down behind the Jeep, Erin pulled her gun and aimed it at Gordy. But instead of pulling the trigger, she handed it to Ailish. "You're up, Mafia Princess. Henrik just saved your ass, now you save his. That's how it works."

Ailish didn't think—she didn't need to. If Henrik was hurt because of her, she wouldn't be able to live with herself. With a deep breath, she let the loud sounds and whispered instructions from Erin melt away, and she pulled the trigger.

The moment Gordy dropped, silence reined. And then they were running. Erin hustled Ailish to Henrik's truck, threw open the door, and urged her inside before jogging back to the SUV.

Ailish only caught a peek at Henrik's livid expression before tires squealed once again and they were zooming down the small-town street toward the highway.

"Are you okay?" Henrik managed through lips gone numb. *Don't think about what would have happened if you'd arrived ten seconds later. Don't think about it.*

If he lived another thousand years, he would never

witness anything more terrifying than Ailish being taken away at gunpoint. His stomach protested, urging him to pull the car over and empty its contents, but he breathed through the nausea and kept driving. They had to keep moving. Who knew what kind of small-town sheriff could be a mile behind them, sirens blaring? Derek held no jurisdiction here, leaving them solidly on their own should they be stopped. Connor had already taken the first exit off the two-lane interstate, obviously knowing law enforcement would be looking for two vehicles and they needed to split up.

Henrik kept the gas pedal pushed to the floor and continued onward, although he wanted nothing more than to pull over and shake the girl beside him. Shake her until he stopped seeing her fear back on that sidewalk. Until the stark, brittle feeling of helplessness left him.

Ailish stared straight ahead, still gulping in oxygen. *Good.* She needed to be aware of the impact of her actions. *Goddammit*, he was pissed. So why did the need to hold her, tell her everything was going to be all right, override his anger?

"I-I just killed a man," Ailish murmured. "I'm no better than any of them. My father, Gordy…"

The desolation in her tone made Henrik's ribs ache. "He was attempting to abduct you, Ailish. You didn't have a choice."

"Yes, I did. There's always a choice, isn't there?" She swiped a hand over her eyes. "Is today the first time you took another person's life?"

"No," he responded quietly. "It's not."

She was quiet for a few beats. "And I was the reason for this time."

It was torture, not being able to touch her. Pull her across the console into the cradle of his arms when she looked so lost. But it was paramount that they drive hard and far before they even considered stopping. "Did you know those men?"

"Yes." She smoothed fingers down her seat belt. "Gordy and Vick. I don't know their last names. Or anything about them, really, except they've worked for my father for a long time." Her voice took on a reminiscent quality. "They weren't allowed to speak to me. No one was. I think today might have been the first time we exchanged actual words."

In Henrik's current edgy state, he knew asking was a bad idea, but nothing would stop him from finding out everything to know about Ailish. It was like an addiction that required feeding. "Why weren't they allowed to speak to you?"

"I inherited my mother's gift of persuasion. That's what I overheard my father tell them. That lies come easy to me." She looked down at her lap. "They wanted to keep their jobs, and that meant they couldn't show me any sympathy. Not that they had it in them, but I guess...I guess that's why they chose to ignore me. They didn't want to think of me as a person."

Henrik realized he'd let the vehicle climb to a dangerous speed during Ailish's explanation and slowed by ten miles per hour. "I won't lose any sleep over putting one of them down, Ailish. Know that. You shouldn't, either."

He could feel her stare. "What was *your* father like?"

It was the way she posed the question. As if she had no idea how an actual father was supposed to behave. God, he was back to wanting to shake her. Hold her. Kiss her. "He was a cop. Retired now." Henrik cleared away the dust in his throat. "He believed in the system, doing everything by the book. One of the good ones."

Had Ailish moved closer? The now-familiar tightening in his stomach that occurred whenever she drew near told him she had. "Did he take you camping?"

"You're killing me over here, Lish," he grated, her wistfulness wrapping around his neck like a boa constrictor. "Can we have this talk later?"

"I don't understand."

Henrik flexed his fingers on the steering wheel, then gripped the leather tighter. "Your father knew what he was doing, telling those assholes not to speak with you. Anyone with an ounce of decency would hear a few words from your mouth and—"

Her perplexity reached him across the seat. "And what?"

He shook his head. "Forget I said that. There was nothing right about what your father did. Not a goddamn thing." *Calm down, man. Reel it in.* "Yeah, we went camping once. It wasn't really our thing, though. He liked to drive me to spots around Chicago where he'd made arrests and walk me through them. Step by step. The decisions he made and why."

Damn if she hadn't moved closer again. Close enough for him to cover her hand with his own? "He must have been proud when you followed in his footsteps."

"At the time, yes. Now?" Henrik tried to focus on the road, the distance they needed to travel before stopping. Anything but the shame in his father's eyes the last time Henrik had gone to visit. "Let's just say I'll be lucky to get a Christmas card this year."

"Because you're...not a cop anymore?" She sighed when Henrik didn't answer. "My father had no use for me until my standardized math test results came back. We had dinner together that night in the backyard. I thought it was so crazy. We were eating outside." Her tone grew so light he had to strain to make out her words over the truck engine. "He gave me two sets of statistics. Two baseball teams and their numbers for the season so far. And then he asked for a probable outcome. I didn't realize until I saw the teams playing on television what his reasoning had been. But I... that was when he stopped sending me to school. I just worked after that."

Henrik wished the man were standing in the truck's path.

To use Ailish such a way…he could never let it happen again. Never. And if he didn't focus on something besides the broken way she relayed her memory, he'd rip the steering wheel off and wreck the vehicle. *Calm. Down.* The wooded landscape on either side of the truck was unfamiliar, making him long for the smog and concrete of Chicago. At least he knew how to hide someone there. Knew how to navigate every inch of those streets.

When Ailish's fingers drifted over his knuckles, Henrik's abdomen shuddered, need sinking low and filling the flesh between his legs. "It's only a matter of time before they start to miss you," Ailish said, rubbing her cheek on his shoulder. "You were only gone one night when *I* started missing you."

His eyelids drooped, the organ in his chest going insane. *Poundpoundpound.* "What are you trying to do here, Ailish?"

"Don't take me back to Chicago," she whispered against his ear, one hand settling on his thigh, drifting higher…higher. "Please. I know that's where we're driving and—"

"Enough," Henrik snapped out. "You think you can seduce me into turning this truck around? Is that really your plan?"

"Yes."

He waited. "Yes? *That's it?*"

Ailish nodded, the top of her head bumping his jaw. "Whenever we touch each other…we start over. Everything that we said or did before stops mattering. There's just us and what's next." Her head lifted and she scrutinized him. "Right?"

The truth behind her words weighed heavily on his shoulders. They'd been in a state of feeling each other out for days, him doling out snippets of information when it was convenient. She'd had reason to run—doubt. Doubt in him that disappeared when they touched, if he understood her correctly. Shit, that was something, wasn't it? She trusted him when their bodies were working toward pleasure. Now he needed to work on the rest.

"Ailish, Chicago is where you'll be safest. You left before I had a chance to explain—"

Sirens.

His pulse dropping to an adrenaline-laced beat, Henrik transferred his attention to the rearview mirror. Perhaps he should have been nervous, being chased instead of chasing. But there was nothing but calm focus, sending a flicker of wonder winding through his mind. Maybe he'd never been meant for the inside of a police car. Had his path always ended at the undercover squad he so resented? "Hold on, Ailish."

There were no visible flashing lights yet, only sound. At the next narrow break in the tree line, Henrik veered off the road and onto bumpy earth. He wound around thick trees, not giving a damn about his suspension, as they would be ditching the truck at first opportunity. After they'd gotten about four hundred yards into the forest, Henrik slowed in degrees, winding his way into a thick fall of branches before hitting the brakes and cutting the truck's engine.

Henrik unfastened his seat belt and removed his gun from the waistband of his jeans, ejecting the spent clip onto the seat. He reached across Ailish and removed a fresh clip from the glove compartment and clicked it into his weapon. "Be ready to move."

Not bothering to unlock her own seat belt, Ailish sucked in a deep, audible breath and held it, her eyes wide, like two hazel moons.

"They won't hear you breathing from the road, baby."

Ailish laughed, releasing a rush of oxygen at the same time. And goddammit if he didn't almost reach for her, fully prepared to lay her out on the front seat, to position her for the fucking of a lifetime. His cock was granite inside the leg of his pants, a product of adrenaline and Ailish being in the same place. There was alarm mixed in, too. Alarm that he could load a gun in preparation for protecting his girl, by fair means or foul, without a single hesitation. Not a single one. This went beyond destroying evidence. These were men's lives he was willing to sacrifice.

He watched Ailish as she scanned the woods. "I bet you wish camping was your thing about now."

Suspicion trickled in at her thoughtful tone, lifting Henrik's antenna. "If you're thinking about running again, Ailish, I wouldn't suggest it."

She actually had the nerve to look hurt. "I'm not."

Tension reigned inside the car, their gazes clashing as the sirens drew closer. At least four police vehicles, if the overlapping wails were any indication. Henrik placed his fingertips on the door handle, and Ailish did the same. To run from the cops? Or him? *Fuck*, he couldn't read her. And there was no time to talk, because the peals of sound were even with them, roaring past the forest as they stayed perfectly still and waited. Waited.

It seemed as if an hour had passed when silence finally greeted their ears. No crunching of forest ground, so Henrik knew the local law enforcement weren't creeping up behind them, either, hoping to employ the element of surprise. Very slowly, so Ailish could see his actions, Henrik applied the safety feature on his gun and slid it back into his jeans' waistband. "Stay right there. I'll come around to get you. Understand?"

"Then what?" Ailish blurted.

"We're leaving the truck and walking. I'll find us another ride."

"And then we're headed to Chicago, right?" Her gaze cut to the forest, then back. "Tell me why I shouldn't try to run again."

"Besides the fact that I'll catch you?" He shoved the door open, but made no move to climb out of the truck. "I've secured you a deal with Chicago PD. If you cooperate in the case against your father—from a distance—there will be no charges brought against you, including your work under the Bookie Cookie pseudonym."

The strain around her eyes eased a bit. "You told the police?"

"I told the captain as much as I *had* to, Ailish." He punctuated the air with a finger. "I put as many necessary cards on the table to get you clear, in spite of everything. But he's a smart man. He made the deal knowing damn well there's more to come." His breath was uneven. "When we give the captain your alternate identity, I needed to make sure he couldn't find a way to use it."

Her hand fell from the door handle into her lap. "What about you? Are you just going to turn me over to your captain and leave?"

"Not for good." He swallowed the golf ball–sized lump in his throat, brought on by the idea of leaving her behind, even for a small space of time. "Long enough to get what we need on Caine from the inside."

"He'll know," she whispered. "He won't be fooled."

Henrik alighted from the truck and paused, looking back at Ailish where she sat frozen in the passenger seat. "Your word won't be enough on its own, especially in light of your arrest. We need something solid."

"And I'm going to help you figure out what that thing is? Is that right?"

The apprehension she was trying to lock behind her bravado made him want to climb back into the truck, pick a spot on the map, and just drive. As far away from Chicago as they could get. But they would always be running, looking over their shoulder. And who was to say she even wanted to run with him? Even now, she wanted to sprint through the forest, leaving him in the dust. This course of action was in her best interest, even if she didn't realize it yet.

"If you want your deal," he said, "Chicago is the answer."

Henrik slammed the door on her response.

They had a vehicle to steal.

Chapter Twelve

Awareness prickled along Ailish's skin when Henrik opened the passenger-side door. His gaze fell to her bare legs, that throat of his working in a way that was now comforting. Familiar. But when she thought he might reach out and caress her skin, he popped the glove box instead and removed a set of handcuffs.

"What are you doing?"

His stoic expression was carved in stone. "I can't risk you running again. We only have another day to get back to Chicago, and there's no room for setbacks at this point." He dipped his chin once. "Get out of the truck and turn around."

It was on the tip of Ailish's tongue to claim she wouldn't run, but it was obvious Henrik wouldn't believe her. Rightly so. But her running now would have had less to do with not trusting Henrik—especially now that he'd relayed his plan—and more to do with keeping them both alive. Caine wouldn't let either of them live once he realized he'd been crossed. No one understood but her, and Henrik was beyond listening.

Seeing no choice but to obey him for now, Ailish turned

and very slowly slipped off the passenger seat, noting the way his nostrils flared when her shirt rode up and exposed her stomach, the underside of her breasts. Lord, she was far from unaffected, too, a fact that obviously didn't go unnoticed as their breath mingled between them. The cuffs dangled at Henrik's side, his head tipped forward so their foreheads were in danger of touching. "Turn *around*," Henrik ordered, his voice rasping like two pieces of brittle sandpaper.

Something in Ailish's chest kicked up a brutal rebellion at the suffering in Henrik's voice, surprising her in its intensity. For just a second, she shut down the dread threatening to run amok in her gut and looked at Henrik. *Really* looked. And listened to the heart knocking against her ribs. This beautiful, protective man had shown up on her doorstep, and while he'd been secretive, he'd put himself at risk to keep her safe. Kissed her, touched her, with such passion, her legs trembled at the sweltering memories of those stolen moments. "Who *are* you, Henrik?"

If possible, his big body went even more still. "Excuse me?"

"How did you get here? With me?" Her mouth opened, closed, opened again. "Why were we in this together from the moment you showed up? I don't understand it even though—"

He snagged her around the waist with a powerful forearm, jerking her into the warmth of his body. But instead of kissing her as she'd anticipated—and yeah, kind of *needed* to go on living—he simply closed the car door and spun her around to face the vehicle. "Even though what, Ailish?"

"I don't understand why we're a team…even though it feels like that's how it's supposed to be." She stared up at Henrik's reflection in the passenger-side window, saw his eyes close and wondered at that response. "Why did we feel like a foregone conclusion when you walked into my cabin?"

"What is this?" Henrik breathed into her ear. "Another

attempt to seduce me so you can get away? I won't let it work. I *can't*."

Ailish's hands were drawn to the small of her back. When she felt the metal closing around her wrists, heard the metallic *clink*, her fate was sealed. So why was she more focused on the man standing so close, breathing into her hair like he'd just run a marathon? Her loins pulsated, body crying out for more contact. Craving it. As if she'd made the plea out loud, Henrik's lap fit against her bottom and they both released pent-up exhales of air. God, she could actually feel their connection, like a spinning, golden flame in her belly that only he knew how to extinguish. She had no idea where the words she said next came from, only knew they'd been unveiled from their hiding place in the back of her mind. "Did you want me that day in the park, Henrik?"

"*Yes.*" He stumbled forward, forcing Ailish up against the side of the truck. "I wanted to undress you, right fucking there. Rip the dress off your tight body. You don't know, baby. You don't *know*."

A moan ripped through her vocal cords, fogging up the car window. She made no secret of being turned on when a man desired her to the point of pain—but the confession from Henrik was utopia. This sexual giant of a man could barely stand under the weight of his need, and it hypnotized Ailish, flushed her head to toe. She reached back into her memory bank and remembered that day…how exhausted and downtrodden she'd been, unable to attempt garnering notice in her usual manner. And he'd wanted her anyway. He wanted her *now,* a fact made unshakable by him pushing his erection into her restrained hands.

"I'm so hot," she whimpered. "I need to have you."

His groan was agonized, but the sound was followed by his tongue licking up the side of her neck. A bite of her earlobe. "We can't. We—you're handcuffed." His palms slapped down on the passenger-side door, caging in her body. "Fuck, you're my *prisoner*, Ailish. Everything is different now."

"It doesn't matter," she said huskily, massaging the bulge of his manhood with what little mobility she could muster. God, she wanted *all* of him. Needed to touch everywhere. *Right now*. "We both know the handcuffs don't mean anything."

Where was this conviction coming from? Ailish couldn't pinpoint the location, only knew it was deep down, where nothing could shake it. She could feel Henrik teetering on an imaginary fence behind her, so close to being pushed to one side, but she couldn't tell which. "We need to *walk*," Henrik growled, negating that desire a split second later by wedging her more firmly against the truck.

"You really think—" Ailish broke off when his right hand cupped her breast and squeezed. *God yes. Touch me. I forgot how to live without your hands on me.* "You really think we can turn this off?"

"Not in this lifetime." Henrik's other hand found her left breast, his thumb strumming over her nipple like she was an instrument to be played. "But you were wrong. The cuffs *do* mean something. They mean we don't trust each other. They mean you want to get away from me. I can't fuck you when you'd rather be running away." His hands released her breasts, sliding down her belly to cup the juncture of her thighs in a double grip—*roughly*—ripping a ragged moan from Ailish. "That would be wrong, baby. So goddamn wrong."

Her legs wobbled, threatening to give out. "I don't want to run. I don't want to run. Please, Henrik. I'm *hurting*."

Was that her voice? Her face? The reflection staring back at Ailish was more sexed-up porn star than almost-virgin. Warmth pooled beneath Henrik's possessive touch, her skin so sensitized that a passing breeze whispering across her cleavage aroused her even more. *Oh God, this is torture.* How to convince Henrik her need was real and urgent? Not a ploy or a bad thing, like he thought.

It took every iota of Ailish's willpower to struggle away from Henrik and shuffle past the front bumper. She immediately mourned the loss of his touch to the point that walking was painful. The tops of her thighs were slick with moisture, her bound position forcing her to walk with breasts thrust forward. Everything about the situation provoked her live-wire senses, but she managed to keep putting one foot in front of the other. "If you want to walk, we'll walk." When her voice wavered, she lifted her chin to compensate. "I'm not going to beg you."

Please, please, come get me.

Ailish heard the crunch of leaves behind her, knew Henrik was fast approaching, and her hormones started to spin in mad circles. "You think you're calling my bluff?" His tone evoked the image of smoking coals. Only a few yards on her trail now. *Closer. Come closer.* "This isn't a game we're playing. I could…" Two big hands grasped her hips, pulling her to a stop. With a crude oath gritted into her ear, one masculine hand slid around and flipped open the button of her jean shorts. His touch descended slowly, delving into the front of her panties. "I could lose the only job I'm qualified for…could compromise the case."

When his index and middle fingers rubbed over her clit, Ailish's thighs shot together, her moan echoing among the trees. "You don't seem that concerned about it," she managed.

"You don't think so?" Having found her atrociously wet, Henrik pushed those two fingers inside her with a satisfied grunt. "I *am* concerned, Ailish. But right now, I'd let the world burn to get my cock inside this tight hole. I'd let it go to fucking ashes, that's how hot I am to come inside of it." He shoved his fingers deeper without warning, putting Ailish so off balance he had to steady her with his body. "*Christ*, I don't even have a condom to protect you with." His tone was agonized, but aroused. So aroused. "How can I *do* this?"

"I'm on the pill," she gasped, her head tossing on his muscular shoulder as her inner walls clenched around his touch. "*OhhhGodsogood.*"

Her permission made something inside him give way. She could feel it happen in real time, answering deep in her middle. "I'm clean for you, baby. Tell me you know that," Henrik muttered thickly, his fingers working in and out, jostling her clit in the process.

"Yes."

His groan shook her. "It's going to be my dick this time. And I'm going to be mean about it, you understand? I wanted to go slow, but you ran. You *ran*." Henrik exhaled in a rush above her head. "I must be one of the bad men, baby, because now that I've caught you, I just want to please that pussy until you're docile enough to *stay the hell put*. Next time I say I'm handling shit, I want you to part your thighs, smile, and ask me if I want a quick fuck first."

Ailish's mouth dropped open on a gasp. No one had ever spoken to her in such a base, sexual manner…and she *loved* it. Being the key to this giant man's gratification, to the point he didn't spare a thought for the world going up in flames around them, sent her on a high so glorious she never wanted to come down. Even though her body was still fully clothed, she felt naked and bathed in blistering sunshine, pressure building between her legs where Henrik's fingers milked in and out, the heel of his hand beginning to grind on her sensitive nub between drives. "Tell me," she husked. "Tell me you're handling—"

"I'm handling shit," Henrik growled right up against her ear.

She didn't know whether Henrik spun her around or if she turned to face him in dire need of seeing his face, but when they locked gazes, pockets of lust seemed to explode in the atmosphere, landing on their skin with a sizzle. "If my hands were free right now, I would rip your stupid shirt off," she breathed, shocking herself. Henrik, too, if his lifted eyebrow was any indication. He sauntered the last remaining step between them, took hold of the T-shirt's hem and lifted it over his head, giving her an up close view of squeezing abdomen muscles, the sexy, shifting patterns they made beneath his skin.

"Thank y-you."

"Stop being so goddamn adorable, Ailish." He twisted both hands in the sides of her shorts and yanked them down to the forest floor, along with her underwear, his gaze devouring the sight of her exposed center. "I said you were getting it mean. Being cute won't save you."

Her pulse clamored through her veins, antsy for more touching. More of his hands. His mouth. Anything she could get. When Henrik lifted Ailish's shirt to expose her breasts, his fingertips grazed the swell of her cleavage, nearly buckling her knees. "More, please. Touch me."

"I'll remind you about asking for more"—he tugged her bra down, allowing her breasts to bounce free—"when you're screaming for me to pull out."

"I can't wait that long."

Looking suddenly agonized, Henrik slapped a hand over her mouth. "*Cute.*"

She kissed his palm. Then licked it, side to side.

With a low curse, Henrik pulled his hand away, but held it in the air while working the button and zipper of his pants, shoving the garment to his ankles, along with his boxers. Then he took the hand she'd licked and used it to lubricate his erection, watching her as he stroked. Hunger for his taste flared to life in Ailish's belly, so intense she started to kneel, but Henrik caught her under the arm, hauling her body upright. "Oh no. That mouth might be the only thing in the world that could make me forget how badly I need to fuck you."

Ailish had no time to prepare for Henrik wrapping an arm around her hips and lifting her body up against his bulk, flattening her breasts against his pecs. Her body moving on instinct to get as close to its pleasure source as possible, Ailish's legs shot up around his waist, granting her the first experience of his plump arousal slipping through her naked female flesh. "*Oh my God*," she whimpered, head falling back on her shoulders. "I need you."

She felt Henrik's hand moving beneath her backside, then his erection was being guided back and forth, dragging over her clit, teasing, testing. "You need this, Ailish?" He took a drag of her mouth, pulling her bottom lip away with him before freeing it. "Tell me how I'm going to give it to you."

"Mean," she whispered, hyperaware of her bound hands, not being able to touch him when he was so beautiful. *Unfair*.

"That's right." Henrik pushed his hard flesh up against Ailish's entrance and loosened his grip on her body, allowing her to slide down and take a portion of his arousal. "There you go," he grated, his breath accelerating. "Take a couple inches and earn the rest."

Ailish barely heard the command because she was too busy marveling over his thickness, the leashed power between her legs. As if her hips were operating on their own, they flicked back and ground forward, the friction against her clit sending a moan flying past her lips. With his erection lodged inside Ailish, his available hand was free to knead her bottom in a hypnotic rhythm, moving in tandem with her undulations.

"There's a good little earner." His palm cracked down on her backside. "Moving like she wants more."

"*Yes. Please.*"

Confusion crept in when Henrik covered her mouth with a big hand, but it cleared a second later—*everything* cleared from her mind—when Henrik seated himself completely inside her with a savage upthrust. Ailish screamed into the meat of his palm, her legs scrambling on either side of Henrik's waist to climb higher...or climb down. Away. She didn't know. Only could process the full breadth of him, pushing against her walls, his unrecognizable voice chanting into her hair. So much. Too much. And yet a sense of completion, of rightness, was there in the background, fighting for attention.

"Calm *down*, Ailish." Henrik's voice shook, his body riddled with tension. "Fuck, I knew you were tight, but...did you lie to me? You a virgin?"

She couldn't speak with his hand covering her mouth, so she simply shook her head. The movement made her nipples slide sideways against his chest, sparking lust in her middle. Against his palm, she moaned, shifting her legs higher. "Feels better." Her words were muffled. "*Ohhh*. That feels better."

Henrik's jaw looked ready to shatter. "Goddammit, I could break you like this. I have to lay you down somewhere—"

"No." Ailish shook her head to dislodge his hand, pride making her brave. No way would she be found too weak for this man. In that moment, he was *hers* and she would satisfy him. "You said *mean*," she murmured before going in for the kill, pushing his lips apart with her own and mingling their tongues together. The hand on her bottom tightened with bruising strength as he joined the dance...then started to lead. A broken sound split from his throat a second before he started to devastate Ailish, angling his head and deepening the kiss. She breathed through her nose, refusing to give up his mouth and its perfection. His erection beat inside her, even that subtle pumping of blood creating enough friction to arouse her even further. But it was nothing compared to when Henrik slid out a couple inches and pushed back in. *Deeeeep.*

"Motherfucker," he growled. "Stop squeezing me. I already need to come."

Unaware that she'd been doing anything but kissing him, Ailish focused on where their bodies joined, relieved that the discomfort had subsided. Pleasure replaced it with every passing second, until she was frantic to buck her hips, which she did, ripping a string of curses from Henrik's mouth. "You feel so good," she whimpered.

"*Me?*" With both hands gripping her bottom now, Henrik lifted Ailish to the tip of his erection and slid her back down, baring his teeth when her body prevented him from going any further. He leaned in and pressed their mouths together, not kissing her, just breathing, breathing, as he walked them backward. Over Ailish's head, Henrik braced one hand on a tree, his hips beginning to move in slow pumps. "*I* feel good, Ailish?" Their lips were flush when he groaned, so she could feel the sound on her tongue. "Men fight wars over pussy like this."

If Ailish's feet weren't already dangling off the ground, they would have lifted all on their own, carried by the knowledge that she could undo this man. This man who caged such incredible strength, it vibrated beneath his skin with the effort to hold it back. He was thick and demanding between her legs, pushing into her wetness again and again with heavy thrusts, but the rest of him was marble. "You won't break me," she said, wrapping her legs more firmly around his waist. "But you're welcome to try."

"Stop." He ground their foreheads together. "Stop talking."

"N-no." Behind her back, Ailish jangled her cuffed wrists, turned on by her own boldness. Thrills raced and snapped along her nerve endings, brought on by the illicitness of their position. Captive and captor, yes, but simply also woman and man. Two people who couldn't stop touching any more than the sun could stop rising. "I'm your prisoner—now what are you going to do with me?"

A shift of intention took place inside Henrik. Ailish could sense it. Where he'd been thrown off by her inexperience in the beginning…she could see the very same thing made him want. Need. His hand slapped down on her backside, the other raking down the tree bark above her head, dislodging wood in its path. Moving on feminine instinct, Ailish arched her back a little more and presented her breasts, an offering Henrik didn't hesitate to take. His mouth moved greedily from one nipple to the other, leaving dampness in its path. And God, although the sensations wrought by his mouth were tantalizing and perfect, they were nothing compared to the new, hurried slams of his hips. "Do I need to cover your mouth again? Huh?" His question alerted Ailish to the fact that words in some unknown language were being moaned through her lips. "Are you the kind of girl who helps men beat off through the thin walls in apartment buildings? Yeah, I think you would be. The little screamer on the third floor."

Another brisk sting of Henrik's palm on her backside had Ailish pressing her lips together to keep from crying out. His drives were coming at a punishing pace now, her teeth being jarred in her head from the force of being bounced high and slammed back down. "Henrik, Henrik, Henrik…"

"Yeah. That's me. I'd be the big man who gets to fuck the little screamer." Henrik's powerful arms banded around her hips, all of his strength now going into riding her body up his unforgiving flesh and grinding her back down. "Lucky man, they'd say. Wouldn't they, baby? You'd be getting the whole building off, but I'd be the only one who gets this tight prize between your legs."

"Yes," she wailed. The desire to touch him rose to a fever pitch at the agony twisting his handsome features. So much pain. All because of her. And that's what facilitated the quickening at her core. The repeated fullness of Henrik's thrusts, hitting some undiscovered promised land over and over *without cease—slapslapslap—*his strangled grunts, the possession in his gaze…those addictive things joined forces to ruin her. The orgasm came on so strong, her body's fight-or-flight instinct kicked in, her legs moving restlessly around his hips, as if she could run away in midair. Her hands strained for release inside the handcuffs; frustration and lust and sweet agony rose in her throat and left in a scream. She came, she came in such brutal fashion, no air would find her lungs. Henrik chanted words against her mouth and somehow they provided enough focus to suck in air, but the thrusting wouldn't stop, and neither would her climax. It poured and poured over her like oil from an upturned jug, washing her in heat until she was burning up, on fire. "Oh God, I can't take it…*don't stop*."

"*Fuck*, Ailish," he growled into her ear. "Don't make me live without this. Feel how you take me, baby? Like a hot glove, three sizes too small?" He moved in a frenzy, a man fighting for his sanity, which would only come with release. "Keep your legs up while I finish. High and tight. Let me get it so goddamn deep, my come seeps out of you for a week."

His final word was cut off by the shaking of his enormous body, his flesh jerking between her legs one final time before warmth flooded where their bodies joined. Ailish watched through the haze of euphoria as Henrik was brought to his knees—literally. He fell into a kneeling position, Ailish still impaled on his erection. He dragged her up and back on his lap in uneven motions that slowed, slowed, along with the quieting of his bone-rattling growls.

Ailish stared at Henrik's heaving chest, his sweat-dappled face, and felt like she'd been through a hurricane. She was in a similar state, her shirt a damp, twisted mess around her collarbone, moisture slicking every inch of her legs and stomach. "I don't want to live without this either," Ailish blurted, horrified to feel pressure welling behind her eyes, an uncomfortable buildup in her tummy. "Oh no. Oh *God*," she panted, still trying to catch her breath. "I'm one of those women who cries after sex. I have a fifth fault now and you seem to be the one bringing them out of me."

A moment passed where she couldn't pinpoint Henrik's expression. It was awe and amusement...but there was dread, too. Like he could see the future and it was so far from inside that forest, he never wanted to leave. No. No, wait, that was *her. She* wanted to stay right there until someone commanded them to leave. Panic over what was to come in Chicago bubbled up in her middle, spilled over into the perfection they'd created together.

Henrik seemed to sense her worry and cut it off with a long, slow kiss that blurred the edges of her apprehension. His hands slid over her hair, gathered some of it in his fists without tugging, just holding the strands, as if for safekeeping.

When he finally pulled away, the edges of her vision sparkled like firecrackers in the night sky. "Ailish, I'm going to take the cuffs off." Another thorough kiss that felt like... good-bye? So much that she whimpered into his mouth. "I'll get you somewhere safe and leave, if that's what you want. I'm not going to force you back to Chicago, baby. I won't do it. I won't see you scared."

This was it. He was offering her freedom. The one thing she'd always wanted, but it would be without him. Was she brave enough to go back to Chicago and face her demons if it meant being with Henrik when it was all over?

Yes. Yes...she'd always been brave enough. But now she had something to fight for. Something bigger than just her. This unseen force pushing her toward Henrik seemed almost detrimental to ignore. This man saw through her, and saw what she could be. It was there in his eyes when they looked at each other. Connection and understanding, heaped with the crazy lust she'd never thought to experience. And yeah, she'd never felt capable of righting her wrongs—and those of her father—before. But going back to Chicago and aiding the undercover squad, it would *give* her that power. It would ease the guilt of what she'd done, bookmaking for the mob while saving her sanity by pretending the consequences of calling in debts didn't exist beyond the desk in her room.

Henrik scrutinized her, holding his breath while waiting for an answer.

"Take off the cuffs," she murmured.

A heavy beat passed as Henrik reached down and tugged the keys out of his jeans pocket. As he wrapped both arms around her and undid the cuffs blind, he laid kisses on her forehead. Good-bye kisses that made her want to cry again, *dammit*, so as soon as the metal was no longer encumbering her hands, Ailish threw her arms around Henrik, tight as they would go. He dropped the cuffs to the forest floor and pulled her close, close as Ailish could get without climbing inside his barrel chest.

"I told you I didn't want to live without this and *then* you give me the option of leaving?" She pressed her lips to his shoulder. "That's very rude, you know."

His body deflated in degrees, but his arms turned to steel. "What should I have said instead?"

This is trust. The weight of the metal cuffs had only been transferred to her heart. She never wanted to be separated from the man holding her so tightly. And she knew—without a single doubt—letting her go would hurt him just as much as leaving would pain her. But he'd do it. Because he wanted her to be happy, more than keeping his job. Or proving himself.

It felt as though the hours spent in interrogation had taken place years ago, but she still recalled the resignation she'd felt. The certainty that she'd be a prisoner soon enough. And yes, there'd been *massive* relief. She would finally be paying for what she'd done. The guilt would no longer be a daily burden she carted around like a pack mule. She'd been blinded by freedom and forgotten about her past deeds. The ones her father continued to commit. Henrik could give her the chance to banish the guilt, stop the violence, once and for all. And he'd be right beside her while they accomplished it together.

"I would want you to say that we're a team. And where you go, I go."

Henrik's gusty exhale blew back her hair. "I want that to be true. I don't think you realize...exactly how goddamn much." He ran open lips up the side of her neck. "But you can't come with me where I'm going. Your father's house. Especially now that I know what you went through there."

She leaned back and met his gaze. "You don't understand. I *need* to go with you. Going to prison...that was my chance to make up for my role in so many—" Saying the word "murders" or "beatings" out loud was too much, but Henrik's eyes told her he understood. "I've survived my father before. I can do it again. We can do it together. I've been sheltered my entire life and I hated it. Don't you sideline me, too. Please. Promise me."

His voice was hollow when he answered. "Promise."

Chapter Thirteen

After they'd stopped and procured a new vehicle—and by procured, he meant stolen—and made the necessary arrangements with Derek, Ailish had held his hand all the way to Chicago. Henrik had lost count of how many awkward ways he'd devised for steering the car without letting go, but there had been a shit-ton. Her hand, so small inside his, had a fierce grip nonetheless, as if she was trying to prove going back to her hometown was what she wanted. Even though the trapped-animal energy radiated from her like a lighthouse beacon. Words kept sticking in his throat. Assurances that nothing would happen to her, even if he was cold and dead in the ground. But the time had come to show Ailish, not tell. *Put your money where your mouth is.*

Rain pelted the truck's roof as they pulled up outside the defunct recreation center, the basement of which was where undercover squad meetings were held. He was grateful for the shitty weather, because he didn't like having her exposed. The fact that nighttime had fallen during the drive only eased that worry some. But the sooner they got this meeting over with and he could get Ailish somewhere safe, the better. Until that happened, he was resigned to his gut grinding nails.

"Who will be there?"

Henrik turned Ailish's hand over, massaging circles into her palm with his thumb. "Captain Tyler." He thought of the phone call with Derek, which out of necessity, he'd made while Ailish used the bathroom at a rest stop. So she wouldn't overhear the conversation. "The squad will be there, minus Erin and Connor, since they're still lying low. No one you need to worry about."

She nodded. "I've never been to this part of Chicago." Rain filled the silence. "I've never been to most of it, actually. Maybe someday—"

"I'll take you everywhere." With an effort, Henrik dialed down the intensity. "Is there one place in particular you want to go?"

"No." She gasped. "*Yes.* I want to ride the train. The aboveground one, you know? Maybe I can read a book or listen to music…or just look out the window. No one rushing me or telling me where to go."

Henrik was capable of holding back only a matter of seconds before capturing Ailish around the waist and dragging her onto his lap. Something about the rain, or the darkness of the Chicago evening, made it okay to drop his head and wedge it beneath her chin, inhaling the scent of summer that lingered on her neck, chest, clothes. Her fingertips traced over his head, the scratchiness of his hair growing back after a week of not shaving. "It might be a while before we're together like this again, baby. You think of me, okay?" His hand slipped up her thigh, straight under the hem of her shorts, toying with the edge of her panties. "You think of me planted inside you. Think of me kissing you. Understand?"

"How could I forget to think of you? We'll be undercover, but I'll still *see* you." Ailish tilted her head, and Henrik wasted no time sucking the skin beneath her ear, lower, savoring her little kitty-cat noises. "You think of me, too. Like this. Understand?"

Even he could hear the guilt in his laughter. "Ailish, I'm already planning all the ways I'm going to think of you."

"Name one." He nipped her ear, making her squeal. "*Two*. Name two."

When his throat started to feel crowded, Henrik breathed through his nose. Goddammit, she felt so perfect on his lap. Why did they live in a world where they couldn't be together without so many gray areas? "I'm going to think of you bandaging my shoulder when you shot me."

Her spine snapped straight. "That is so *rude*."

Henrik twisted a hand in her hair and tugged, *tugged* until her head fell back on a gasp. "You didn't mind the rude things I said when my cock had you five feet off the ground."

That sweet ass shifted around on his lap. "N-no, I didn't. Is that the other thing you're going to think about?"

He let his hand travel to the valley between her legs, nudging the seam of her shorts with his knuckles. "Being tucked inside this pussy? I'll never stop thinking about it. Thinking about how to get back in. When. How."

"Do we have to go the meeting right this minute?

Henrik breathed through a laugh, but it was edged with misery. "Yeah, baby. We're already an hour late because of the traffic."

Ailish nodded, but made no move to get off his lap. "Why do you want to think of me bandaging your shoulder? Isn't me shooting you a bad memory?"

"No...uh. That was the first time I saw you up close... longer than a few seconds. You were muttering about people creeping up on you and..." He blew out a breath, knowing he was revealing too much, but not giving a shit. Might as well go for broke. "Christ, Ailish. I forgot I'd been shot at all. I just wanted to go on looking at you, baby. Letting you fuss over me. I'd get shot all over again if I got to replay seeing you up close for the first time." She looked up at him, mouth open, obviously stunned. And she stared for so long, Henrik's nerves started poking at him. *I said too much.* "And we both know you checked out my ass, too," he rumbled, scratching the back of his neck.

Ailish lunged for Henrik's mouth and he caught her just in time, groaning when she turned and straddled his lap.

"Ahh Jesus, Lish." His cock was already hard as a rock, straining against the fly of his pants. *Want. Want. Want.* "We can't."

"Yes." She reached between their bodies and unzipped his jeans. "Yes, we can. I need you."

They tore at each other's mouths, kissing each other the way people do in the throes of an orgasm. Without a thought to finesse or propriety. Tongues meeting in the middle to lick, teeth snapping, hands gripping whatever they could find. Ailish's hands made a quick job out of unfastening his pants, drawing out his cock and looking at it like Sunday dinner. Getting inside her as fast as possible became his ultimate goal, his waiting colleagues be damned. Without bothering to unfasten her shorts, Henrik pressed Ailish back against the steering wheel, yanked her knees up under her chin and pulled the tight material down over her curved ass, ripping off and tossing the garment away.

Then they were back to scrambling, Ailish sliding her sexy goddamn thighs wide on the seat, poising that pussy right over his distended dick and taking him to the hilt, with a maddening little sob of his name. Henrik's balled fist bashed into the truck's ceiling, the tight slide of Ailish's flesh robbing him of rational thought.

"I'm going to starve without you." He lifted his hips and gave Ailish a few sharp thrusts, rolling those hazel eyes back in her head. "Going to starve without juicing you like this. This sweet redhead pussy, baby. It's all for me. I'm a fucking monster for it."

Just as he'd recognized in the woods, Ailish loved being spoken to in a manner that simultaneously ashamed him and felt righteous as fuck at the same time. He coveted the right to speak about her body with ownership. To know how special she was on the inside, while detailing every foul male activity his body needed to complete with hers. And she *loved* knowing he hurt, the gorgeous brat. Loved knowing she could climb on top of him anytime, anywhere and he'd be fucking powerless to turn her down. It was her tease's nature and God, he wanted to cultivate it. Wanted her to tempt the hell out of him, as long as she granted him the heaven of being inside her afterward.

Just like every time they touched, Ailish was wasting no time making his balls feel heavy with the need to empty. Her nails dug into his shoulders, tits thrust out, hips flicking up and back like a working girl. Her thighs were so far apart, he had the perfect view of her pussy struggling to take his entire cock with every swift, rocking movement. And yeah, he wanted to throw her down onto the seat and pound like a motherfucker, but watching Ailish perform, watching her battle pleasure, was something he couldn't pass up.

Henrik settled a hand on her ass so he could feel her pump, as well as see it up close. "God*damn*. You're working overtime on it like you've got something to prove." An easy slap, just to hear her cry out. "How does that dick feel? How does it feel knowing you control it? Crook your little finger and get me hot, don't you?"

As if his words had wet Ailish up even more, she moaned at the ceiling, her ass cheeks clapping against the inside of his thighs as she rode him. "I—yes, yes. It feels so good. I love it. It's *mine*."

Without an order from his brain, Henrik's hand shot out to grasp her jaw, bringing their faces close together. "It is yours, Ailish. Yours to care for. And you better take that job seriously, because your tight pussy has ruined me for my own hand. What the fuck else am I going to do but take it out on your body?"

Her eyes were bright, lust-glazed. "I'll t-take care of it."

Henrik released her jaw and fell back against the seat, allowing his touch to travel up her inner thigh, finding the little pink bud there and rubbing it, using the pad of his thumb. "I take care of this, too. Always. When you need it. And sometimes when you don't realize you need it." A groan spilled from his mouth when she worked herself on him faster, her lips, thighs, hands starting to shudder. Flesh slapped; breath grew choppy. *Close. She's close.* "When this is over, Ailish? The first time we're alone together? I'm going to take everything off my bed except a fitted sheet so I can plow you like a goddamn field without a single damn thing in my way. Nothing for you to grab on to but me. You be ready, understand?"

His sincere warning did it, sent her into oblivion a few seconds before Henrik followed, powerless to stop the tumult when her walls clenched around his hurting flesh. Sticky moisture pooled where their bodies met, but it only seemed to turn Ailish on more, his not-so-innocent girl grinding down into the wetness with a reveling cry, another trembling wave passing through her body and hitting him square in the soul.

There were words fighting to leave his tongue, but he pressed his lips together and held them back. With what was to come inside the meeting room, though, she would hate him all the more if he vocalized the feelings storming inside his chest. So instead, he tugged Ailish down onto his chest, wishing for all the world he could absorb her, carry even a small part of her around with him over the next couple days. Knowing they only had a few more minutes of being close, existing without betrayal, Henrik stroked her red hair, breathed her in.

"I have something for you."

She sat back and looked down at his lap. "Something else?"

Henrik wanted to laugh, but couldn't quite manage it. Nor could he manage to tear his gaze off Ailish as he reached into his jeans pocket to remove the jewelry box he'd been carrying around since yesterday. Eagerness hit him, so intense he couldn't wait for Ailish to open the gray suede box herself, popping it open between them. He held his breath as she looked at the contents, pressing delicate fingers to her mouth, but not quite stifling her gasp.

"You bought me a necklace?" She took the box, running a light touch over the silver charm. It was in the shape of a key. "It's beautiful, Henrik. Thank you."

He took the box and removed the necklace, memorizing the way she bit her lip and lifted her hair, excitement dancing in her eyes. "This key means something. It's the key to your freedom. You understand, Ailish? I need you to wear it and remember I'll never let someone lock you away ever again." He managed to fasten the tiny clasp, not an easy feat with big, blunt fingers. "As long as you're wearing it, you're acknowledging that. Okay? I hope you never take it off."

Cloaked in quiet trust, she shook her head. "I won't."

Forgive me for what I have to do, baby.

When Henrik and Ailish walked into the squad room fifteen minutes later holding hands, impatience hung in the air like humidity. Derek paced behind his desk, fists flexing at his side. On one end of the room, Austin and Polly leaned against the cinder-block wall, speaking in hushed tones. Bowen and Sera were tucked up in a corner, Sera perched on her boyfriend's lap as usual, writing in her notebook while Bowen read over her shoulder.

The quiet scene in the room changed dramatically when Henrik and Ailish walked in—five pairs of sharp eyes landing on Ailish, making judgments and gauging her usefulness. When Ailish released his hand, crossed her arms, and sized them up right back, Henrik's pride in her expanded more than ever.

On cue, Sera gained her feet and glided across the room with a hand out. "I'm Sera. Sorry for the lack of warm welcome. We're actually not so bad once you get to know us." She treated each of her squad mates—including Bowen—to a raised eyebrow. "Maybe they just need a reminder you're here to help?"

A chair scraped back, Bowen the first to take his wife's less-than-subtle hint. Henrik bit down on the urge to drag Ailish into his side as the ex–gang leader approached to shake her hand. "Bowen. And we *are* that bad." He pecked a kiss onto Sera's cheek. "Except this one."

Ailish's expression softened. "Oh, another couple." In what seemed to be an unconscious move, Ailish uncrossed her arms and took Henrik's hand again, while still addressing Bowen and Sera. "Do you double-date with Connor and Erin?"

Bowen's laughter bounced off the walls until Henrik silenced him with a scowl. "We're not too social," the former Brooklynite explained. "But do me a favor and ask Connor that same question next time we're all together. Just so I can see his face."

"Sure," Ailish returned. "But I'll lay odds on a frown."

"Funny you should mention odds," Derek cut in, approaching to their right. "Since information about your father's gambling operations is why you're here."

Irritation pulled at the top of Henrik's spine, and this

time he did draw Ailish up against his side. No help for it. His nerves were starting to fray at the inevitability that was fast approaching. "You think she could shake off the rain before you start interrogating her?"

The captain was unfazed. "If you weren't an hour and a half late, I would consider it." He went back to his desk. "As it is, however, we don't have a lot of time for introductions, so take a seat."

"Was there a please in there?" Ailish wanted to know, not budging an inch and making Henrik want to kiss her pouty mouth until she ran out of air.

Clearly well used to working with strong women—not to mention being married to one—Derek gave a single nod. "Please take a seat, Ms. O'Kelly. We're on a time crunch."

Henrik reached for the nearest folding chair, dragged it over, and grunted, indicating that Ailish should take it. Before she sat down, she went up on her toes and whispered in his ear. "Henrik?"

"Yeah, baby," he rumbled, letting his hand settle on her hip.

"I won't ask you for a please since you just rocked my world."

When Austin gave a discreet cough across the room, Ailish's cheeks turned pink and she quickly dropped into the chair in front of Henrik. "Well," the con said. "That clears up the mystery of why they were late quite handily, doesn't it?"

Polly elbowed her boyfriend in the ribs, but the hacker was definitely battling a smile. "I'll start, since I'm"—she shrugged, glancing around the room—"the best. I mean, let's not sugarcoat it."

Austin nodded in agreement.

Bowen's eye roll could probably be heard two states away.

"I tracked the man who stole Ailish's money in Wisconsin—Eamon Lindt—and found him in Miami, because *that* wasn't an obvious choice." Henrik watched Ailish's shoulders stiffen at the information relayed by Polly. When she'd told him about Eamon—or Cubs Cap, as she'd referred to the man—he'd been collecting information to keep her safe, but she would see his sharing it with the squad a breaking of confidence. And there was nothing he could do about it. "Since Connor and Erin are keeping their heads down anyway," Polly continued, "we sent them down to bring Captain Obvious back. They should be on a plane as we speak."

Henrik sensed Ailish staring up at him, knew there would be questions in her eyes, so he couldn't look. "So we should be good to go for tomorrow morning?"

Polly gave him a thumbs-up. "You can thank Austin for taking care of designating a safe house for Ailish to cool her heels while you're on the inside with Daddy-oh. No one will be able to find her, except me. So be glad I'm not looking."

Ailish's spine had gone straight. She started to speak, but Derek's voice boomed before she got the chance. "Bowen and Sera will be guarding you, Ms. O'Kelly, replaced by Polly and Austin every other day until this is over." He ran a hand over his day-old beard. "You have nothing to worry about."

"I don't?" Henrik couldn't ignore Ailish this time. She stood and turned, confusion swirling in her beautiful eyes. When he offered no immediate explanation, she paled a little more, facing Derek again. "Why are you bringing Eamon back to Chicago? I don't understand."

Derek and Henrik exchanged a glance, the captain correctly interpreting what lay in his expression. He hadn't told Ailish the actual plan. Derek leaned back on his desk and sighed. "Henrik is going to take Eamon as an offering to your father. He was in possession of the money you stole when Connor and Erin found him in Miami. Henrik hands over the thief, the stolen cash, and he's in."

Over her shoulder, Ailish pinned Henrik with a shaken look. "You said you were using *me* to get in. You"—her voice dropped—"you promised we were in this together."

Henrik wanted to claw his skin off just witnessing the pain flashing lightning bolts across her face. His heartbeat had dropped to a dull, lifeless beat at the loss of her. He'd lost her, just like that. "I can't take you in there, Ailish. If something goes bad with me, suspicion will land on you by association. Don't you know I would do anything to prevent putting you in danger? *Anything*."

"Including lying to get me back here." The remaining color leached from her face. This time when she whispered, it was for Henrik's ears alone. "Were we…was it real? I—"

"*Yes*." Henrik gripped her shoulders and shook, unable to control his own body or the sick feeling permeating his gut. "You can't actually be doubting that. *Look* at me. You *can't* be."

She opened her mouth, closed it, before tugging out of his grip and taking in the room, as if through fresh eyes. It didn't go unnoticed by Henrik that she hadn't given him an answer. Oh no. It was an uncertainty that made him wish for a quick death. "So what? You leave me with them, while you go to work for my father?" She shook her head. "I don't want to be protected anymore. You *know* that."

"As soon as you tell Henrik what he's looking for inside the house, he'll spend the night preparing," Derek answered quietly, addressing only the first of Ailish's questions. "Although in this case, there isn't much for him to prepare for, considering he's just playing himself."

"Sometimes that's the hardest part to play," Austin interjected, with a nod at Henrik. "We have a longer night ahead than you think. Best get started."

Sera moved toward Ailish. "We can take you to the safe house, make sure you get cleaned up and have something to eat." She laid a hand on Ailish's forearm, her tone comforting. "Tomorrow is soon enough for Derek to speak to you at length, but for now, just give Henrik an idea of the lead he's looking for. That's all we need tonight, then you can get some rest."

Henrik couldn't see Ailish's face, but when her shoulders squared, he knew what was coming. Knew it better than anyone in the room. Ailish might have lived her life according to everyone else's rules and plans, but she sure as shit wasn't playing the docile daughter now. Even in the midst of the swamping dread, Henrik was proud as hell of her. Wished their connection hadn't been severed, so he could share the moment with her. Beg her to reconsider afterward.

Ailish dropped into the folding chair and crossed her legs. "I'm not telling Henrik anything. Or you," she said, nodding at Derek. "I'm not cooperating. And I'm not going to any safe house. So why don't you go ahead and put me in a cell?" She held out her wrists, an invitation to cuff her. "Congratulations, you have the Bookie Cookie in custody."

Even though he'd expected an extreme reaction from the captain, seeing the hardening of Derek's jaw—along with the added interest from his squad mates—made Henrik question his decision to bring Ailish back. Question his decision to trust the captain's word.

"We had a deal," Henrik reminded Derek. "It. Stands."

Derek laughed without humor, scrubbing both hands down his face. "Christ. This squad is going to fucking kill me." The captain was quiet for long moments. Too long. Moments that tempted Henrik with scooping up Ailish and making a run for the door. Taking her somewhere and explaining what it would do to him if she were harmed under his watch. Or worse, if he was *responsible* for her being harmed. She would have to understand if he explained his actions—his reasons for lying— enough, right? Finally, Derek spoke, breaking the silence in the dim basement. "You go home, Henrik. Take Polly and Austin, get ready for tomorrow." He lifted his head. "My word stands. She'll be safe, and she'll walk out of here without a record. But you sure as hell better bring me my man." A pause dragged out. "Or you'll be taking her place in the cell. We clear?"

When Ailish turned her attention on Henrik this time, he saw beneath the wall she'd thrown up. Saw her alarm at the idea of him going away on her behalf…and God, he almost laughed. *Baby, you have no idea.*

"Clear as crystal," Henrik grated. "I don't think I have to tell you that if something happens to her, I'll paint this town with blood. Do I?"

"Yours or ours?" Austin drawled, calculation in his eyes.

Not deigning to answer, Henrik took one final look at Ailish, so beautiful and out of place among the harsh lighting and filthy walls, and strode from the room, painfully aware that he'd left his heart beating in the dank basement.

Good thing where he was going, he wouldn't need it.

Chapter Fourteen

Ailish refused to break Derek's stare as he paced back and forth behind the dented metal desk. After Henrik had walked out of the meeting room, Derek sent everyone packing, saying he wanted time to speak with Ailish privately. Well, he could ask repetitious cop questions until his face—which she could grudgingly admit was quite handsome—turned blue, and she wouldn't budge. She'd been in this position before, but nothing about being the subject of a law enforcement member's scrutiny felt the same now. In the last few weeks, she'd fended for herself, finagled her way out of two kidnappings, and been betrayed by a man. So Derek could bring it on for all she cared. At the moment, she didn't have capacity for anger or fear. The numbness kept everything else locked out.

Every time Ailish thought of her rambling speech in the forest about Henrik and her being a team, being on the same side, shame coated her stomach. How could she have been so far off? Henrik knew how badly she wanted independence, how much it meant to make her own decisions, but he'd made the ultimate choice for her. Put her in a chair across from his captain as an asset, a means to an end, instead of an active participant. And she'd been blind enough to let it happen.

Go to your room Ailish, let the men talk business. How was that sentiment from her father any different than Henrik leaving her behind? She had wrongs to make up for, and it wouldn't happen now. She'd never get the chance to make up for her transgressions, because he'd left her behind to be protected. Guarded. Talk about déjà vu. The princess was right back in her ivory tower where she belonged.

Fine. After being deceived, however, she wouldn't put her chin up like a good girl and help their cause. If the police failed, she would find another way to atone for her sins. Implode Caine's operation by herself. *If* the police indeed let her walk away, as Derek had promised. She had no reason to trust his word, although some stubborn part of Ailish believed. *Because Henrik wouldn't let it be any other way.*

Ailish shifted in her chair, irritated at the conviction she still held over Henrik's trustworthiness. How could she still have faith when he'd blindsided her so thoroughly tonight? Left her behind without so much as a good-bye. *Again.*

"I had questions prepared, but that was before I knew who you were," Derek said, breaking the relative silence of the squad room. Water trickled along the asphalt ground outside, which stopped a few feet from ceiling level. "So forgive me for taking my time."

Right. He doesn't even think I realize it's a tactic.

"I just didn't want you to think I was stalling on purpose." He stopped pacing and faced Ailish. "Like a tactic."

Okay, so Derek was a way better cop than the one who'd interrogated her last time. Perfect. She still had nothing to say, but it was hard not to answer the man when he was speaking directly at her. It was rude to ignore people, after all. A reminder of all the times she'd called Henrik rude made Ailish's throat hurt, so she curled a hand around it and breathed through her nose.

Derek's sigh just about blew away every piece of official-looking paper he'd stacked on the table, his demeanor changing right before Ailish's eyes. He pulled out the folding chair tucked under his desk and sat heavily, folding blunt-fingered hands on the scratched surface. "You're lucky I have a soft spot for women who take off with a boatload of cash trying to find a better life."

Ailish buried her surprise. "Yeah? I'm stuck in a basement with two choices. Rat out my father or go to jail. I don't feel so lucky right about now."

"I can see that."

When the captain didn't elaborate, Ailish's curiosity got the better of her. "Your wife?"

A brisk nod. "She raised herself, her sister. Saw an opportunity for a fresh start and took it. I can sympathize with that. I've only spent a short while in your company, and I can see you're not your father's daughter." He leaned back in his chair. "And despite what Henrik did to land on my squad, I trust his judgment."

Hearing Henrik's name made the stupid, traitorous organ in her chest leap into a sprint, winding her in mere seconds. Once again, a weight pressed behind her eyes, fury making her stomach burn. Too much. So much. And he wasn't even there for her to shout at. She could feel Derek watching her, assessing, and didn't want to take the bait by asking about Henrik. But who knew when she would get another chance to fill in the gaps? "What *did* land him on your squad?"

Derek's stoic expression didn't change. "I wondered if he'd told you."

A flashback to her walk with Erin in the woods chose that moment to crop up, replay like a homemade movie. Hadn't Erin said something similar? Just how heinous was Henrik's crime? "I've met Connor and Erin. The rest of your team tonight." She shook her head. "He doesn't belong here."

"He does. He made a choice."

"Yes. So did I. I made them every day." Ailish could see the desk in her bedroom, the gambling debts of unknown men spread across the surface like a bloody battlefield. Could see the remnants of her eraser, hear the scratching of her pencil. "But sometimes hard choices are all that's left."

"Don't I know it?" Derek remained silent a few beats before leafing through the documents on the battered desk. "You're not going to tell us what we need, what we should be looking for and where. I can see that."

"No. I agreed to cooperate if Henrik stayed away from my father." She massaged her aching throat again. "He lied."

"He made the only decision he could to keep you safe and get his spot on the force back."

The flow of Ailish's blood slowed. "Get his spot back?"

Derek blew out a breath. "I might be to blame for some of the secrecy between you and Henrik. I asked him to treat this case like a job, when it was clear from the beginning he's not objective where you're concerned." He paused. "I assured Henrik I'd do what it took to have him reinstated if he—"

"Brings down my father." She swallowed the stone in her throat. Getting back his badge would mean everything to Henrik. Everything. And she'd been his ace in the hole to gain entry to Caine's world. But he hadn't taken it. Not ready to feel sympathy or be reasonable, Ailish pushed to her feet and paced toward the small ground-level window. "I've been kept safe my whole life. Lied to. I'm tired of it. He should have been honest. I just want people to be *honest* with me."

"Be careful what you wish for."

Ailish turned. "What's that supposed to mean?"

Another industrial-strength sigh from the captain. "Look, I need you in that house. You've been inside, know where everything is located, and that's information no one else has.

It could whittle this operation down from indefinite to one damn day. And that means fewer people die by your father's hand."

Her legs turned to lead. "Henrik would never agree to let me inside."

"He and I made a deal." Derek stood, pacing behind his desk once more. "You remain safe and walk out of here without a record. I'm already working on the former, and there's no safer place for you than with Henrik. Trust me on that."

"No." Frustration welled so severely inside Ailish, it spilled over like an erupting volcano. "*No.* I won't blindly trust you. Or Henrik. I've been brought here on a lie. *You're* lying to Henrik, despite how you justify it to yourself." She lifted her arms and let them fall at her sides. "And I'm done being in the middle of everyone's deception. It's a terrible place to be."

To the captain's credit, he didn't appear unaffected by her speech. Far from it. But there was still determination in the set of his jaw. "I would like to let you walk out of here, free and clear, Ms. O'Kelly. Free to start over. But I'm responsible for a city. And that city is at risk as long as your father's operation is up and running. My family lives here. Millions of families. So I'll do what's needed. That's the burden I accepted when I took this job." He looked away a moment, hands propped on hips. A ditch opened in Ailish's stomach, but she didn't know where the sense of impending doom came from until he continued. "Do you ever wonder why we released you from police custody?"

Say no, a voice whispered at the back of her head. But it would have been a lie, and she'd just got done voicing her distaste of liars. The captain would see right through her, and she'd be a hypocrite. "Yes. I've wondered every day."

"Henrik." Derek shuffled the documents into a stack and shoved them into a manila folder before lifting his gaze to

Ailish again. "Henrik destroyed the evidence we had against you. It's what lost him his badge. What put him on this squad."

The lava that had been flowing inside Ailish turned to cement, hardening immediately. She couldn't catch a breath. Couldn't believe her ears. "W-what? Why would he do that? I-I don't understand."

For the first time, Derek looked slightly uncomfortable. "That's a question for Henrik to answer." He cleared his throat. "But sometimes there's no explanation for what a man will do for a woman. It just is."

There was no stopping the tears from spilling down her cheeks this time. "Did you tell me this so I'd cooperate? So I'd go undercover in my own father's house?" Derek didn't answer. "Why didn't he tell me?"

The captain propped a hip on the desk. "Again, that's a question for Henrik. But I suspect because he didn't want you to owe him anything."

"But you're counting on me seeing it that way, aren't you?"

Rainwater trickled against the windows, running along the concrete outside, filling the silence. "I have a city to keep safe," Derek said finally. "Are you going to help me, Ms. O'Kelly?"

Ailish thought of Henrik alone in the lion's den. She knew what would get him out of the house as soon as possible, before her father figured out Henrik was an informant. Knew where weapons were located to keep them both safe, should that become necessary. She couldn't leave Henrik to contend with her father indefinitely. Or it could very well end in his death. Fear pushed into her indignation, but she didn't allow it to fester. Now was the time to focus, and maintaining her anger would be paramount. There was no denying a responsibility to Henrik, even after he'd lied. Locked her out. But this mission needed to be about her. Righting the wrongs she'd committed. Calling her father to the floor for taking lives with her handiwork.

She was going home. And when she walked out, hopefully she would finally leave the guilt and pain behind, once and for all.

Yes, she would focus on that. Not the fact that the man she craved was in danger. How would she cope otherwise?

"Yes," she whispered. "I'll help."

Henrik rolled his neck, trying to work the kinks out. Last night, after hours of poring through files with Austin and Polly, learning everything there was to know about Caine O'Kelly, Henrik went a few rounds with his punching bag. There'd been no sleep to be had, because every time he closed his eyes, there was Ailish. Looking stricken, sold out…afraid.

His grip tightened on the steering wheel, making the leather creak. *Breathe, man. Breathe.* If he went into this operation thinking about Ailish, it would be unsuccessful. He would fail. But God, not being near her was torture on his soul. His mental state. His body. Everything.

If he didn't have a man hog-tied in the trunk of his car right now, he might have given in to the urge to go see Ailish. Just for a few minutes, without anyone else around, so he could apologize for lying. Explain to her that putting her in harm's way would be equivalent to burning his skin off with acid. *How romantic.* All right, he wasn't exactly Casanova, but putting himself in the line of fire so Ailish wouldn't have to go be an informant or be interrogated past her breaking point? That was the only way Henrik knew how to show her how he felt. So that's what he would do, and hope she received the message. Or cared enough to look for it.

Late last night, he'd received a call from Derek, letting him know Ailish wasn't cooperating. She refused to aid Henrik in his search for evidence, meaning Henrik would be on his own. He'd blocked the hurt, telling himself Ailish's reticence was justified after his dishonesty, but as he headed into the fray, the hurt couldn't be subdued. It might take a while without the intel she could provide—hell, months—but he would gain O'Kelly's confidence and get the job done. And hope with every ounce of his being that Ailish would speak to him when it was all over. That was all he had.

That. And a criminal stuffed into his trunk. A suspiciously quiet criminal, at that. Derek had shown up with the vehicle half an hour ago at the designated meeting stop, tossing Henrik the keys and instructing him to climb in and drive. And while Henrik hadn't appreciated being ordered around—especially since his ass would be on the line during the operation—he'd needed to prevent himself from asking the captain about Ailish. Was she comfortable? How many times had she cursed him to hell?

Up ahead, Henrik saw the gated grounds of O'Kelly's house, manicured lawn running the perimeter. A suited man with an earpiece stood just inside the gate, watching Henrik approach. Expecting him? Hard to tell. There'd been no set schedule with O'Kelly. Hell, they'd barely made an agreement. Henrik pushed the car into park and waited, tapping his fingers on the wheel as the guard spoke into his earpiece. When the man finally approached the car, he gave Henrik a once-over and signaled him to roll down the window.

"Morning," Henrik drawled.

The guard grunted. "Mr. O'Kelly was expecting you to bring a package."

Henrik forced himself not to stiffen at hearing Ailish referred to as a package, but he *wanted* to wrap the man's tie in his fist, yank down, and slam his head against the car door. The fact that it wasn't actually Ailish in the trunk might have saved the guy a concussion. "I have what he's looking for in the trunk."

An impressed eyebrow lift. "Go ahead and pop it. We'll have a look."

Henrik removed his sunglasses. "I'm not popping shit out here on the street. After the trouble I went through to find what he wanted, he'll be letting me in."

Earpiece backed up a few feet and spoke quietly into the device. Henrik stared at the backseat through the rearview mirror, wishing he'd taken the time to introduce himself to the motherfucker who'd robbed Ailish's money, leaving her high and dry. Connor had called Henrik upon landing in Chicago, giving him the particulars on Eamon Lindt and assuring Henrik they'd been discreet, not giving the man a single reason to believe they had ties to law enforcement. Which was key, seeing as Henrik would be opening the trunk and presenting the man to O'Kelly in a matter of minutes.

Earpiece approached once more, coming close enough to the driver's side window that Henrik itched to go for his gun. But after a final, scrutinizing once-over, the guard gave whoever was on the other end of his earpiece the all-clear, smirking as he issued it.

Henrik eased past off the street onto the pristine brick driveway, painfully aware that he was crossing into enemy territory. Three black luxury cars were parked in a row near the entrance, two guards having a conversation by the double-door entrance. Something about the grounds struck Henrik as looking like a movie set, a perfect replica of what a gangster's home should look like. He stared out through the windshield, imagining it through Ailish's eyes. Prison. It would look like prison to a young girl, especially one with so much life inside her.

I miss her. I need her. She hates me.

Henrik hit his brakes with a little too much force and

hoped it jostled the man in the trunk. Why should he be the only one in pain this fine goddamn morning, right? After throwing the car into park, he climbed out and waited by the driver's side, lifting his arms up automatically when the two guards—their conversation now finished—swaggered over to frisk him. They removed the piece from inside his jacket pocket and slid it across the hood, out of his reach. He'd anticipated being unarmed, at least in the beginning. He didn't like it—not even a little bit—but it was par for the course with a paranoid criminal like O'Kelly. Having his fists to work with in a pinch gave him some comfort. There wasn't a man on the grounds could take him in a fight. He had that going for him at the very least.

When the guard finished checking Henrik for ankle-holstered weapons, he whistled, and the front door swung open. The first thing Henrik noticed about O'Kelly was the sweat on his forehead. He descended the steps looking jumpy. A man who'd had a few lines of cocaine with breakfast. God. *God*, Henrik had never been more relieved to have Ailish somewhere safe. Never been happier to have destroyed that evidence and given her a chance outside this life. Unfortunately, he had to deal with this tenser version of O'Kelly and explain that while he hadn't found Ailish, he'd brought him someone else appealing.

"Where is she?" O'Kelly asked, running a finger along his upper gum line. "Trunk? She give you any problems?"

Henrik reacted to the manic, rapid-fire questions with a casual demeanor. "Yeah. More than a few. As in, I couldn't find her."

Two men pulled weapons on Henrik, but he didn't flinch. "Relax. I didn't come empty-handed." He held up his left hand and pointed at the interior of his car, with the right. "I'm going to reach in and pop the trunk. Sound good?"

Caine's responding laugh was semi-maniacal. "Still talks

like a cop, this fucking guy. All right." He clapped his hands together. "All right. Let's go. Let's see what you got."

As Henrik ducked down, he watched two of Caine's men exchange an odd glance before training speculative eyes on their boss. Dissension in the ranks? *Good to know.* He hooked his finger beneath the plastic lever and pulled. Before he could fully straighten, Caine was already rounding the car. When he looked into the trunk, he gave that disturbing laugh again, the sound ricocheting through the stiff brick courtyard. "He might be a cop, but he's got a sense of humor."

Caine dropped a hand into the trunk and pulled out—

Ailish.

Chapter Fifteen

That haunted house scream from Henrik's youth tore across the landscape of his mind, eroding mountains, whipping through his self-control like a destructive tornado. A harsh sound escaped him and he just managed to disguise it with a cough into his shaking fist. *No. This is part of the movie. It's not real. She's not here, being manhandled by her drugged-up father, yanked out of the truck like a piece of luggage. She's not here in the middle of several loaded weapons, when I don't even have one. No, baby, please don't really be here.*

"How did you find her?" Caine asked, but the older man's voice sounded tinny, as if it flowed out through a spinning vortex of white noise. Henrik's mouth was too full of wet sand to answer, so he pulled together a lethargic shrug. Something that hopefully said *I have my ways*. And then came very close to vomiting on his shoes.

Ailish was wearing a yellow sundress, and it seemed so out of place among the black suits and brick walls. The strain around her mouth told Henrik the grip Caine had on her elbow was way, way too fucking tight, and there was nothing

Henrik could do about it. The man beside him snickered, breathing the word "bitch" close to Henrik's ear, as if they were buddies commiserating about last night's baseball game. *Fuckfuckfuck.* He couldn't do this. Not with Ailish on the line.

"Welcome back, daughter," Caine said. "Have a nice vacation?"

Her hazel eyes fired bullets at O'Kelly. "Yes, I did. When I wasn't being kidnapped, anyway."

"Oh, come on now." He tilted his head. "What's a little kidnapping among family?"

Ailish went white as a sheet. Whatever was going on—whatever Derek had gotten them into to further his cause in bringing down O'Kelly—Ailish wasn't acting. That much was clear. She was genuinely distraught over being addressed with such open hostility by her father. Did that mean his behavior was unusual? The few times Henrik had allowed himself to imagine their father-daughter relationship, he'd pictured quiet resentment from both sides, but maybe he'd been wrong. And he'd been so worried about his own reaction, he hadn't asked Ailish about it when he'd had the chance.

"Why couldn't you just let me go?" Ailish asked her father, her soft words carrying on the wind to pummel Henrik in the chest. "Why?"

Ailish jolted under her father's hold. *Too tight. Too tight. He's hurting her.* Henrik felt the other men scrutinizing him and schooled his features with a considerable effort. "I might have let you go, daughter, if I hadn't gone through the books and found out you've been screwing me seven ways to Sunday."

When Ailish cried out in pain, Henrik took a step forward—and the guns lifted again. That was the fist time Ailish met his gaze. The disgust he encountered there made him feel like a wounded animal brought down by a hunter. But there was something else. Something that glinted from its position against her throat.

She was wearing the necklace he'd given her.

Something was wrong. Ailish had known it the moment her father opened the trunk. His eyes were glassy in a way she hadn't seen since her mother still lived in the house. Drugs. He was using again. And for the first time—through the eyes of an adult—she wondered what had prompted him to stop the first time. More importantly, why was he back at it?

In addition to Caine's twitchy behavior, he was…livid. Disgusted. With her. She'd expected serious animosity from her father, being that she'd taken a heap of money and run away. She'd expected even more intense lockdown than usual. But there was a glint in his eye that had nothing to do with the drugs, and he'd never manhandled Ailish in her entire life. Never. Something was most definitely wrong.

It had taken Henrik a good few minutes to get his bearings after she'd made her appearance, but he was on his game now. Arms folded across his broad chest, he looked just as irritated as everyone else that she'd crashed the party. It only made her want to kiss his face, his mouth, his neck all the more. Then she wanted to smack him good. Pretty much how she'd always felt looking at him before, except now she knew he'd thrown his career away, all for her. A total stranger. So the simultaneous kissing and smacking felt like necessity now, instead of a mere urge. No telling which would happen the first time she got him alone.

One thing was for certain, though. She would have an explanation. A satisfying one that didn't skirt a single truth, the way their dealings had been up until now. The cards were on the table, they were undercover together with the same goal, and she wanted to know Henrik's mind. Every complicated corner.

First, though, they had Caine to deal with. Evidence to collect and an exit to plot. She might not even have a chance to be alone with Henrik until they were free of the house, which would require Ailish to be on her toes. To look for cues from Henrik and be ready to go at any time.

"Let's head to my office, shall we?" her father said, already turning Ailish with a firm hand on her shoulder. "I'd rather have this reunion without an audience."

Having a hard time maintaining her balance with both hands bound, Ailish stumbled on the brick steps. "Can someone untie my hands first?"

Over her shoulder, Ailish watched Caine produce a pocketknife from his pants, flip it over in his hand, and slide it beneath the cable tie keeping her wrists locked together. Father and daughter met eyes as he twisted the knife, snapping the plastic tie—but cutting into her skin at the same time. Ailish sucked in a breath and kept walking, her heart chugging like a freight train inside her chest. Without even looking at Henrik, she could feel his rage gathering, a storm waiting to break. Oh God, what was happening? She'd assured Derek that her father would be irritated, would place her under constant watch, but would never physically harm her.

Obviously, she'd been wrong. There was only one reason she could fathom that would put her father in this extreme a rage. And if that were the case, they were in far bigger trouble than she'd anticipated.

Ailish's hands were free, but still asleep, so they dangled uselessly at her sides, making her feel helpless as she led the way toward her father's office. His men, including Henrik, had followed them into the familiar, dimly lit foyer. Ailish vibrated with the need to turn around, lock eyes with Henrik, but she couldn't. Couldn't glean comfort from him or warn him that something was off. She would have to face Caine alone for now. Although the man matching her stride down the hallway was noticeably different from the Caine in her memory.

Just before they reached the office door, her father stopped short. "Mr. Vance, come on in and join us?"

Ailish was thankful no one could see her face, because there was no way to hide the relief. She almost sank down into the carpet with it. Just having him close would be enough to keep her calm, keep her focused. Caine reached over her shoulder and pushed open the office door, giving Ailish a nudge between the shoulder blades to make her move. Her father was determined to express how little regard he had for her comfort, and she knew without a doubt what was coming.

Thank God she hadn't fought Derek on the listening device around her neck, hidden in the necklace Henrik had given her. If everything went south in the next five minutes, at least they had a backup plan. Chicago PD was on high alert should their lives be in danger, but she couldn't proceed with that crutch in mind. They needed good, solid evidence to convict her father, and obtaining it was Ailish's only option. To stop Caine from hurting anyone else, from plaguing the streets of Chicago. But it wouldn't hurt to let everyone listening know that Caine wasn't acting his typical self, to keep Derek and the team vigilant.

Ailish sat in a leather armchair facing Caine's desk. "Can I have a tissue…or a Band-Aid? My wrist is bleeding."

Caine fell into his high-backed chair. "Let it bleed."

She could feel Henrik walk into the room at her back and shifted, as if uncomfortable to have him there. "What do you need him here for?"

Her father still held the pocketknife he'd used to free her wrists. Now, he tapped it against the desk's edge, creating little indentations in the wood. There were hundreds of the same markings, as though it wasn't the first time he'd abused the piece of furniture. Instead of answering her question, Caine addressed Henrik, the amusement clear in his expression. "When I told you to get my daughter home by fair means or foul, you took it to heart. You've got balls bringing her home inside a trunk."

"That's why I'm here, isn't it?" Henrik sounded like a different, darker version of himself, and the goose bumps that rose along Ailish's skin in response were authentic. "I got sick of hearing her beg me to let her go somewhere around Grand Rapids."

A snort left her father. "Runs away just like her mother... begs just like her mother..." Caine's focus landed on her, harsh and condemning. "Has no regard for hard-earned money just like her fucking mother."

Ailish was paralyzed in her seat. Blood from her injured wrist had trickled down into the palm of her right hand and—without thinking—she wiped it on the skirt of her dress, creating an ugly red streak. "What does my mother have to do with anything?"

Again, Caine ignored her, giving his attention to Henrik. "I've had a lot of time to think since my daughter took off. A lot of time to look back. Review." He poked himself in the temple with his index finger. "I've got a few irons in the fire. Running odds and collecting bets isn't my only operation. Maybe that's why I didn't see it."

"See what?" Henrik said, sounding almost bored.

Caine leaned forward, slowly—then he lifted the pocketknife and stabbed it full-force into the desk's surface. "Didn't see my own flesh and blood had been ripping me off."

Ailish had seen it coming before they'd walked into the office, but still. She'd been so careful. Covered every single base. "What do you mean?" she mumbled, uselessly, still half praying she was wrong.

"Drop the bullshit, daughter. I found the second set of

books." Having rendered Ailish speechless, he left the knife sticking out of his desk and leaned back. "Took me about a week." He tapped his nose. "But I could smell something rotten. You thought you were clever, didn't you? Keeping them taped inside the vent in your closet. *In my own goddamn house.*"

She couldn't move, was afraid to breathe. With the fire roaring in his eyes, Caine was angry enough to kill her. Money. She'd messed with his money. The one thing he could never forgive. "It was only a few…shuffles," Ailish whispered, wishing Henrik were free to settle his hands on her shoulders. Anything. Just some form of contact so she wouldn't feel so cold. "You didn't even miss it."

"Oh yes. You certainly are your mother's daughter." Her father tugged open the center drawer of his desk, removing a yellow legal pad and slapping it down beside the embedded knife. "Four hundred thousand, six hundred and twenty-nine dollars. That's how much money you cost me. *Bookie Cookie*," he sneered. "At least, that's what I have so far. I've only gone through one fucking book."

Ailish started to shake. She'd never actually added up every cent she'd managed to hide from Caine by moving around funds, creating fake names with false entries. Breaking apart giant debts that could spell a man's death sentence and whittling them down, spreading them out until they were nothing. Debts too small for Caine to take notice. Ailish could remember the morning she'd begun fudging the books like it had taken place only last week. Having woken to the sound of shouting, she'd gone downstairs and found a man kneeling, begging for his life in the backyard. She'd remained hidden at the base of the stairwell, but she'd watched her father take a man's life that day. Watching the light go out of someone's eyes. All because he'd bet too much money on football games.

Days had passed before she'd been able to open her

ledgers. They were no longer just numbers written down on the pages, but life-and-death wagers. Ailish had been the one to pass on notice of the dead man's debt to her father, having naively assumed—what? That he would put the man on some kind of payment plan? She'd been so stupid. So blind. And she'd immediately started to atone, creating a different set of books with more names, ways to spread out the amounts owed. She'd asked her father for a more active role and began working directly with the bookies via a separate phone line. Caine had trusted her, and she'd lied, day after day, in the interest of saving lives.

Now her own life had come into the equation.

"What you were doing…I couldn't let it be on my head," Ailish said, thankful for the note of steel in her voice. Thankful for the shadow Henrik's big body cast over her father's desk as a reminder of his presence. "It wasn't fair for you to put me in that position without my knowing the consequences."

Caine appeared surprised she'd spoken up. Which was fair, considering the only stand she'd ever taken had been behind the scenes, in secret. Never to his face. After a pause, her father's surprise turned into disgust once again. "That there? That's another thing your mother never understood. You earn your keep in this house. No one gets a free ride. You had a gift with numbers, so I put it to good use. In return, you got all the shit I never had. Private school, food, a house." He ran his tongue along the inside of his gums. "Good news is, you're going to make it up starting now."

Dread balled up in her stomach. "How?"

"I don't have time to go through every line of chicken scratch you made over the last five years. I want to know whose debts I have to call in—and you've got two days to give them to me. Every last one." Caine shot forward, pointing a finger at Henrik. "You. You obviously don't take her shit. Maybe I should have taken a page out of your book while raising her, huh?" Her father didn't wait for an answer. "You make sure she's working. Getting me those names and figures. If you get a sense she's slacking off, you have my permission to shake her until the information I need falls out of her pretty little head."

Henrik saw everything through a filter of deep red. Ailish stormed down the hallway in front of him, putting on a show for her father, who watched from his office door, laughing at the display of spirit. Henrik could just about achieve an even gait, just about keep his fists from turning to stone at his sides. As they rounded the corner at the hallway's end, Henrik turned and gave Caine a serious nod, letting him know Ailish wouldn't get away with any nonsense on his watch. When he really wanted to charge the motherfucker and put him down.

She looked so fragile, her blood-streaked sundress fluttering around her thighs in a breeze entering through the window up ahead. A window overlooking the pool. Tearing his gaze from the injured Ailish—which took a concentrated effort and a vow to fix her wound as soon as humanly possibly—Henrik took the opportunity to scan each room they passed. All available exits. Possible weak spots of Caine's superior security system.

Ailish stopped at the final door lining the hallway, still not looking up at him. Good. She wasn't taking any chances. Derek had no doubt impressed the importance of maintaining cover at all times, but that didn't stop Henrik from wanting to throttle his captain. No matter what it took, Henrik would get her out of this situation alive. If he had the same luck—throttling notwithstanding—it would be his last mission with the squad. No one put Ailish in danger's path and maintained his loyalty. He would complete the mission, but he would do it for *her*.

Henrik followed Ailish into her bedroom, hold-ing up a finger when she opened her mouth to speak. His willpower was already maxed out, but throw her husky voice into the mix and he'd have her out of that dress before she knew what hit her. When Ailish nodded, Henrik began moving around the perimeter of the bedroom, relieved by its size. She might have been held captive inside her own home, but at least she'd had space to breathe. While discreetly checking for cameras on the ceiling, bookshelves, fire alarms, Henrik couldn't help but register everything else. The pastel pink bedspread. Pictures on the nightstand of a young Ailish swimming in the backyard with a pretty woman, no doubt her mother. Everything in her closet had been thrown into a pile at the room's center, probably left there after Caine had found Ailish's hidden books.

Wordlessly, she picked up an armful of discarded clothes and disappeared into the closet. It took Henrik a few more minutes to ascertain the lack of cameras before he joined Ailish in the unlit closet where she stood on her toes, stowing a stack of clothes on the upper shelf. When his body blocked the muted light shining in from the bedroom, she turned. Waiting. Fingers picking at the hem of her bloody dress. Until that moment, he'd managed to keep the reality of their situation at bay, but now the fear streaked across his sky like jagged lightning—and he went for his girl. Went for her like a man who'd been robbed of sanity.

Just before he reached Ailish, he somehow remembered to hold a finger to his lips—*quiet, baby*—and attempted to sweep her up into a hug.

She dodged him. Feinted to the left to avoid his embrace. And his senses were immediately confused. His lungs were full of summer scent, but he couldn't *feel* her. Couldn't *see* his smiling Ailish in her closed-off expression. There was no mistaking the betrayal swimming in her hazel eyes. Or the fact that she'd withdrawn from him. "I had to cut you out." His whisper felt harsh leaving his throat. "You don't know how far I would go to keep you from being hurt."

"Yes, I do." She stepped back even farther, dislodging his heart. But there was awareness in her demeanor that hadn't been there before. "I do know. I know…everything."

The evidence. She knows about the evidence I destroyed. A multitude of reactions speared into Henrik at once. Relief that Ailish finally knew about his sacrifice. He no longer had to downplay his instantaneous devotion to her, to keeping her out of prison. A place she could never belong in a million damn years. But there was also royal fucking rage. She'd been coerced into aiding him in the mission. "Derek shouldn't have told you that."

"No, Derek shouldn't have. *You* should have." Energy snapped in the air between them. "You made a major decision for my life, dictating it with your actions—and I'm not going to pretend I'm not grateful, because being free is *better.* Better than I ever thought it could be—"

"Ailish." The way her voice cracked almost dropped him to a kneeling position. "I don't need you to be grateful, I just need you alive and safe."

She squared her shoulders. "What about what I need?" For a moment, she stared off into the bedroom, memories almost visible as they played inside her head. "When you gave me this necklace, you said you'd never let me be locked away again. But that's exactly how I felt when you abandoned me last night."

His equilibrium dipped under the assault of her softly spoken words. "No. No, that's the opposite of what I wanted."

When she looked up at him again, her eyes were wet and luminous. "We were supposed to be on the same side and you shut me out. It wasn't the first time, either. Or the second time. You moved me around like a chess pawn, and I didn't even get a say." She traced a finger down the bloodstain on her dress. "So you don't get a say in me being here. Do *you* understand?"

Henrik wanted to turn away from her disapproval, but forced himself to dwell in the face of it, even though acid speared up from his stomach. "I hate you being here, Ailish. I hate it. But I'm glad as hell you're not here because you feel indebted to me. For what I did."

She spoke in a whisper. "I *can't* let myself feel that way. Not yet. If I think about it, I'll want to ask why you did it. And if you tell me…I might get a little less pissed. I don't want that, because I've spent my life being treated like a pawn, and I won't accept it anymore. I *won't*. Especially not from you."

God, she was murdering his soul. He could feel it being battered around like a hockey puck. "Why especially not from me?"

Ailish shook her head, letting him know she wouldn't be answering. "I'm here because it's the right thing to do. I have to fix what I've done." She shifted forward as if she might come closer, but stopped, burying him in disappointment. "For now, we're still on the same team, so let's talk about what we need to do."

A huge part of him admired the hell out of her just then. She was fierce and beautiful in her staunch fury. But how could she expect him to strategize with their relationship on such thin ice? *Goddammit.* What choice did he have? Keeping her safe inside the house was his number one concern. When they got out of this alive, he would beg, borrow, and steal to get her back. Whatever it took. "The room could be bugged," he managed, the words sounding strangled. "When you talk to me, I'm the man who kidnapped you. Brought you here against your will. You understand? At all times." He bracketed his hands behind his head, paced away and came back, his stomach lining on fire. "What if they'd sent someone else in here with you? What would you have done?"

Apprehension rippled across her features. "I don't know. This is unusual, to say the least." Her eyes lifted to his and flitted away. "You're the first man who has ever set foot in this bedroom. That includes my father."

It took a serious effort not to be turned on by that news, and he still failed. *Focus.* Pacing the short length of the closet, he replayed the meeting with Caine. "So you've been feeling guilty all this time about reporting gambling debts to your father, when in reality you've probably saved hundreds of their miserable lives by making two sets of books. That right, Ailish?"

"Doesn't change anything," she insisted with a headshake. "I'm still complicit. I could have done more. Could have gone to the police."

"Ailish, you couldn't move an inch without eyes on you. Going to the police would have endangered your life." Henrik thought of the way Caine had stabbed the knife into his desk, dilated pupils like lasers on Ailish. "Same way your life is in danger now, dammit." He closed his eyes. "I take it from your reaction that Caine isn't normally so volatile?"

"No," she whispered. "That's new. He's always been ruthless, but it was controlled. Now…"

Henrik swallowed the agony of knowing they were surrounded by enemies. How outnumbered he was if it became necessary to protect her in earnest. "So we have two days until Caine expects those names and figures. Can you get through the books by then?"

"Yes." Ailish stared into the bedroom. "But I don't want to give those names and debts to my father. He'll *use* them. And it'll be on me. Again."

He'd reached his limit on seeing Ailish battle guilt. "Let's get something straight. A man makes a deal with the devil, he knows the consequences up front. You're just the messenger. None of this has ever been on your head, baby." He couldn't tell if his words were sinking in and hated it. Hated the connection she'd blocked between them. "Either way, we won't let Caine use those names. We have to get you out before handing them over, though. Because once you do…"

"I might be disposable."

He breathed through the dizziness inflicted by saying the words out loud. "That gives us two days to retrieve the evidence. I'll have to work fast to make sure we get an opening. And find a way to make contact with Derek."

Ailish's cheeks streaked with color. "Did I forget to mention there's a microphone in my necklace?"

Henrik arched an eyebrow. "That would have been nice to know." He lifted the key necklace—their skin shocking upon contact—and brought it to his mouth. "Start looking for my replacement, Derek. You can consider this my notice."

Wishing like hell they could remain in the closet indefinitely, where his body could block Ailish from danger, Henrik forced himself to wrap up their conversation. If someone entered the room and found them together in the closet, unfortunate questions would be asked. "We don't have a lot of time to pull this off. I'm not convinced Caine put me in here just to play babysitter. I don't think he's ready to have me roam the house just yet." On reflex, he reached out to cup Ailish's cheek, but it turned into a fist and dropped before making contact. "Tell me what we're looking for. Tell me what evidence we're here risking your *life* for."

She opened her mouth and closed it again. "I'll tell you when the time comes. I can't risk you cutting me out again." When Henrik started to launch a protest, she cut him off. "My father has two offices. The one where he brought us, and another in the basement. You need to get me to the basement office."

Henrik's head tipped forward. "You're asking too much of me, Ailish. Do you know what will happen if we're caught together stealing from your father?" He eased closer. "I'll protect you with my life, my body, but I won't be able to get you out safely if I'm—"

"Don't say it," she breathed, alarm transforming her features. "Please."

Hope caused the broken pieces of his heart to stir. "You're still my girl, aren't you, Ailish?"

Her lips parted on an almost inaudible sob, but she blinked and stepped away. "You need me in that office because I'm the only one, besides Caine, with the combination to the safe. And everything we need is inside."

Chapter Sixteen

Ailish stared into the blue depths of the swimming pool, watching her feet glide back and forth as if they were someone else's legs. Growing up, the swimming pool had been her escape, but now she found that laughable. It was surrounded on all sides by three stories of the prison she'd called home. Towering over her little slice of normalcy, blocking out the sun and casting long shadows. At one time, the ivy climbing the walls had been beautiful to her. Now the strands of green medallions only appeared to be making a break for freedom.

The sound of the gentle ripples created by her feet were drowned out by her father's men inside the house. Henrik would be with them. Blending in as best he could as a former police officer turned to the criminal lifestyle. She hadn't spoken to him since the early afternoon confrontation in her closet. After immediately getting down to the sickening business of drafting a veritable murder list for her father, Henrik had left her bedroom to stand guard in the hallway, opening the door to check on her once an hour. Too many hours of her life had been spent in that bedroom, working over her desk, trying to spare as many lives as possible. Because of her numerous attempts to run away since becoming a preteen, a guard had always stood sentry in the hallway. She didn't want Henrik to take the place of those men. It made her ill.

And whether or not it was rational, it made her mad.

Ailish was inside the walls of her own doing. She'd allowed Sera to bind her, allowed Derek to help her into the trunk. This was *her* decision. And while having that control put her a great distance from the powerless girl she'd once been inside those walls, the memories were too potent. The male shouting and laughter in the distance built a churning whirlpool of disgust and indignation within her. Every time she heard clinking ice cubes in a glass or the crack of pool balls, she wanted to scream. Maybe if she screamed loud enough, she could crumble the walls out of sheer force of will.

When she sensed someone joining her in the pool area, Ailish didn't even glance up. She knew that tread, knew that quiet restraint by heart already. Henrik. The whirlpool turning in her stomach moved a little faster, fast enough to drown out the way her pulse ticked up forty notches at having him nearby. A tiny twinkle of guilt tried to wedge itself in the whirlpool's path, grind it to a halt, but she wouldn't allow that. She'd been given the option of freedom in that forest. But she'd chosen to come back to Chicago, to fight her father's evil side by side. That decision had taken so much. The overcoming of fear, a giant leap of trust. He'd squandered that trust, and there would be no running into his arms or forgiveness. The hurt was too fresh.

Ailish slipped off the side of the pool, letting the cool water engulf her. She turned upside down, letting the tips of her toes point toward the sky, and rejoiced in the absolute silence. Air started to run scarce, so she pushed back to the surface, unsurprised to find Henrik standing at the pool's concrete lip. She registered the worry lines between his eyes, the tautness of his body, as if he were preparing to dive in after her. It made Ailish feel a little desperate. Made her ache. But her newfound stubbornness galvanized and overcompensated, kicking any sympathy for Henrik to the curb and making her want to lash out.

I thought you could be my future, but now you're just blending with the past, abusing my trust like everyone else. A familiar, helpless feeling was overtaking her, and she met it head-on. The only way she knew how.

Ailish's eyelids grew heavy, warmth growing heavy in her belly. She braced her hands on the pool's edge and climbed out, aware of the water running down her body. Over her breasts, loosely contained as they were in the teal-green triangles of her bikini. When she'd chosen it out of her dresser drawer, pride had prevented her from admitting the hope that she'd run into Henrik. Now her pride presented itself in a different way. She wanted some control back. There was a way to accomplish that. Recognizing and embracing the need to act out physically was just like slipping naked into cool, crisp, silk bedsheets.

Night was falling, the encroaching darkness accelerated by the surrounding walls of the house. Only the barest amount of moonlight shone in, giving her an excuse to be bolder, more daring than she would be in the daylight.

Henrik stepped back as Ailish exited the pool, throwing a look over his shoulder toward the house before giving her his full attention. "Are you…" His cautious gaze ran the length of her without moving his head, the deep voice of his emerging as if scraped over a bed of nails. "How are you?"

Ailish gathered her wet hair and squeezed out the excess moisture. Then she stretched her arms up, piling the tresses on top of her head, swaying slowly as she secured a bun. "I'm just fine." She watched Henrik follow the droplets of moisture coasting down her stomach, absorbing into the thin material of her abbreviated bottoms. "Did you need something?"

His throat muscles shifted. "Your break has gone on long enough. Time to head back."

She blinked away the red screen that dropped in front of her vision. "And you're going to escort me back to my cell?"

"You're safer indoors," he answered in a low tone. "Wrap a towel around yourself and get inside."

Henrik was right. She knew that. Since she'd run away, a shift had taken place at her father's house, and the landscape wasn't entirely the same as it had been. The energy was uncomfortable, clinging to the walls in every room like the ivy she'd stopped appreciating. If the men were no longer ruled by fear of repercussions from her father, Ailish was in more danger than ever. But it was hard to reason with herself under the influence of a thrumming pulse, excitement tickling up the inside of her thighs, and Henrik looming so close, clearly wanting to devour her. "I'm not ready to go inside."

"Do you need to be carried?"

He didn't want to do it. Didn't want to take away her free will—that much was plain in his expression. But he would if she pushed him far enough. And the secret, wicked part of her wanted to taunt him. Force him into cracking. Being just that much more like everyone else. Ailish dropped down onto the lounge chair where she'd laid a towel earlier, smoothing her feet up and back the terry cloth material. Up and back. Up and back. Stretching her thigh muscles out, then drawing them back in. Watching Henrik through half-closed eyes, she let her fingers dance on the propped-up tops of her knees, slowly dragging them down toward her center, arching her back as they traveled.

"Goddammit, Ailish." Henrik stepped closer to the lounge chair. "Stop this. They're downstairs now, but they could come looking for me."

Fingers playing around the edge of her bikini bottoms,

Ailish trapped a moan at the bright gold brilliance of tempting a man. *This* man. Being angry or disappointed in him didn't remove the need. He'd purchased property in the circle of her desire and couldn't be evicted. But she could harness the lust, direct it where she chose, and regain some of the power that place took away.

And yes, *yes*, she wanted Henrik to break. Wanted his hands on her body, even for just a few stolen seconds. It was no use denying it. Henrik's touch had gone from craving to requirement. And she wouldn't consider that a weakness, as long as Henrik had the same requisite need for her. His shallow breathing and barely audible groans as she toyed with the scant material of her bottoms was proof enough. "If they come looking for you, they won't be surprised to find me being bad. As long as you don't give in, you're not breaking any rules."

His shin bumped the chair. "I've been inside you. I know you treat my cock like your own private fuck toy. So *not* breaking the rules is going to be a lot harder for me than any of these pathetic motherfuckers."

A flush blasted over Ailish's skin, head to toe. "It's a good thing I left the necklace in my room."

"It's *not* a good thing," he growled. "You should have it on you at all times."

Undeterred by the reprimand, Ailish trailed her fingers up her rib cage and slipped them beneath the barrier of her bikini top. Her skin was still wet from the pool, making her breasts slick as she cupped them, massaging in a slow rhythm. "Feels so good. I haven't touched myself since the cabin."

"When?" Henrik asked hoarsely. "Tell me exactly when it was, damn me for asking."

Victory collided with lust and streaked through her middle. "The morning you left. Right afterward, when I was still—"

"Still *what*?"

She peeled back her top, allowing her breasts to pop free. Then she walked her fingers down, past her belly button, to tease the material of her bottoms. "I was still so wet," Ailish breathed. "I moaned your name into a towel while Erin and Connor were right outside."

"*Enough.*" He dropped a knee onto the chair, making it creak and undermining his command. *He's so huge.* His body blocked out everything but the wild, spinning desire for him to crack. To drop his weight down onto her and admit defeat. "You don't have a fucking clue what you look like, laid out all wet and naked, do you? Tits bouncing around. Those bottoms so wet, I can see the slit between your thighs." He raked a hand over his open mouth, all while perusing her body with sexual intent. "If we were anywhere else, I wouldn't be acting right, Ailish. I'd have a hand slapped over your mouth and I'd be using you up without a hint of gentle. You understand?"

"Yes," she whispered, tossing her head back on the chair. His words were rough, but she was hugely turned on by the image they conjured. Henrik covering her mouth while pumping out his frustration between her splayed legs. Hard. Maybe even enough to make her scream against his palm. "I understand."

When she attempted to slide her fingers beneath the low waistband of her bottoms, Henrik snagged her wrist. "*No*," he grated. "I know you're angry. I *see* that." His gaze strayed to the wet teal triangle covering her private flesh. "But you're going too far. I'm fucked up, okay? Knowing you hate me only makes me want to fuck you more. Fuck you *harder*. Makes me want to win your body back, right here and now. You'd like that, huh? If I gave you my cock hard enough to bust this chair?"

Unable to draw a decent supply of oxygen, Ailish only nodded.

Henrik released a low string of curses, before crouching down...and leaning in. His mouth hovered above her belly button, releasing hot puffs of air, creating goose bumps on every inch of her damp body. His lips opened, tongue licking out to stroke a devastating circle around her belly button—and the voices in the house grew louder. *Closer.* Henrik's body tensed, but neither of them moved. Until footsteps could be heard in the distance, treading over the tile floor of the kitchen, which led out into the pool area.

"Shit," Henrik grated, tearing himself away from the slick temptation of Ailish's body and rising to his full height. "Put your top back on."

Thankfully, Ailish didn't need to be told. She was already replacing the triangles over her breasts and tightening the knot at her nape. It was unfortunate that Henrik couldn't hide the evidence of their dangerous foreplay quite so easily, however. His cock was solid and ready, shoved up against the zipper of his jeans. God, if the men hadn't returned from downstairs, would he be fucking her right now? Out in the open where anyone could see them?

Yeah. He would. Logic was sorely lacking in anything involving Ailish. Even now, when they were seconds from having company in the pool area, he wanted to strip the bathing suit bottoms off of her and get a few thorough licks of her pussy. Just to get the taste in his mouth. Maybe he could even accomplish it before the men came outside.

You're a sick man. Yes, he was growing more ill with every passing moment he couldn't have her. She was the sickness *and* the elixir.

Henrik closed his eyes and focused on breathing deeply. If anything could loosen the hold of arousal, it was replaying the conversation he'd heard take place among the men inside. Just before coming out to find Ailish. To say they were antagonistic toward their boss's daughter was an understatement. They resented her for having what they considered a cushy lifestyle and squandering it. Wanting to better herself. *She thinks she's so much better than us, huh? Too good for this life? I'll show her the only thing she's good for.*

Yeah, that was all it took for rage to filter in. "Get up," Henrik growled, just as they men stepped outside. The sounds of lighters flickering echoed off the walls, accompanied by small flashes of flame. He saw those flames in Ailish's eyes, which was pretty appropriate, considering her temper had visibly risen with his command.

"I'll come in when I'm ready," she gritted out.

Aware that the men were watching, Henrik gripped her elbow and tugged Ailish onto her feet. "You have work to do."

He reached behind her to retrieve the towel, holding it out to her, but she refused to take it. Instead, her face transformed with a smirk and she sauntered past him. In nothing but the barely-there bathing suit, she strolled past the group of men, her footfalls the only sound to be heard. Henrik followed closely behind her, giving the group a conspiratorial headshake.

Not that any of them were looking at him.

It didn't matter that Ailish was playing a part. Flaunting herself in a way that brought men to their proverbial knees, the way she'd once done as daughter of the house. It didn't matter that he understood why she'd chosen to act out in such a way. No, none of it mattered when men who'd so crudely discussed Ailish's body before were now all but drooling as she passed. And he wanted to swing his fists until they were in a fucking pile on the ground.

"Back to work, little girl," one of them taunted.

Another one leaned close as Ailish passed, entering the house through the sliding glass door. "Make Daddy proud."

Henrik ground his molars together—hard—shoving his right fist into his jeans pocket so he wouldn't snap and use it. How much of this could he reasonably take? And this was just another sign that they'd lost respect for their boss. They'd never spoken directly to her before, according to Ailish, meaning there'd been a rapid shift in their behavior. God, he needed to get her out soon. *Tomorrow night. Just have to make it to tomorrow night.*

Following Ailish down the hallway toward her bedroom, Henrik tried to rein in the jealousy that made his blood boil. *Mine. Mine.* His brain repeated the word in time with her soft footsteps. A primitive beat played, beginning in the recesses of his chest, booming louder. Louder. When Ailish reached the door, she turned to meet his gaze, her lips parting on an intake of breath, obviously witnessing the results of what took place in his head. Too bad she was still pissed at him. It was there in the stubborn set of her jaw, the jerky way she opened the door.

"Coming?" she whispered, pausing with a hand on the jamb. God, that bikini was riding a little too low for his peace of mind. Any lower and the top of her slit would show. Had she tugged it down while they were walking?

"You know I can't," he rasped.

Henrik watched in slow motion as Ailish dipped a finger into the front of her bathing suit bottoms and slid it back and forth, tugging them down farther with every sensual journey. "Just to the closet?"

He couldn't do it. Couldn't take just a few minutes with her, could he? The men were drunk off their faces downstairs. He could still hear their shouting and laughter from outside, the scraping of metal chairs telling him they weren't coming back inside any time soon. *Stop trying to justify it.* "Get inside and lock the door," Henrik said, adjusting his erection with a muffled groan.

Ailish was breathing too fast, her cheeks bright pink. She was enjoying his torture, but there was apology in her eyes, too. His girl had a kink, and he was the target. Not something to be sorry about, but she'd chosen a damned inconvenient time to play. Jealousy had done something funny to him. Made him want to be aggressive with her, even more than usual. Made him want to claim her in rough fucking fashion.

Common sense had Henrik moving backward down the hall, but he'd only taken a few steps when Ailish peeled off her bathing suit bottoms and tossed them into the dark bedroom. She turned slightly in the doorway, just enough to give him a view of her ass, before slipping into the room. "Suit yourself."

Need choked Henrik, propelled him forward. Into the room. He had blinders on, couldn't see right or left, only straight ahead. The closet was pitch black when he entered, closing the door behind him with as much ease as he could muster. "Where are you?" he grated. "*Ailish.*"

"Here."

Just a breath away. His hands lifted, running over the curve of her hips, higher to strip off the bikini top. *Soft.* So smooth and soft. She moaned as Henrik spun her around until she faced away. "What do you want all this teasing to lead to, huh, baby? What are you hoping I'll do?" Henrik held his hips away from the temptation of Ailish's ass, otherwise he'd never be able to walk out of there. Not without feeling the tight stroke of her inner walls along the ridges of his cock. Not without listening to her beg. So instead of fitting her against his lap, Henrik rubbed his palm in circles on her backside. "Answer me."

"I'm not sure," she said on a shudder. A hand closed around Henrik's heart, a symptom of the honesty in her voice. She was pushing that sweet ass into his hand, going up on tiptoes to accomplish it, and he battled between the urge to continue on his quest to fulfill a need he sensed in Ailish—and turning her around, holding her until their pulses steadied. "I just want you to need me. So bad that you can't stop yourself from...taking."

He pressed his face into her hair. "I passed need weeks ago. Need is just a word. I *am* my starvation for you, Ailish. It rules me."

Her breath released in an excited rush. "Show me what it does to you."

Like a red flag being waved at a bull, Henrik gripped her ass cheek so tight, she gasped. "It makes me want to discipline you for teasing me." Letting go of her taut flesh, he pulled Ailish's hair to one side so he could speak directly against her ear. "That's what you've been asking me for, isn't it? You haven't been naughty for the sake of being naughty. You want repercussions."

"I-I don't know. I've never—"

"Hands on the wall, cock tease," Henrik ordered, tugging on the strands of red hair he'd snagged with deft fingers. The sound of her whimper was accompanied by clothes being shoved aside, hangers squeaking on the rack, the barely audible *thud* of her hands connecting with the wall. "We're going to find out, aren't we? See if you flashed that ass at me for a reason."

"*Yes.*"

Muscle memory kicking in, Henrik inserted his boot in between Ailish's bare feet and shoved her legs apart. "I wish like hell the lights were on so I could see you spread." He stroked a hand down her spine, around her hip, and up her rib cage. Back down and around. Over and over. "Those nipples hard, baby? Tell me."

He sensed her nodding a second before she whispered, "Y-yes."

"Good. I want to think about them bouncing when I spank you. Want to think about your pussy giving a little shake from the impact, too."

Ailish began to pant. "You're going to spank me?"

"Until you're dripping down the insides of your legs."

Henrik angled his body to the side, reared his hand back, and slapped the flesh he'd been in need of touching to the point of pain. His cock reacted to the cracking sound, filling and expanding in his boxer briefs. *Jesus. Christ.* He'd never spanked a woman before. Had never thought he'd find it appealing. Or maybe it was only an activity that could be pleasurable with Ailish, because—*fuck*—he loved the image in his head. Ailish in a frisking position against the wall, being punished by his hand. But his concern began to mount when Ailish remained silent, after her initial gasp.

"Baby." He smoothed his hand over the place he'd landed the light blow, tending the supple flesh with an up-and-down rub. "You want some more?"

She tilted her hips, arched her back. "*More.*"

Henrik held tight to his grip on the lust when it tried to run rampant. This was why he shouldn't have followed her inside. How was he going to walk out in a matter of minutes? *How?* He swung his hand in an upward slap, glancing off her left ass cheek. Harder than the first time, due in part to his frustration. He could hear Ailish's fingernails scratching on the wall as he delivered another smack. Another. "No more teasing while we're inside this house. *No more.*" *Smack.* "I can't fight two wars at once."

"Fine," she sobbed. "No more teasing."

His relief only made a brief appearance before he shot back toward blanketing desire. "When we get out, you can make me miserable all you want. When putting my cock in your pretty body won't get us both killed."

The next spank was firm and brooked no dissent. Ailish's

low moan had Henrik running a hand up the inside of her thigh and finding dampness. She tried to slide her legs back together with a sound of protest, but he kept them spread. The muscles of her backside flexed in his hand, an annoyed sound coming from her mouth. A solution occurred to him in that moment. An undesirable one, but a solution he sorely required. The only way he would make it out of Ailish's room without giving in to the endless need to be inside her was to make her angry. Or *keep* her angry, rather. *Shit,* he didn't want to do it. Having her mad and disappointed in him was like being strangled with fishing wire. Pushing her further away would be a hundred times worse. Still.

Think beyond the moment. This closet.

"Remember what I told you in the cabin, Ailish?"

When her answer emerged slurred, Henrik wanted to slam his head against the wall. She needed him. She needed him, and he had to leave. "W-which…what thing?"

He gave her one final glance of his palm, which shot her into a tiptoe position with a soft yelp. "You're not the only one who can tease," Henrik breathed in her ear before forcing himself to step back. Away from the warm, pliant perfection of her body, positioned as she was for a dirty, hot fuck.

"Get out," came her voice in the darkness. When he made it to the bedroom door, he refused to let himself acknowledge the tears in her voice. If he acknowledged them, he would go mad. Would never escape the need to hold her. Make everything better.

"Lock the door behind me and stay put," Henrik commanded, even though there was little point in directing her. Not when the only way he would leave his position outside her door was in a body bag.

Chapter Seventeen

Father and daughter stared each other down across the dining room table. Caine was an early riser, so Ailish had thought it safe to venture downstairs for something to eat, but he'd surprised her by walking out of the kitchen just as she entered. Whistling. Looking far less on edge than he had the prior afternoon, but just as mean. His *good morning, daughter*, had been nothing short of mocking. The old Ailish would have grabbed a bowl of raisin bran and scurried back upstairs. She wasn't going to retreat, however, so there they sat. Waiting for the other to speak or eat or move first. Perhaps it shouldn't have felt so unexpectedly exhilarating.

Oh, but it did. She'd finally succeeded in getting away the last time. And even though Caine didn't know she was back home of her own volition, *she* did.

I'm not your weak-willed lackey anymore.

Yes, she certainly hadn't anticipated breaking bread with her father ever again. Nor had she expected to find Henrik standing sentry outside her bedroom door upon exiting. The sight of him had brought her up short in the doorway, heart leaping, body crying out to make contact with his sturdy, reassuring form. She had just spent half an hour beneath the shower spray, wincing as the hot water cascaded down the raw flesh on her bottom. *Loving it.* Loving the knowledge that he'd been pushed far enough to inflict the delicious kind of pain. Hating what had come after. *Would he apologize? Would he whisper that he missed her?* But he'd only looked at her head to toe, his gaze full of meaning she couldn't interpret, then turned and disappeared around the corner of the hall, the outline of a gun at the small of his back.

Ailish had been out of line last night. She could admit that. In the light of day, she saw her behavior for what it was. A desperate attempt to recapture her sanity. Her independence and control. The darkness of night and the racy new desires Henrik had coaxed to life had made her reckless. Letting go of her anger toward Henrik's high-handed betrayal wasn't an option, not when it felt so imperative she remain true to her decisions, hard as they were to keep. They were all she had. And this case deserved her full attention. Communicating with Derek was first on her to-do list. And while they'd planned on Henrik being the one to leave the house to make contact, she felt the pressing need to take initiative. To be useful.

She'd started by working through the need. Getting as far ahead as possible on Caine's list, just in case he dropped by to check. Truthfully, it would be no sweat delivering what Caine wanted by tomorrow. Her father had always demanded she keep their dealings on paper, paranoid about hard drives being confiscated or hacked, but he hadn't made that specification this time around. Ailish was inputting the data with one hand into a spreadsheet, which performed most of the calculations for her, speeding the process along considerably. She was already much further ahead than Caine would expect by this point.

With that assurance in mind, she picked up her cereal

spoon without breaking the staring contest. "I need to go out. To pick up some things from the drugstore."

Since she'd anticipated Caine's amusement at her request, Ailish didn't even flinch when his laughter filled the dining room. "You've gained a sense of humor, too? Will wonders never cease?"

"I've always had a sense of humor." She dipped the spoon into her bowl, nudging the golden-brown flakes into tiny islands. "Maybe we just don't think the same things are funny."

Her father inclined his head, as if to agree. "I always found your little attempts to run away funny, so you're probably right." He scratched his chin absently. "Henrik says he found you in Michigan, living in a cabin. How long do you really think you could have pulled that off?"

Ailish's throat felt tight. "What do you mean?"

"I mean, you have no survival skills." He flattened a palm on the table and leaned forward. "Not like me. You're nothing like me. You don't know how to start with nothing and turn it into paper. *Money*. You would have been returning home in another week. Maybe I should have just waited. It would have been even more satisfying than pulling you out of a trunk."

"I would have starved first." Another echoing laugh left Caine, but Ailish spoke through it. "If I have no survival skills, it's because I wasn't allowed to learn any. You're not a father, you're a prison warden."

Henrik walked into the dining room with that sentiment still hanging in the air. Just inside the arched entry, he stopped, his expression one of boredom. As if hearing that a man had kept his daughter imprisoned meant exactly nothing. Same shit, different day. It was a convincing act. One that she envied. On the tail of hearing her father claim she had no survival skills, doubt trickled in. She'd gone undercover knowing the score, yet she was doing a horrible job of coping. Keeping up

a pretense while being confronted with her past confinement.
Pull it together.

As Henrik moved through the dining room toward the coffeepot, Ailish picked up her glass of orange juice and took a healthy sip. "Am I allowed to leave the house today, or not? There are things I need." Her pulse tripped over itself. "Or are you even going to keep me around long enough to need anything?"

The energy in the dining room had been tense before her statement. Now? It pulsed with renewed life. Caine wiped his mouth with a napkin and laid it down carefully. "You want to go out?" He tipped his head in Henrik's direction. "You take Vance, there. You try to run and he feels the need to put you in another trunk? I might take a little longer to open it next time."

She kept her features schooled, but any remaining connection she'd once felt for her father severed in two, lancing her in the sides as it toppled. "Fine," she managed, ordering her hands to stop shaking. "I'm used to being escorted around Chicago by your henchmen. It'll be just like old times."

"Now that's where you're wrong. The old times have come and gone. You'd do well to remember that." Caine winked at her. "You have a job to complete. Don't be long. Or we'll have a problem."

As ashamed as she was to admit defeat in the battle of words with Caine, Ailish had to leave the dining room. It was one thing to have suspicions that your father found you dispensable, but being presented with a confirmation instilled a new kind of fear, so different from the fear of being confined. Fear for her life.

Ailish took the stairs two at a time to her room. There, she let her robe drop to the floor and changed into a modest light pink sundress. She slid her feet into a pair of white flats and began to pace. She couldn't appear too overeager to get out of the house with Henrik, but waiting was brutal. Like running out of air with an oxygen tank just within your reach. When half an hour had passed, Ailish opened her desk drawer and peeled her emergency fifty-dollar bill off the inside frame, where she'd taped it months earlier. She tucked it into her bra and went downstairs.

Henrik leaned against the foyer wall, holding the folded *Chicago Tribune* in one hand, a mug of coffee in the other. When he caught sight of her at the top of the stairs, he sighed and set both objects down on a nearby console table, heading out the front door without another word.

"Where do you need to go?" Henrik asked, once they'd both climbed into the vehicle. And although his tone was long-suffering, he laid a finger briefly to his lips, reminding her of what she'd already suspected. Between the time they'd arrived yesterday and now, her father could have had the car wired.

"The drugstore."

As they pulled through the gate and out onto the road, Ailish couldn't help but stare at Henrik's large hands on the steering wheel, watching the leather glide through his fists and remembering the way they'd treated her backside the night before. Firm, biting, but somehow…affectionate. As if he enjoyed spanking her—a lot—but cared more about satisfying something inside her. Without any conscious thought, Ailish shifted in the seat, loving the twinge of pain wrought by the friction.

Henrik shook his head without looking at Ailish. His eyes were in the rearview mirror constantly. Checking to see if they were being followed? The realization pushed a frisson of alarm leapfrogging through her thickening blood, but it was snuffed out when Henrik reached over and squeezed her thigh. On cue, Ailish's head fell back on the seat, her hand covering his touch. She silently begged him to move higher, to explore beneath her dress, but he clenched his jaw and focused on the road. By the time the chain drugstore finally came into view, Ailish had become embarrassingly wet between legs, soaking through her panties. Just from that big, rough hand warming her leg. God.

Scenery rushed past in a blur on either side of the car, but they were in a secluded world, restricted though they were. Even Ailish's breathing had to be regulated, and it was obvious Henrik made the same conscious effort, although the frequency with which he shifted in the driver's seat told its own tale.

When they reached the parking lot, Ailish expected Henrik to park somewhere near the entrance, but he surprised her by rounding the huge strip mall. Driving past the Dumpsters to an alley lined with back entrances for each business. He pulled the car parallel with the wall—Ailish's door only a few feet from the cinder block barrier—before shutting off the engine and climbing out. She could see him striding around the back, mouth set in a purposeful line. Hard. Commanding. But nothing prepared her for Henrik to throw open the passenger side door and haul her out, not even allowing her feet to touch the ground before she was wedged up against the car's side, aligning her with every ripped, devastating inch of him.

"Goddamn, Lish." His hips jolted her up the car's exterior. "I'm hard up for a fuck between your pretty thighs, but we have no time. No *time*."

She framed Henrik's face with her hands, bringing him forward, close to her mouth. Right there. "I don't understand."

"What? What don't you understand?"

Her tongue brushed his bottom lip. "How I can be less angry with you...after you spanked me. And left. I should want to kill you."

"No, baby." He ground their hips together. "You don't

want that. Don't say that to me when I just heard your father threaten you, *dammit*. I'm barely holding on here. I almost strangled him."

"I'm sorry. I'm sorry." What was she apologizing for? What she'd said? Or…everything? Pushing him away. Teasing him. She didn't know. Only knew just then, in that filthy alley, she wasn't scared. He was comfort. Salvation. Although the dress was cut modestly, his proximity had swelled her breasts over the neckline, and she thrust them up for his perusal. "Please. I need something."

He made a sound halfway between a growl and a moan. "We need to talk. I shouldn't be touching you when there are so many questions between us."

Yes. She wanted to talk. Wanted everything explained from the moment she'd approached him in the park until now. It was getting more and more difficult to pretend she could survive without that information. But another more significant part of her didn't *want* to know. Didn't want to find out how her path had been dictated, when all along, she'd thought she was setting her own course. With their mouths pressed together, Ailish locked her ankles at the small of Henrik's back and slid her core up and down his distended fly. "We have time for me to take care of that. Don't we?"

Defeat crumpled his expression for a beat before hunger rushed in. Different from usual, more extreme. Depraved. "This alley is patrolled regularly, Ailish. I've patrolled it myself. You know why?"

"Why?"

"Men bring women back here." He fit his erection into the notch of her thighs and bounced her. *One, two, three*. "To perform certain acts. You following me? I'd never let you go down on your knees in this place." He dragged his tongue up the side of her neck. "Much as I need you to service my hungry cock, I would rather go without coming for a year."

The crude speech she'd come to crave elicited a breath-stealing squeeze in her loins. But she disregarded most of it and focused on *much as I need you*. Need. So much need. "If someone comes down the alley, we'll hear them. And I'll stop."

His big hand framed her jaw, applying pressure until her mouth popped open. "And I'm just supposed to pull out after you've taken me down the throat, is that right?" He shoved his thumb between Ailish's lips, pressed down on her tongue to keep her mouth open. "Once I hear those sweet little sucking noises you make, I'm staying in until the job is over. I would rather shoot whoever comes down this alley than stop before I come in your mouth. Is that clear enough?"

She was burning from the inside out. Couldn't remember a time when she wasn't in pain from lack of Henrik. Inside her. Touching her. Speaking from just above her mouth like a master. Every ounce of her femininity screamed toward the hand cradling her jaw, savoring the single connection like a lifeline. "Please. I'll do it so well. I remember the vein...what you like. I'll make sure it doesn't take long."

"No." His hand turned punishing on her jaw, and the pressure echoed between her legs, so severely Ailish whimpered. "*God,* I fucked you twice before we went in. Didn't I?" Henrik moved his mouth against her ear, licking, raking his stubble side to side on her sensitive flesh. "You're never going to give me a chance to sleep, are you? I can see you now, climbing on top of your man at all hours, begging to dry me out again. Know what I think?" His hand dropped from Ailish's face to her breasts, where he squeezed without mercy. "I think your pussy is sweet as fuck, but a little selfish for what I got. Isn't that right?"

"Yes." Ailish gasped when Henrik stepped back, enough for her to slide down the car, her feet meeting the ground. She braced her palms against the warm exterior, afraid to move as his hand vanished beneath the hem of her dress, blunt-tipped fingers slipped down the front of her underwear. When the pads of two fingers smoothed over her clit, Ailish arched with a muffled scream. "Oh my God."

His mouth moved in her hair, his arousal pressing against her hip. *Need to touch*. But when she tried to cup his erection, he jerked his hips back with a warning sound. "No, no, Lish," he rasped. "You'll give it up again later when I'm not watching for the police or worrying for your life. Remember this. I'm getting you off now, but later? When you take my hard-on deep, I'm going to make sure you feel the payback in your stomach."

Her nod was jerky against his shoulder, her thighs moving restlessly on either side of his hand. "Okay, yes, please, oh God."

"Couldn't even make it a couple days, could you?" His fingers were relentless on her clit, rubbing without gentleness one minute, plucking the nub of flesh between thick knuckles the next. Two fingers dipped into her clenching center, Henrik groaning in her ear at the tightening and releasing of her female flesh. He must have sensed she was closing in on her orgasm, because the pleasuring touch at her breasts vanished and a hand clamped over her mouth. "Sweet, sexy, selfish girl, all for me. I'm going to get back inside this pussy soon, Ailish. *Soon*."

"Soon. Yes. Please." She didn't recognize her own voice, the words she released into his palm as her body went through a dizzying round of spasms.

Moments later, his fingers slipped out of her satisfied flesh, trailing dampness up and down her thigh. "You better?"

"Yes," Ailish managed, collapsing against his chest.

"Good," he breathed out, planted a kiss in her hair. One, then another. "Now we're going to have a conversation."

Henrik needed every minute that Ailish spent in the drugstore to calm himself down. After he'd driven around to the main entrance, he'd escorted Ailish into the store, bought a disposable phone for the call he needed to make, then left her in the store alone, as a sign of trust. He planned to talk to her when she emerged. *Only. Talk.* God, if he got his hands on her again, they would scandalize an entire parking lot full of customers.

More pressing than his mounting male urges, he'd witnessed Ailish's apprehension at the word "conversation" and thought he knew why. Getting them back on the same page was imperative, because time was running short. Caine's threat to Ailish this morning meant they moved tonight, and it meant they moved as a team, whether he liked it or not. She had just as much skin in the game as he did. Could make her own decisions. If he wanted another chance with Ailish, he'd have to accept that. Remember it for the future.

He leaned against he front bumper of his stolen, more-than-likely bugged car and called Derek. The captain answered on the second ring.

"Captain Tyler."

"It's Vance. I've only got a few minutes."

A chair creaked in the background. "Better talk, then."

Henrik's crack of laughter held no humor. "You have nerve, I'll give you that. Unfortunately, I don't have time to remind you why this is my last case with the squad." He pinched the bridge of his nose. "We need to move tonight."

Scratching sounded down the line. A pen moving on paper. "What do you need from me?"

"Backup. Ready to come in locked and loaded, if we need it. If me and Ailish manage to get out without alerting anyone, we'll need transport waiting along the south side of the property. I want medical outside, waiting. Just in case." It got more difficult to inhale, the more he talked about the danger Ailish would be in. "Caine is volatile. Especially when it comes to Ailish. I don't think he plans to…" He held the phone away from his face as he breathed through his nose. "He doesn't plan for her to see past tomorrow morning."

Silence. "She assured me that wasn't the case. That he was protective. I wouldn't have sent her in there otherwise."

"Yeah? Well, she sees good things in people. Sometimes when it's not really there." Frustration burned in his sternum. "Why do you think she gave me a chance?"

The sound of a plastic bag dropping to the ground had Henrik whirling around, reaching for his gun. Ailish stood between two parked cars, watching him with wide eyes, her mouth parted. As if she'd heard him. But he couldn't find the wherewithal to care, because God, she was so beautiful against such a mundane backdrop. Sun shone down on her head, making the red glow like gold dipped in wine. The universe kept conspiring to take her away, and he resented it. Hated it for introducing him to the embodiment of happiness and then trying to snatch it back.

With a serious effort, Henrik turned away and braced his hands on the car's roof. "There's a safe in the basement office. Ailish has the combination. She's in it." He dropped his voice. "Just make sure she gets out. No matter what it takes."

"Consider it done." Derek said nothing for a few beats. "It might be impossible for you to trust my word right now, but I'll say this anyway. When she walked into the squad room, she became one of our own. I don't take that responsibility lightly."

Henrik's spine went rigid. "She's *my* responsibility."

"Yes, she is." Even through the phone, Henrik sensed Derek wanted to say something more, but the captain cleared his throat instead. "Let's end this tonight."

Henrik disconnected the line. "We have to get ba—"

Ailish wrapped her arms around him from behind. Fresh

scent colored the air around him and he sucked it in, sucked it in like a starving man. Her embrace—whatever the reason for it—restored his equilibrium. Allowed his chest to expand for the first time in days.

"You okay?" he asked gruffly, looking over his shoulder but only seeing the top of her head. "Lish. Give me your face."

When she lifted her head, Henrik swore the answer to every question he'd ever asked in his life was right there dancing in her eyes. She dropped her arms and—in a move that swelled his heart—she wedged herself between him and the car. Not a sexual maneuver, just an *I-want-to-tuck-in-here* maneuver. "Thank you for saying what you did. About me seeing the good in people." She laid her head on his chest. "I saw good in you when you arrived on the porch of my cabin. And I still see it. No matter what."

He rested his chin on the crown of her head. "I'm not going to lie, I'd love to be facing tonight without you. You have no idea." He knew she had a lifelong vendetta to settle, but that didn't change anything. Didn't make her any less of a liability. To his heart. His sanity. "I can't concentrate with you here. All I can see is that knife your father stabbed into the desk. What he said to you this morning. I thought it was over before it started, Ailish. When he brought us into that office, I almost killed him for nicking your wrist. You don't have any idea what it cost me to stand there while you bled. What it cost me to hear him threaten your life."

"I know. I could feel it was hard for you." She reached down and slipped her hand into his bigger one. "I'm sorry, Growler."

"But I know it cost you just as much. Maybe…more." When she stilled against him, he knew he'd surprised her. "This is your fight as well as mine. And you're strong, baby. Stronger than me—or anyone—has given you credit for. I'm sorry for not building you up when you needed support.

That's on me."

She tucked her head beneath his chin, but not before he saw the dancing of emotion cross her face. It was a while before she spoke, her question catching him off guard. "What you did to have me released from police custody…why? Why did you do that for me?"

God, he was weak right now. So weak. After having his hands on her in the alley, he was starved out of his mind. And yeah, there was a hint of fear that he would fail tonight. Fail her. The mission. Leaving her without an explanation. "That day in the park, Ailish. You asked me for help. Maybe not with your words…but when you looked up at me? I…I haven't seen anything but your face since." He closed his eyes and thought of her, dressed in green, dark circles under her eyes, but surrounded by sunlight. "I didn't know who you were until you showed up in the interrogation room. But I *knew* you were good, baby. And I needed to *be* what you needed. I still do. It's like a never-ending ache. Need to be Ailish's man. Protector. I want to cut down everything in your goddamn path. And then I want to take you to bed knowing I earned it."

She looked up at him, stunned, sending his heart sprinting fast enough for a one-minute mile. "What about me earning you?" Her voice shook. "You haven't given me the chance to earn you yet."

Was this woman for real? "I don't require earning. I require you to keep breathing."

Her thumb brushed over his wrist, over his hammering pulse, and she made a comforting sound. "I remembered more about the park. I remember thinking you looked as alone as I did." She kissed his T-shirt-covered chest. "You might be the first person who ever listened to me at all…and you heard things I didn't even say. Thank you."

"Ailish—"

"Wait." She pressed a finger over his mouth. "You saved me. I'll never forget it. But now you have to let me be part of something bigger than me. You've asked me for trust so many times. Now I'm asking for the same." A heavy pause as she scrutinized him. "Don't try to cut me out tonight. No matter what."

"Dammit, baby," he leaned down and grated against her lips. "If someone hurts you, I'll level that fucking house with everyone inside it. You know that?"

"Yes. I know that."

She opened her lips and accepted his sweeping tongue, so ready to allow more that Henrik had no choice but to tear his mouth away, positive he would die of sex deprivation before the day was over. "Our time is up."

"No," she murmured, giving him a final peck on the mouth. "It's only beginning."

Heart in his throat, Henrik watched the girl—who'd so casually insinuated they were together for the long haul—walk to the passenger side and climb in. She wanted him, just as he was, but the need to be worthy poured on his head like torrential rain. Could he get them both out alive, with the evidence to earn him back his badge? Make him a man of honor once again?

Only tonight would tell.

Chapter Eighteen

Henrik paced the guest room floor, his gaze straying to the digital bedside clock for the hundredth time that hour. The four tastefully painted walls of the bedroom felt like a cage, and he needed to break free. He hadn't seen Ailish alone since that morning, one of the armed men accompanying him every time he'd gone to prod her on Caine's behalf and check on the progress of her work. The hostility radiating from the men in Ailish's presence was almost too much to take without using his fists to swell their eyes shut. So they couldn't look at her anymore. Couldn't show so much disdain for her. They made his skin crawl.

The only thing allowing Henrik to maintain his sanity was the plan to move *tonight*. To collect Ailish, retrieve what they needed from the basement safe, and get the hell out of Dodge. Any longer in this house with her in jeopardy would have been more than he could bear. Completing the mission after only two nights in the house was beyond risky. He hadn't been given time to lull Caine into a false sense of security. But with Caine's behavior so erratic and his newfound knowledge of Ailish's second set of books, they were already out of time.

It had to be now.

Thankfully, Henrik had watched Caine drink his weight in bourbon tonight and take several trips to his upstairs office, presumably to add cocaine to the mix. Most of his posse had followed suit, but seen fit to drive home in their identical black cars anyway. A blond woman had shown up just before Henrik went up to bed, accompanying Caine to his upstairs bedroom located one floor above Ailish. So at the very least, Caine was occupied for the time being.

One o'clock in the morning now; Henrik needed to move. He double-checked his weapon, sliding it into the inside of his jacket pocket as he strode for the door. Having already checked to make sure the door didn't squeak, Henrik slowly eased it open—a figure stood just outside in the hallway, partially obscured by darkness. His weapon was drawn before he'd registered it was Ailish.

Both of her hands shot up as she fell back a step. "It's me," she whispered.

Henrik couldn't drop the gun fast enough, his every nerve ending scorched by the tremor in her voice. He yanked her into the room with his free hand, closing the door behind her and locking it. "I told you to stay in your room."

"I know." She tucked a lock of stray hair behind her ear. "But I figured we would meet at midnight, and when you didn't come, I thought maybe…"

"You thought I went without you." He cupped the side of her face, groaning inwardly when she turned her head, those lips plumping as she kissed his wrist. "I told you I wouldn't do that."

Stepping past him, Ailish removed the necklace from around her neck, tucked it beneath one of the bed pillows, and returned to her place in front of him. She rolled her lips inward, restless energy drifting off her like mist. "Henrik, I don't want anything left…open. Between us." A frisson of unease wormed in when her meaning wasn't entirely clear, but she stepped closer…and closer, until her tits met his stomach, forcing him to relax. Until she laid a hand on his belly, let it drift lower to settle on his belt buckle, and his dick lifted to meet her hand. "I've been pushing you since we got here and I want—no, I-I need—to make up for it. I don't like knowing you eased me and I didn't…you didn't…"

"Come." Lust flowed out from every corner, pushing at all the walls he'd managed to build, making his muscles flex of their own accord. "Is that what you're trying to say?"

Ailish nodded, her hand trailing down even more to grasp his erection, momentarily blanking his mind. She elevated herself on tiptoes, her tongue licking around the hollow of his throat. "You need to be what I need, don't you?" Her torturing hand slid to the base of his arousal and back up. "I need you to use me to clear your mind. Use me to ease your frustration before we go. And do what we came here for. I need the same."

Base, original lust that meant claiming his woman couldn't be delayed any longer. He'd stripped Ailish of her nightshirt before the impulse fully registered. The bra came next, those two candy-flavored nipples pointing up at him, begging for the kind of cheek-hollowed sucking only he would ever deliver. When he saw the shorts she'd had the audacity to wear outside of a bedroom, little sparks went off in Henrik's palm with the need to slap her ass. Without holding back. They were black, a cross between underwear and spandex shorts, ending only a quarter-inch from where they cradled her pussy.

"What the *fuck* are those?"

"They're just like all my clothes." Starting at her belly button, she trailed her index finger down to her pussy, sliding it between her folds. "Made for you to take off of me."

"That might be the best answer I've ever gotten." He plowed his fingers through Ailish's hair, gripped the strands, and turned her around to face the door. "Bite your lip, baby. This is going to sting."

God*damn*, the girl ever spread her legs like she was about to be frisked. While that idea was tempting as hell, the way her ass cheeks hung out of the bottom of those shorts demanded his full attention.

He dropped his open palm in a downward arc, glancing off her left cheek, groaning into her hair when the flesh jiggled just right. "If I wasn't hard enough to break through steel, I'd be owning that pussy from behind right now."

"When are you ever not that hard?" she said on an exhale.

"Are you back-talking me?" He twisted his fist in Ailish's hair, laughing when she only tilted her hips and whimpered the word "more." "I'm too hungry not to take what you're offering, Ailish. You want to take me on hands and knees like a beggar? So be it. But you know what I want first." Roughly, he shoved his hand into the back of her shorts, kneading her ass. "Go down on me like it's the last time."

As soon as his grip loosened on Ailish's hair, she turned and fell to the floor, working the buckle of his pants with desperate fingers. His stroked the crown of her head, brushing back the red hair that kept getting in her way, chanting *yes, yes, yes* in a tone reminiscent of torn-up concrete. When she'd finally released his cock, Henrik's legs almost buckled at the freedom. Christ, he'd been thick behind the fly since fingering Ailish that afternoon and he *needed*. Needed to be handled.

"Be rough with it." He covered her stroking hand and squeezed—*hard*—so hard that Ailish gasped. But when he showed her how fast, how irreverently he needed to be jacked off, she wasted no time following his instructions. She balanced the head of his cock on her tongue and beat him off, her hand moving in a blur, strangling him root to tip better than he could do it himself. "That's right, baby. You won't hurt it. Pretend you're angry with me. You want to make me mad so I'll take it out on you when we finally get down on the floor and fuck. Choke it off—" He growled into the crook of his elbow when she added a wrist twist on her ascent to his plump tip. Still propped on her tongue, Henrik hooked a finger into the side of her mouth, drawing her lips wide and thrusting halfway into that addictive warmth. "Ahhhh. *Shit.* Suck me in between your teeth. Rake them over me."

God, she was eager. Loving up and down his package like she was sick and his come was the antidote. Henrik leaned forward so he could see her ass in the shorts, the shorts he would be taking off her very soon. To bang her breathless. But he'd sure as hell remember to take them along with him when they got out. She'd be modeling those things for him until they became so threadbare, they wouldn't stay on her hips anymore. All of it would take place in his apartment, where there wouldn't be any distractions. No time limits. Just the thought of having unlimited access to Ailish made his balls pull tight.

"All right, that's enough." She wouldn't stop. Taking him down her throat until her eyes squeezed shut, then releasing him with big, gulping breaths. Red hair stuck to her cheeks, feathered her nipples. She was the hottest fucking sight of his lifetime. "I can't take anymore," he groaned, wrapping a hand around her hair and tugging her away from his aching dick.

"I need you. I need you," she whimpered.

There was a bed right behind them. He could get her there. He could—

She turned around, right there on the carpeted floor, falling forward onto her elbows and putting her ass on display. He was tempted to claim the shorts were his downfall, but it was all Ailish that had Henrik dropping to his knees behind her. All Ailish that had him feasting on her ass cheeks with wide, openmouthed kisses. All Ailish that had him outlining his handprints with the tip of his tongue, his palms smoothing over the tight, bent-over flesh, his mouth making a meal of her backside.

"Take off the shorts. Show me where I'm going to sink in." Face pressed to the floor, Ailish reached back and slipped the slinky material down her angled bottom, exposing *everything* to Henrik without hesitation. Telling him without words that she would be his playground until they were both spent. "If I forget myself and take you too hard, baby, you *tell* me." He let his middle finger travel over the pucker of her back entrance, lower, through her folds to play with her clit. "Something about this position that makes me feel a little fucking ruthless. You understand?"

She spread her thighs wider. "Yes. I understand."

Jesus. If he didn't know any better, he'd think Ailish wanted to kill him. She was tight, slick temptation just waiting for him to take. And waiting wasn't an option. Not when she was already so wet and begging for it with discreet glances over her shoulder. "You're my woman, Ailish. And I'm going to give you a filthy, sweaty bang under your father's roof to make sure you know it."

His cock made it halfway inside Ailish before she clenched and resisted him, a soft cry leaving her lips. Having met the same struggle before, though, Henrik knew once he pushed through and gave her time to adjust, she'd be fine. She wouldn't be hurting then; she'd be begging for some rough. So he reared back with his hips and pushed deep, almost blacking out the first time his balls smacked against her. *Damn. Damn. Damn it's so tight. So sweet.*

Henrik slid a hand up Ailish's spine, burying it in her hair and tugging her head back. "Tell me when you're ready to be ridden."

She wiggled her hips around, thighs flexing, issuing soft expulsions of breath toward the ceiling. "I'm ready. I'm ready."

With a closed-mouth growl, Henrik propped up his right leg beside her hip to give him added depth. And he scooped his hips up, pressing deep, *deep*, letting Ailish know what she was in for. Her features went slack as he ground himself inside her, buried to the hilt. "Feel where I'm touching? I'm the only one who'll ever reach that part of you. Mine. I claimed it. I'll claim it every day."

Her nod was jerky. "The only one. Every day."

"Good girl." Already the tide was rising inside Henrik. But it was darker and more powerful than usual. Having Ailish in such a vulnerable position signaled that she trusted him and shared this animal lust with him. He wasn't alone in wanting to fuck like two desperate creatures. Not if the sweat pooling at her lower back, the wheezing quality of her breath, was any indication. Her hips were jerking up and back now, her body insisting without words that he take. "Yeah, you want it. Don't you?" He pushed her hips up to the tip of his dick and slammed back to the hilt, sliding her knees forward on the carpet. "Want it so bad, but you barely let me in."

"Yes, I can," she moaned, the flesh of her backside shuddering with every blow of his hips. "So *good*."

Needing to hear her voice right up against his ear, Henrik fell forward, planting his knees on either side of Ailish's hips and holding her still with an arm wrapped beneath her torso. He dropped his chin down onto her shoulder to give himself a nice view of her pretty bouncing tits. And he pumped like he'd never get another chance. Ahhh shit, she was sopping wet between her legs, turned on but never once making it easy for him to go balls-deep. Every thrust was a struggle, and something about making such a rough effort over and over set loose a riot of his darker desires, pounding in his temples, shaking under the muscle of his abdomen. Their size difference only exacerbated the need for aggression. The need to make his unique mark on this woman. *His* woman.

Each time he managed to sink the full way inside, she made this gasping hiccup sound and it was driving him out of his mind. It blew around his head like leaves in the wind, echoing louder with every revolution. "Henrik," she sobbed. "Don't…I can feel you're holding back. Don't."

Was he? *Yes.* Yes, dammit. He was so used to keeping himself in check, he didn't even know what it felt like to let himself go. "I want to go harder. I *need* to. Need to make that pussy sore, then soothe it with some hot come. Need to make you a slave to this dick. You want that, Lish?" His pace kicked up a notch. "You giving your man a tight little place to spill himself, no matter how mean he gets?"

Ailish's breath whooshed out near Henrik's ear when he pushed her down onto the carpet, the elbows she'd been using to prop herself up now pointing out at her sides. Henrik slid his arm down from beneath her belly to jerk her hips up—just her hips—into his groin area as he continued driving between her thighs. With her cheek flush with the carpet, he could see her profile. The red staining her cheeks, the little O her cock-tease mouth formed. Pinned. Being taken. Watching her fingernails dig into the carpet, while the sound of his balls slapping her flesh played like an erotic overture in the room. He was growling into her neck, the sight of her tits jiggling in sync with his thrusts driving him high, so fucking high. *Mine. My woman. My body to pleasure myself with. My woman to orgasm as I see fit. Mine. All for me. All for her.*

Henrik vacillated between lust and love, ownership and wanting to be owned. Until those two heavy sides meshed together and fell over him like a net. "I couldn't let them take you away from me, Ailish. I was already in love with you. I was already your man in the park. And they wanted to put you away. No. *No.* I wouldn't...I couldn't ever let it happen, baby. I need you."

God, if he'd thought simply explaining his actions was a weight off his shoulders, telling Ailish he loved her was like digging his way free from a pitch-black ditch into the sunlight. He'd never admitted it to himself before now, but somewhere in between that chance meeting with her in the park and now, he'd let himself fall. He was still falling, though, reaching out for a precipice to grab on to. Ailish. It was her. Always her. With a gritted curse, Henrik pulled out of the perfection between her legs, flipped her onto her back, and fucked into her again.

While muffling her screams with his mouth, Henrik gave her the full weight of his hips, his cock, pressing her down into the ground. "Look up here. Look at me, Lish. I want to make sure you know I mean what I say." Still pushing deep into the heaven of her pussy, he fell forward onto his elbows, capturing the sides of her face with his hands, kissing her with tongue. "I'm in love with you. This is how I show it." He slid his cock out halfway, then bucked forward. Back and forward. Stealing her little whimpers with his lips. "I show it by killing anyone who tries to hurt you. And trying to fill you up…the way you make me feel so damn full. Just in a different way. Understand me?

"Yes," Ailish whispered unevenly, stroking his cheekbones with her thumbs. "Yes, I understand you. Show me anyway."

As Ailish said the words, she locked her ankles behind his back, but Henrik shook his head, telling her without vocalizing that he needed more. "Over my shoulders, baby. You're going to get a deep fucking."

Those sweet pink lips of hers fell open as she complied with his order. With what looked like very little effort, she bent her body in half, her ankles meeting in a crisscross behind his head. "Like this?" she breathed.

Henrik tested the new angle and hissed out a breath at the incredibly narrow space he had to work with. The wet friction. "Goddammit, you're a flexible little thing, too. Aren't you?" She clenched her inner walls around him, forcing him to stop and regroup, lest he climax before she got hers. "It's going to be a while before we go out in public, Ailish. Or somewhere I can't get you in a dark corner to take my cock. I'm a fucking fiend for this pussy."

"Good—" Her response broke off into a closemouthed scream as Henrik braced his hands on the ground, her ankles on either side of his head. And essentially began executing push-ups. Up and down. Lowering his dick into the squeeze of flesh between her thighs and drawing back out. Again and again. With each push-up, Henrik became more forceful until their sweaty flesh was slapping against each other *slapslapslap*. "Oh my God," she choked out, her head tossing side to side on the ground. "I'm…I'm coming. I'm coming."

As if he couldn't feel it. When her core tightened up and started to shudder around his pained flesh, Henrik had to push extra hard to go deep. It spelled the end for him, an end so goddamn fulfilling, his hearing cut out before returning amplified. "Fuck. *Fuck*. Me, too. Spread your legs for it." He didn't wait for Ailish to comply, grasping both ankles tensed up on his shoulders and yanking them wide, delivering his final pump on a growl, teeth bared against her ear. "You feel it all?" He heaved the words, his body convulsing. "My body wants to make you pregnant, baby. *I* do. And I *will*. You feel it?"

Her answering nod was vigorous, sweat dripping down her temples as her own orgasm continued to sweep through her body, milking him in the process. As drained as he felt when his climax passed, Henrik forced his eyes to stay open. To watch her. She'd invited him to clear his head by making love to her—and Henrik could admit it had worked, but well beyond what Ailish had likely intended. As he looked down at the beautiful woman with a matching heart beneath him, he could see his future. *Their* future.

He would annihilate anyone who tried to deprive them of it. And he had a bad feeling it might happen sooner rather than later.

Chapter Nineteen

Ailish could admit to being a little shell-shocked as she leaned against the wall of Henrik's room, waiting for ten minutes to pass before joining him in her father's basement office. Henrik had wanted to make sure the house was clear before she left the general safety of the room, making sure she had a weapon to protect herself while they were separated. Her body felt sore, with twinges in her buttocks, thighs…and more private regions. Every time she moved, she could feel his hands, his breath bathing her neck and shoulders. His rigid flesh sinking into her body. The sense memory felt *amazing*. The act of belonging to another person. A person who understood her, had seen something good inside her during the barest of encounters. Knowing Henrik belonged to her, too, was even more incredible.

…the way you make me feel so full…

She did that to him, when she'd never felt the capability to make another person love her enough to stay. Not her mother or friends. Her father's odd brand of affection had only ever been conditional. He provided it as long as Ailish was useful.

Henrik was the opposite of those broken relationships. He'd barreled through all her faults, her past, with a bulletproof vest on and seemed almost anxious to take on any obstacle on her behalf. The gravity between her and Henrik had always been there, waiting to be fully explored, and tonight? They'd explored. Or *marauded*, to be precise. Ailish felt conquered. And like a conqueror all at the same time.

Henrik loved her. Whatever trust issues she'd had upon leaving Chicago hadn't just disappeared. Maybe they never would. They were still a part of herself she needed to work on, grow around, and overcome, but when Henrik said he loved her? There wasn't a doubt in her mind he was telling the truth. She'd wanted to say it back, but craved the same experience he'd had. Of doing it his own special way. She wanted that chance. To make it something they would remember. Once her feelings were out there in the world, she would probably never stop saying the words. She had years to say them.

But first, they had to get through tonight.

Ailish checked the digital clock and added some steel to her spine. Time to move. As Henrik had asked—with an unprompted please—she held the necklace up to her mouth and spoke. "We're moving now." She breathed through her nose, trying to get a handle on the adrenaline spiking in her blood. "There are three men and one woman in the house, including Caine. The men are armed."

Praying that Derek had heard her and the listening device hadn't malfunctioned, Ailish opened the door and crept through without a sound. She focused on the heel-toe sequence of every step, careful to avoid floorboards she remembered being creaky. When Ailish reached the living room, she crept along the living room wall and opened the basement door, taking the stairs slowly. Just before she reached the bottom, Henrik appeared, waving her down. "We're all clear down here, baby." He pulled her into his arms and planted a kiss on her forehead. "Let's get this done so I can get you out of here."

"I'm getting *you* out of here, too."

The right side of his mouth tipped up. "Yeah. You are."

He stooped down and lifted, bringing Ailish with him so she could kiss him on the mouth. And she did. With what was probably an inappropriate enthusiasm level for a woman who'd just been given the orgasm to top all orgasms upstairs.

Henrik pulled away first, shaking his head. "I can't wait until there's no time limit on how long I can kiss you." He tilted his head to suck her earlobe between his teeth. "How long I spend tasting you."

Ailish felt his erection against her belly and swallowed hard. "How long I get to taste you, too," she murmured.

His chest vibrated with a laugh. "This equal measure stuff really works for me. Have I mentioned that?"

"I love you," she blurted, only catching a fleeting glimpse of his dumbstruck expression before wedging her forehead between his neck and shoulder. "Dammit. I was going to wait for a special time. You ruined it."

A long pause paused. "How did I ruin it, baby?"

She lifted her head and blew out a breath. "By looking at me."

"I'm not going to stop doing that anytime soon."

"I'm not going to stop loving you anytime soon."

"Equal measure," he rasped, running his gaze all over her face. "Don't tell me you love me again until we're safe. I want every bit of motivation I can get my hands on."

Ailish could feel Henrik's regret as he stepped back. "Let's get this done. I want to get to a place where my need for you only makes us late for work or miss dinner reservations. Okay, baby?"

"Yeah." She couldn't help but stare at him after those beautiful words, but somehow found the wherewithal to precede Henrik into her father's darkened office. It was a far cry from the swanky digs upstairs, more functional than anything else. A desk with one rolling chair, another identical one facing it. Ailish had always harbored suspicions that her father brought men down there to be interrogated. Had they been tied to that rolling chair while she slept upstairs?

Guilt trickled inside Ailish's throat as she moved to the far wall where built-in cabinets were located. She opened the far left door and crouched down to look over the familiar metal box housing countless secrets. Ailish opened her mouth to tell Henrik she required more light to enter the combination, but he beat her to the punch, shining a key-chain flashlight at the numbered silver knob, illuminating it.

Ailish closed her eyes and recalled the set of numbers she'd housed in her brain so long. It was the date her mother had left: 09-23-08. Her fingers moved right to left, muscle memory kicking in on the second revolution, until she heard the *click* and the safe door bumped ajar.

Henrik squeezed her shoulder. "Well done, Ailish." His praise eased the pressure inside her chest somewhat, making it easier to reach for the plastic freezer bag full of documents and photographs. "What is it?" Henrik asked.

"It's blackmail." She swallowed. "Every cop, every politician in Chicago, and even some baseball players who've had dealings with Caine. He always makes sure there's something to use against them if they try to renege or back out." Ailish closed the safe and stood, holding the bag out to Henrik, who shone the thin beam of light over the bag. "Caine never leaves behind anything. No one ever talks. But we can use these people to testify in exchange for a deal. Kind of like I did."

Henrik jostled the bag to get a good look at the contents and whistled under his breath. "I already see a few faces that sure as hell won't want to be recognized." He turned off the light and focused on Ailish. "I need to make sure you're good with this, Ailish. He's your father, bastard or not. I wouldn't expect you to feel nothing about giving him up to the police."

Running a finger over the plastic bag, she thought back to the years she'd spent confused about sick, violent words overheard spoken between men in her house. The unsafe feeling. The conflict and guilt over bookmaking for Caine. There would always be a bond with the man who'd fathered her, but a daughter's loyalty could only go so far. And with the discovery of her second set of books, she would be responsible for untold pain, and this time, it could kill her. "I'm good, Growler."

"All right, Lish." Henrik shoved the bag into the back waistband of his pants and removed his gun from the inner pocket of his jacket, checking the clip and replacing it with a metallic slide. "On the way out, you need to stay right behind me. Always behind me, unless I tell you different. *Please.*"

She went up on her toes and kissed his mouth. "Right behind you."

Henrik gave Ailish one more long, memorizing look before leading her up the stairs. The silence was so heavy, it weighed down on her eardrums as they paused at the top of the staircase, staying perfectly still while listening for sounds in the house. Then they were moving again, traversing the entryway, her focus on Henrik's hand where it rested on the butt of his gun. They passed the front door, heading for the side entrance instead which would let them out onto the south side of the property. Where hopefully Derek and the squad would be waiting.

As soon as they entered the kitchen, Ailish knew something was wrong. She lunged forward and laid a hand on Henrik's back, his muscles tensing beneath her touch. Alarm buzzing along her nerve endings, Ailish turned in a circle, trying to locate the reason for her prickling sixth sense.

On the kitchen island was a half-eaten apple that hadn't gone brown from exposure to air yet. Which meant—

"Midnight snack?" Caine's voice snapped from behind them.

Before Ailish could even register fear, Henrik had wrapped an arm around her waist and slung her backward, behind his body. Since she couldn't see over Henrik's towering frame, Ailish turned her head to the side, watching the horrifying scene play out in the kitchen window's reflection. As Henrik backed her up against the marble island, his gun was already drawn, pointing directly at Caine. But her father's stance was identical, his own weapon leveled in Henrik's direction.

"No," she whispered, curling her hand in Henrik's T-shirt. *Please don't let this be happening. Please.*

Caine wore jeans and no shirt, his aged tattoos seeming to sag in the murkiness of the reflection. "My own daughter, huh?" His laughter made goose bumps break out on Ailish's skin. "You know, I'm ashamed to admit I didn't see this coming. Didn't think you had the backbone for it."

"She has more backbone than you do. Must have gotten it from her mother." Henrik's voice was steady. "Put your gun down, Caine. It's over. There are two of us. If you fire on me, I will still put you down, and Ailish will get out with everything the police need to eliminate your operation."

"Funny you should mention her mother. And bones." Her father's smile was almost melancholy, but it didn't match his mocking tone. "All those hours spent swimming in the pool, Ailish. Back and forth. No idea your mother was buried just a few feet from the diving board the whole time."

The scream began in Ailish's belly, but grief made it lose momentum on the way to her throat, emerging as nothing more than a half wail, half sob. Her knees tried to buckle behind Henrik, but he reached behind with the arm not holding his weapon, grasping her to his back in an upright position. It felt as though her insides were pouring blood, but through sheer force of will, she commanded herself not to lose even the twisted respect she'd earned from her father. *Later.* She could rail over the unfairness of her mother's death later, when their lives weren't at stake.

Swallowing a lung's worth of oxygen, Ailish slid her own weapon free, stepped to Henrik's right, and aimed the barrel at Caine. Without looking at Henrik, she could sense his surprise, but addressed only her father. "Weren't expecting that, were you?"

His cocky expression slipped, but snapped back into place. "This morning I might have been surprised. Now?" He backed up a step. "Not so much. Considering I was woken up by the arrival of someone you might just recognize."

The lifted gun entered the kitchen first, pointed at Ailish. Henrik made a broken sound to her left, but she could only stare at the man who joined them in the kitchen, walking with noticeable difficulty, a permanent wince on his face. Gordy. The man she'd shot in Michigan. "Hey there, little girl."

Caine traded a look between Henrik and Ailish. "Thought I was losing control of my men, here. Every time I sent them after you, they didn't come back. Turns out I passed a little thirst for violence on to my daughter." Mind rebelling over her father's words, she didn't notice Henrik trying to sidle closer, until her father shouted at him to stay put. Then he turned his head slightly to address Gordy. "Is that the man you saw Ailish with at the campsite?"

"Yeah. That's him." Gordy made a rough noise and clamped his non-gun hand over his side. "They were inside together for a while until she split. That's when I followed her." He cocked his gun with a sneer. "That's when the bitch shot me. And he took down Vick."

Beside her, Henrik stood still as a statue, but Ailish sensed a building need to act. Could sense his fear on her behalf. "Caine, she's your *daughter*. You sent these men to kidnap her. You can't blame her for defending herself." His chest lifted and fell slowly. "You're not going to let him kill her over it. She's your *blood*."

"No, I was thinking I'd do it myself," Caine answered, transferring his gun from Henrik to Ailish.

With a bellow, Henrik dived for Ailish, firing his gun at Caine as he closed the distance between them. The bullet struck Caine in the collarbone. He staggered, but didn't go down, only taking a too-brief second to lift the gun again. When Ailish saw Gordy take aim at Henrik, she tightened her finger on the trigger of her own gun—

The kitchen...exploded. At least, that's how it seemed, as Ailish went from a slow-motion existence to rapidly moving reality. Connor and Derek appeared in the doorway behind her father and Gordy, holding black gun muzzles to their heads. The door behind her was kicked open, Bowen storming in with a ruthless expression on his face, Erin close on his heels looking gleeful.

"Drop the guns and slide them toward Bowen." Derek shouted. "Bowen, raise your hand."

Bowen picked the half-eaten apple on the island and took a bite. "That'd be me," he said around a mouthful. "Send 'em on down."

When her father and Gordy laid the guns down, Relief blew in like a gale wind, smoothing out the daggers in Ailish's chest. *Safe.* They were safe. It was over, and her father couldn't hurt anyone anymore. Especially not in her name.

Ailish let her weapon fall to her side and reached out for Henrik.

And then her world slowed down again. In her periphery, she saw her father dive for his discarded gun and lift it—but instead of aiming it at her, he pointed it in Henrik's direction. Her father's body jerked with the impact of two gunshots, fired from where, she hadn't a clue. She only knew the next bullet fired was coming from Caine's gun and it would hit Henrik. The man she loved.

Without another thought, Ailish moved in front of Henrik, white-hot pain tearing through her body almost immediately upon surrounding him in the broadest embrace she could muster. The agony was so consuming, she couldn't tell where the bullet had struck, only that it felt like a hundred bullets instead of one, clawing at every layer of skin, setting her on fire. Henrik's arms were around her, though, and that somehow made the pain worth it. He was yelling her name, interspersed with curses, his voice breaking, and hell…at least that meant he was alive.

Henrik was alive, so their love couldn't die. Even if she might.

That was Ailish's final thought before everything went dim. Then black.

Henrik wouldn't sit in a chair. Didn't want to experience anything comfortable. *Refused* to. *Ailish is hurt. Ailish is hurt. Ailish is hurt.* He longed to slam his head back against the hospital waiting room wall he'd slid down hours before, slipping into a state of numbness on the outside and World War III on the inside, grenades being launched from smoking trenches. Other people were there, too—Derek, Bowen, Erin, Sera, Polly, Austin, Connor—moving like ghosts people catch just before falling asleep, in that space of semiconsciousness. Voices droned from different corners of the room, but he wanted to hear only one voice. Just one. And if they hadn't gotten Ailish to the hospital in time, he might never hear it again.

Misery blanketed him, rendering his limbs useless. He

could only replay what had taken place in the kitchen, again and again, because reliving the horror is what he deserved for letting his girl get—

Fuck. She'd been *shot*. Her blood had been spilled when he'd been only a couple feet away. How? Henrik buried his face in his hands and let the scene gather for the thousandth time. Caine's weapon had been down. Out of his reach. Connor had already been in the process of handcuffing Gordy. Ailish's father had been almost subdued, his body slumping, one hand reaching up to cover the bullet wound Henrik had inflicted. But then he'd just...come to life. He'd dived across the floor and fired the shot in under a second. And the quickest one to react had been Ailish.

To *shield* him.

Henrik's lungs struggled to draw air. If he lost the woman he loved tonight, not even the knowledge that Caine had died on the floor of his own kitchen would avenge her. There was no vengeance to be had. *There's nowhere to go from here.*

"Son."

The familiar voice broke through the wall of agony Henrik had erected around himself, but it was only a minor puncture. Something firmly ingrained in his being—a learned respect—had Henrik lifting eyes to his father. But he only nodded once and began to replay the scene. Again. A sigh came from above, and Henrik registered his father dropping to the floor beside him, leaning against the wall.

"I might be retired, but I still hear about most things." He tapped a fist on his knee, a mannerism Henrik associated with family breakfasts, church services. "So you can be sure I heard what you did tonight. Earned your badge back, Captain Tyler tells me."

Henrik said nothing. But he glanced up long enough to realize his mother and sister were in the waiting room, too. His mother held a bouquet of roses, but he could only envision them being laid on a grave.

His father shifted beside him. "This girl—Ailish O'Kelly—she's the one you lost your career over?"

"I'd do it again." His voice was hoarse from shouting. "Or I'd find her sooner. Take her away so none of it would've happened. Not like this."

They were silent for long minutes before his father spoke again. "What you did—I would've done the same for your mother. And I should have trusted that you were good. I shouldn't have turned my back." The older man gained his feet with help from the wall. "We'd like to meet her when she's better."

When she's better. When she's better. Those words echoed for God knew how long. It could have been hours or days before the doctor entered the waiting room. Everyone in the room stood. The squad, his parents. The doctor removed his glasses and rubbed tired-looking eyes with two fingers before replacing them. "Ms. O'Kelly is in recovery." He scanned the room, as though looking for someone. "She's asking for someone named Growler."

Henrik was moving through the room like a launched cannonball before the doctor even made it to the nickname. Barreling through the hospital corridor, he didn't allow relief to accumulate. Hadn't he felt relief just hours ago, with the feeling ending in Ailish being shot? No. He wouldn't relax until he felt life pulsing beneath her skin. Until her hazel eyes laughed back at him.

"Lish." Henrik said her name as he turned the corner into the recovery room. And he halted. Because even with breathing tubes in her nose, color missing from her face, she was the most incredible sight he'd come across in his life. "Lish. I'm sorry. I'm so sorry."

Ailish reached out a hand and smiled.

Henrik lunged across the room to take it, falling to his

knees beside the hospital bed and bowing his head over her prone body. When he felt her light touch stroke over his neck, thankfulness flowed through his veins like an antidote.

"I would do it again," she murmured, her voice partially obscured by the beeping machines. "Before you say anything, I want you to know that. And I'll never change my mind."

Hearing the words he'd spoken to his father in the waiting room, Henrik could only stare at the girl who'd become his entire damn world in a short space of time. Until that moment, with their shared sentiment hanging in the air, he hadn't fully understood what it *meant* to love someone, beyond the soul-wrenching shock of it. What it meant to love someone strong and capable and kind and brimming with potential. His Ailish. She'd wanted equal measure — *demanded* it — and giving it to her meant accepting that measure in all forms, good or bad. Always.

"Baby…" He blew out an uneven breath, checking the instinct to lecture Ailish or demand she never endanger herself again. "Thank you for saving my life."

Her smile could have powered Chicago for a year. "Thank you for saving mine, too." A laugh tumbled from her mouth, but there were tears shining in her eyes. "I love you so much."

"That's a good thing," Henrik managed around the manacle choking his throat. "Because you can't get away from me so long as you're in that bed. And I'm not budging until you can budge with me." He shook his head. "I have a feeling I'm going to be a worse patient than you are."

Tears shone in her eyes. "Because you love me, too."

Henrik leaned down and kissed Ailish, rejoicing over the warmth — the life — that greeted him. In his mind, an image rolled like an old home movie. Ailish walking toward him in the park, wearing her green dress. Except this time she smiled wide and opened her arms to greet him. "You're damn right I love you."

Epilogue
Four months later

Ailish was nervous. Which was ridiculous. In a handful of months, she'd survived two attempted kidnappings, a gun battle, and a fiancé who—although he'd taken some convincing that she was *actually*, fully recovered—couldn't seem to stop dragging her into their bedroom every chance he got. She could admit, however, that surviving two hundred and fifty pounds of solid, groaning, aggressive male wasn't exactly a hardship.

Speaking of her fiancé, he was next to go up on stage at the Chicago Police Department induction ceremony. At Derek's urging, the department had been prepared to reinstate Henrik as one of their own the week following their stint undercover with Caine; Henrik had been adamant about waiting until Ailish had recovered from her gunshot wound and could attend the ceremony.

"I need you there with me to give it meaning," Henrik had said the morning Derek dropped in to deliver news of the department's decision. Knowing how much having his badge back meant to him, Ailish had urged him to take the honor as soon as possible, but true to his word, he'd been more concerned with her comfort at the hospital. Making sure the doctors were attentive, bringing by her new friends—Erin, Sera, and Polly—to entertain her.

Which had promptly backfired. Listening to the exciting stories of their undercover squad adventures had sparked an interest in Ailish. The possibility of being a part of a team was something she'd never allowed herself to hope for. But she'd had something to offer. Maybe the girl she'd been while growing up within the walls of her father's home wouldn't have thought herself capable of adding to such a group of skilled individuals—criminals or not—but she wasn't that girl now. When she'd brought up her idea to Henrik, he'd looked seasick, but warmed to the idea upon realizing Ailish wouldn't be in harm's way.

Ailish was now the accountant for the undercover squad, a position that had become necessary thanks to the department's influx of funding after they'd not only broken up Caine's operation, but implicated over twenty local politicians in his various schemes. Now that the team members were being paid a salary, they even turned to Ailish for advice sometimes. Some of them, thanks to their growing families.

Case in point, Bowen and Sera, who had just walked into the auditorium. Bowen guided Sera into the empty seat beside Ailish, even more protective than usual because of the baby she carried in her belly, three months along. "Sorry we're late," Sera whispered. "Did we miss it?"

Ailish shook her head. "He's going up soon."

Bowen winked at Ailish, then went back to staring at his wife. Ailish smiled to herself, thinking back to the squad meeting when Sera had announced she was pregnant—out of necessity, since the ex-cop couldn't work in the field until the baby was born, or risk Bowen's sanity.

Sera had gotten queasy during a case breakdown and Austin had handed her a wastebasket, casually asking her when she was due, effectively blowing Sera's surprise. Bowen hadn't been capable of speech for the better part of an hour, simply holding Sera on his lap and speaking in low, urgent tones against her ear, his eyes suspiciously wet.

Speaking of Austin, he and Polly were in the back row, closest to the exit. They weren't in a place just yet where trusting a roomful of cops was in their repertoire. The pair had become something of a legend among the department in the last few months, their undercover disguises and fabricated identities known for being airtight, putting them in high demand.

Erin and Connor, hovering near the auditorium window, were still Ailish's favorite, though. She and Erin had continued their tradition of taking nightly walks in various locations around Chicago, while their boyfriends sweated out their absence at home. Now Erin sent her a pinkie wave, then gave her the universal sign for hand job, while Connor smiled down at her fondly. Ailish didn't keep any secrets from Erin. She'd confided the trials of her childhood to Erin and in return, the blond escape artist had told Ailish enough. Enough for now. And they got a little further every day. One secret she hadn't related to Erin had something to do with the ring box in Connor's pocket—containing the sapphire engagement ring she'd helped pick out. But come tomorrow, hopefully that secret would take care of itself.

Yes, Ailish had a family now, and they were more than she could have asked for. They were loud, challenging, and loyal to a fault. She loved them all. But it was nothing compared to the love contained inside her for Henrik. As if she'd called his name across the crowded room, her fiancé found her gaze through the audience and smiled that bedroom smile of his. The one that said, *we're going to lose everything but the fitted sheet tonight, baby.*

Ailish cooled her cheeks with the backs of her hands. Henrik had proven to be…creative. *Understatement.* Since that stolen night when he'd given her a spanking in the closet of her old house, they'd discovered new things about each other and themselves. Things that involved a lot of teasing. And a whole heap of discipline. Things she *craved*. No matter where they were. Even a long-awaited induction ceremony where her future in-laws were occupying the row in front of her.

Applause broke out around Ailish when Captain Tyler was announced on the podium. The whispered conversations taking place around her ceased immediately, an air of respect and fascination falling over the crowd. Derek had become a revered icon among his peers, and it showed in their silent deference. Not only had he quieted the naysayers who'd doubted his ability to handle a squad of criminals effectively, but his investigation into Caine had created a ripple effect around Chicago. With the evidence produced by Ailish and Henrik going undercover, Chicago had the lowest crime rate recorded in decades. The captain ruled the city with an iron fist, daring anyone to doubt him again. Well, he ruled everyone but his wife, Ginger, and toddler daughter, Dolly, who both beamed up at him from the front row, clearly ruling the captain with ease.

"I'm not going to make a speech," Derek started. "I have to get back to work. But I'm proud to say Officer Henrik Vance will be getting back to work with me. Even honest men makes mistakes, and Vance is as honest as they come." The captain tipped his head toward Ailish's stoic fiancé. "Vance. Come get your damn badge back."

"If we weren't engaged, I think my mother would actually try to adopt you," Henrik muttered into her neck as their elevator ascended to the fifth floor. When Ailish had been restless from spending far too many hours in a hospital bed, she'd made a few decisions. After having her mother's body excavated from the backyard and given a proper burial, Ailish sold Caine's house. She and Henrik had used some of the money to buy a two-bedroom condo near Connor and Erin's apartment. Her very own home she could decorate herself and roam about at will. The second bedroom would be occupied by their future son or daughter, but for now, Henrik's parents occasionally spent the night. Making up for lost time, they called it.

"I thought they were going to follow us home from dinner." Ailish laughed. "But your father definitely caught you making slashing motions behind his back."

Henrik lifted her off the ground, sighing in satisfaction when Ailish locked her heels around his waist. "He'll get over it. I needed you to myself tonight."

Her back met the elevator wall on a gasp. "I need that, too."

When the doors rolled open, revealing the fifth-floor hallway, Henrik stepped out into the dimness, moving toward the very last door along the wall. Their home. Ailish smooshed her grinning face onto his shoulder as they walked inside, greeted by the familiar scent of gardenias, which she kept in a vase on the dining room table. Henrik's hands slid along the outsides of her thighs, gliding beneath her dress to cup her bottom, and she forgot all about homey scents. Ailish shifted and felt his need where it grew between his thighs, eager to be planted inside her. Her limbs growing simultaneously languid and tight from arousal, Ailish dragged her teeth down the side of Henrik's neck and listened to his growl of approval.

"You're officially engaged to a cop after today," Henrik said, laying Ailish out on the bed and stripping the damp panties down her legs, leaving them forgotten on the floor. "How do you feel about that?"

"I'm engaged to you, no matter what you are." She sat up, moving to a kneeling position so she could divest Henrik of his tie and dress shirt. When the final button had been undone and the garment fell, she ran a flat palm over the fresh keyhole-shaped tattoo over his heart. The one that corresponded to the shape of her necklace perfectly. "Do you remember what I said to you that first day in the park?"

"I'll remember it until I leave this earth," he said, his voice gruff. "You said, 'Do you ever wonder whose side you're really on, Officer?'"

Ailish nodded. "I know the answer now. We're on each other's side. We already were that day, weren't we?"

"*Yes*." Henrik hissed the word as Ailish stroked his need, hard, the way he liked it. "I'm hungry, Lish." He plowed his hands into her hair, wound the strands around his fists. "I liked the way you looked at me today."

Looking up at her fiancé through the shield of her eyelashes, Ailish undid the fastening and zipper of his pants. "What way is that?"

"Like I was a man you could be proud of. That you *are* proud of." His grip on her hair increased just enough to part Ailish's lips. "Now I want you to look at me that other way. Like you need to tell me I'm being a little too rough, but you can't form the words."

"Oh. That way," Ailish breathed, drawing his erection out and massaging the whole of him with both hands. "Can I tell you I love you before I stop being able to speak?" She pressed their foreheads together. "I love you, Officer Vance."

Ailish was flat on her back in seconds, legs held apart. "I love you, Ailish O'Kelly—" Pushing deep inside her, Henrik broke off on a groan. "Forever."

Acknowledgments

I'm very sad to see the Crossing the Line series end. Really, it's not just the end of *one* series, but the final note of my Line of Duty series, too, because we're saying good-bye to Captain Derek Tyler, who helped me thread two unforgettable groups of characters together. And no one could have done it but him. He's been with me since the beginning, and I love him dearly. I can't tell you what it meant to me, leaving him on the stage, a legend among the department.

There are other (real) people who were vital to the existence of the Crossing the Line series. But number one will always be the readers who spent their hard-earned money on each book and allowed me to tell them a story. Thank you for trusting me and taking journey after journey with me — I promise I'll never take it for granted.

Thank you to my husband, Patrick, and daughter, Mackenzie, for getting me through every day. Sometimes I worry about things outside my control and then I look at you guys, and realize you're the only thing that matters.

Thank you to my editor Heather Howland, at Entangled Publishing, for encouraging me to spin off the Line of Duty series and being all-around invaluable when making my words make sense.

About the Author

New York Times and USA TODAY bestselling author Tessa Bailey lives in Brooklyn, New York, with her husband and young daughter. When she isn't writing or reading romance, she enjoys a good argument and thirty-minute recipes.

www.tessabailey.com

***Find out where it all began with
Tessa Bailey's Line of Duty series...***

PROTECTING WHAT'S HIS

OFFICER OFF LIMITS

ASKING FOR TROUBLE

STAKING HIS CLAIM

PROTECTING WHAT'S THEIRS

UNFIXABLE

THE STORY CONTINUES IN THE CROSSING THE LINE SERIES...

RISKIER BUSINESS

HIS RISK TO TAKE

RISKING IT ALL

UP IN SMOKE

BOILING POINT

ALSO BY TESSA BAILEY

BAITING THE MAID OF HONOR

OWNED BY FATE

Exposed by Fate

Driven by Fate

Crashed Out

Thrown Down

Worked Up

Wound Tight

Discover more Entangled Select Suspense titles...

HEALING LOVE
by Abby Niles

Doctor Ella Watts wants her old life back. Desperately. Personal trainer Lance Black is the man to help her gain confidence in her MMA abilities. Not only is he toned, muscular, and gorgeous, he's patient, a great teacher, and willing to treat her like a worthy opponent. Except his size makes her freeze whenever he gets too close.

There's more to the mysterious blonde ninja than a beautiful woman determined to improve her MMA skills, and underground fighter Lance Black plans on finding that out. If he can get to know her outside the gym, all the better. As long as she never learns his secrets.

FADE INTO YOU
by Tracy Wolff

When Wyatt Jennings rejoins his rock band Shaken Dirty after a stint in rehab, his demons are never far behind. Until he meets Poppy Germaine, the band's new social media consultant. Even though she's with the label—and therefore off-limits—he craves her. Needs her. Except Poppy is actually the daughter of the label's CEO, sent undercover to keep Wyatt from falling off the wagon again. Proving herself to her father is Poppy's only goal—until she finds herself in Wyatt's bed. But if Wyatt discovers the truth, it could send him spiraling all over again…

BURNOUT
by Tee O'Fallon

Sexy-as-sin Police Chief Mike Flannery knows the new arrival to Hopewell Springs is trouble; he's been a cop too long not to recognize the signs of a woman running from her past. But he can't resist her quick wit, smoking-hot body, and the easy way she embraces their close-knit community. NYPD Detective Cassie Yates is on the run. Armed with fake ID, her K-9, and a police-issued SUV, she flees to this quiet upstate town to avoid a hit. When the hired assassin hunts her down, Mike's past comes roaring back and secrets are revealed in an explosion destined to tear them apart—if not destroy them.

HONOR RECLAIMED
by Tonya Burrows

An interview with a runaway Afghani child bride lands photojournalist Phoebe Leighton in the middle of an arms deal. Forming an unlikely alliance with a ragtag team of mercenaries, she meets Seth Harlan, a former Marine sniper with PTSD. He ignites passions within her she thought long dead, but she's hiding a secret that could destroy him. Racing against the clock, Seth, Phoebe, and the rest of HORNET struggle to stop a ruthless warlord bent on power, revenge…and death.